THE RED LOCKED ROOM

D1714553

THE RED LOCKED ROOM

Tetsuya Ayukawa

Translated by Ho-Ling Wong

The Red Locked Room

This book is a work of fiction. The characters, incidents, and dialogue are drawn from the author's imagination and are not to be construed as real. Any resemblance to actual events or persons, living or dead, is entirely coincidental.

First published in Japanese in *Hōseki and Tantei Kurabu*, between 1954 and 1961.
THE RED LOCKED ROOM
Copyright © Sumiyo Koike
English translation rights arranged with Sumiyo Koike c/o Tokyo Sogensha Co., Ltd.
English translation copyright © by John Pugmire 2020.

Cover picture: one of the "Eight Hells of Beppu" hot springs, Japan

For information, contact: pugmire1@yahoo.com

FIRST AMERICAN EDITION
Library of Congress Cataloguing-in-Publication Data
Ayukawa, Tetsuya
[Seven short stories]
The Red Locked Room / Tetsuya Ayukawa
Translated from the Japanese by Ho-Ling Wong

CONTENTS

Introduction
Taku Ashibe

Anthony Boucher famously wrote "Ellery Queen is the American detective story," and if one were to borrow his saying, one could also claim that Tetsuya Ayukawa is the Japanese *honkaku* mystery story.

The Japanese word *honkaku* on its own translates to 'orthodox' or 'standard.' The term '*honkaku* mystery fiction' on the other hand corresponds to 'classic fair-play mystery' in the English-language world. In the past, mysteries were grouped together with tales of horror, fantasy and adventure under the common term *tantei shōsetsu* (detective story), but the classic mystery novel was eventually differentiated from the other genres through the introduction of the word *honkaku*. It was mystery author Saburō Kōga who first coined the phrase in 1926.

It was also around that period that the S.S. Van Dine boom in the United States reached Japanese shores. Van Dine's writing style, which focused solely on a core mystery plot and eliminated all other redundant story elements—save for snobbery and pedantry---was considered both surprising and refreshing.

Translations of the works of the writers responsible for the Golden Age of Detective Fiction in the west followed. Stories by Ellery Queen, Agatha Christie, F. W. Crofts, E. D. Biggers, E. C. Bentley, A. A. Milne and others helped solidify the shared idea of what a *honkaku* mystery story entailed. However, the time was not yet ripe for Japanese authors to follow.

Neither Edogawa Rampo, the father of the Japanese detective story who had quickly grasped the charm of *honkaku* mystery and realised it would become the mainstream style of the genre, nor Saburō Kōga, who had created the term *honkaku mystery*, were able to switch over to this new style. They had been influenced strongly by Sir Arthur Conan Doyle and Maurice Leblanc and had already obtained a certain reputation as mystery writers, so this new change would have made it necessary for them to alter their writing style.

The first to embrace this new trend was the new generation, which included writers like Yū Aoi and most notably Keikichi Ōsaka, a collection of whose short stories is already available via Locked

Room International. Despite their efforts, *honkaku* did not become the mainstream style because the upcoming World War nipped the movement in the bud. Ōsaka died in the war, while his mentor Kōga died of a sudden illness while travelling, due to scarcity of medicine.

Ironically, losing the devastating war in 1945 actually liberated the Japanese literary scene. During the war it had been forbidden to write detective stories, as they were considered subversive literature, but once the war was over writers could start publishing their stories again, including *honkaku* mystery fiction.

Seishi Yokomizo, who had been an editor before the war, as well as a writer of fantasy and thrillers, brought much foreign mystery fiction into Japan. He had read John Dickson Carr's works during the war, which now inspired him to write *The Honjin Murders,* quickly followed by other masterpieces such as *The Butterfly Murder Case* (*Chōchō Satsujin Jiken*) and *Gokumon Island* (*Gokumontō*). Together, they made Yokomizo one of the pioneers of the *honkaku* mystery novel. Many of the genre's major works were written in the early post-war period. Kikuo Tsunoda, who had previously written romantic and mysterious period stories, published *The Tragedy of the Takagi Clan* (*Takagike no Sangeki*) featuring Superintendent Keisuke Kagami, and Ango Sakaguchi, a pure literature author belonging to the *Buraiha* Decadent School, wrote *The Non-Serial Murders* (*Furenzoku Satsujin Jiken*).

Much was expected from the younger generation. Edogawa Rampo, who by that time was mostly focusing on genre research and criticism, was so impressed by a manuscript sent to him that he convinced a major publisher to print it. This was Akimitsu Takagi's *The Tattoo Murder Case.* The mystery, which involved the discovery of a female corpse minus the torso in a bathroom locked from the inside, could not have been written before the war, or by anyone of the older generation.

The unique circumstances in Japan at the time were an important factor in the growth of the genre's popularity. Due to the long war and the controlling society that had facilitated it, people had been starved of books, whether about philosophy, art or plain entertainment. Period novels were popular among the wider audience, but publishers were hesitant because they were thought to promote feudalist and anti-democratic ideas. On the other hand, mystery stories, which embraced the novelties of the new era, were welcome. (Parenthetically, the Allied occupation forces had established clear regulations for films. Actors who had once starred as heroic samurai warriors were thus forced to play police detectives, coast guards or private detectives.)

Although Tetsuya Ayukawa did not stand out at first, he slowly made his way to the forefront of the new era and remained loyal to the *honkaku* mystery story to the end. Even when the genre was abandoned and even dismissed, he kept on writing stories of mystery and logical deduction, and with time he became a peerless figure, respected by readers and younger writers alike.

Tetsuya Ayukawa (real name: Tōru Nakagawa) was born in 1919 in Tōkyō. When he was in elementary school he was forced to move to mainland China, because of his father's job as an engineer for the South Manchuria Railway Company. Most of his life between boyhood and adolescence was spent in Dalian, a city in Northeast China, although he did return several times to Japan to go to school in Tōkyō. Dalian was a unique metropolis, where Chinese, Japanese and Russians lived together, a melting pot between East and West, the past and the present. The exotic scenery of that city, which would disappear with the end of the war, indubitably made a tremendous impression on young Ayukawa.

When he was in middle school, a senior student told him about the stories of Sherlock Holmes. He was captivated by them and soon thereafter he went on to read R. Austin Freeman's Dr. Thorndyke stories. After that he could not find anything more in local libraries and was obliged to travel to neighbouring towns or even faraway cities to read the translated tales of Poe, Chesterton and Van Dine.

In the beginning he liked stories where a brilliant detective would solve a tricky case, but after reading Croft's *The Ponson Case,* he realised that having a normal detective patiently solving a case through simple trial and error also had its charm. After coming across the timetable of the South Manchurian Railways and noticing the interesting manner in which certain trains connected, he decided to write a mystery story himself.

Ayukawa's family had returned to Japan before the end of the war, so he did not experience the tragic fall of Manchuria, but he did lose the manuscript of his story in the chaos following Japan's defeat. He also found himself suffering from a lung disease and had to spend time in recuperation, only working sporadically. With his creative urge growing, he started submitting stories to magazines. He made his debut in 1948 with an exotic fantasy short story titled *Tsukishiro*. In the same year, he published his first mystery story *The Snake and The Wild Boar* (*Hebi to Inoshishi*.)

Soon afterwards, the post-war detective story boom offered him the opportunity of a lifetime. He had entered an important novel competition organised by the magazine *Hōseki*. His novel *The Petrov Affair* (*Petrov Jiken*), which he had submitted under his real name Tōru Nakagawa, won first place. The novel was a rewrite of the manuscript he had lost in the war and it would become the first novel starring Chief Inspector Onitsura, a Japanese police detective who at the time was in the police force of Dalian.

The alluring story brimmed with nostalgia and exoticism and was set in an international metropolis long gone. The skilled manner in which the complex, perfect alibi was broken down in the tale was a bellwether of the arrival of a new generation of *honkaku* mystery writers.

Unfortunately, the publisher of *Hōseki* could not pay him the prize money due to financial problems. When he protested, he was sent packing and his book was not published.

Ayukawa turned his hand to writing short stories for the several second-rate magazines in existence at the time and he also tried to strengthen his ties with societies of mystery aficionados.

Meanwhile, he continued to work on his second full-length novel. Back then it was rare for a no-name newcomer to have a full-length novel published, but his never-ending efforts would pay off. In 1955, publisher Kōdansha was publishing a series of newly written detective novels. The final volume *The Thirteenth Seat* was open for submissions from newcomers, and his submission, *The Black Trunk* (*Kuroi Toranku*), won. It was the first time he had used the pen name Tetsuya Ayukawa, and his second debut had been a rousing success.

Shortly thereafter, *Hōseki* also had a restart, and this time it had Edogawa Rampo aboard as well. He invested his own funds, devised a renewal plan and even sought new talent to write for the magazine. One of the new stars of *honkaku* mystery he had his eye on was Ayukawa.

The mystery genre in Japan had seen tremendous growth, thanks to authors like Seichō Matsumoto and Etsuko Niki, but in their hands the emphasis changed to the motive for the crime and the psychology of the criminal. The former openly disapproved of stories about brilliant detectives solving fantastic crimes by pure logical deduction, and as a result, readers' interest shifted to realism and contemporary issues.

Despite this change in readers' tastes, Ayukawa remained focused on *honkaku* mystery and kept on writing impressive, high-quality works. His earnest work attitude earned him the trust of his readers and would also influence later generations of writers. It can be confidently stated that there is not one writer belonging to the *shin honkaku* movement who does not hold Tetsuya Ayukawa in the utmost regard. The fact that all the titles on the following list of Ayukawa's novels are true *honkaku* mystery stories is absolutely stunning.

The Petrov Affair (*Petrov Jiken*, 1950)
The Black Trunk (*Kuroi Toranku*, 1956)
The Villa Lilac Case (*Rira-sō Jiken*, 1958)*
A Fossil of Hate (*Zō'o no Kaseki*, 1959)
White Fear (*Shiro no Kyōfu*, 1959)*
The Black Swan (*Kuro no Hakuchō*, 1960)
What People Call Love Suicide (*Hito Sore wo Jōshi to Yobu*, 1961)
Gravestone in the Shadows (*Kage Aru Bohyō*, 1962)*
Castle of Sand (*Suna no Shiro*, 1963)
The Fake Grave (*Itsuwari no Funbo,* 1963)
Whipping the Dead (*Shisha wo Muchi Ute*, 1964)*
A Deadly Scenery (*Shi no Aru Fūkei*, 1965)
Destination Unknown (*Atesaki Fumei*, 1965)
The Semi Express Nagara (*Junkyū Nagara*, 1966)
A Tower of Blocks (*Tsumiki no Tō*, 1966)
A Door Without a Keyhole (*Kagiana no Nai Tobira*, 1969)
Testimony of Wind (*Kaze no Shōgen*, 1971)
What Did the Inugami See? (*Inugami wa Nani wo Mita Ka*, 1976)
A Box of Silence (*Chinmoku no Hako*, 1979)
The Last Writing in Blood-Red (*Shu no Zeppitsu*, 1979)*
Find the King (*Ō wo Sagase*, 1979)
Seat of the Dead (*Shibito no Za*, 1983)

The titles feature Chief Inspector Onitsura, except those marked *, which either feature the amateur detective Ryūzō Hoshikage, or don't belong to any series. Ayukawa also wrote a series starring the bartender of the bar Number 3. He had been working on the Number

3 series' first novel, entitled *The White Birch House Affair* (*Shirakabasō Jiken*), when he died without finishing the novel.

If one were to point out the characteristics of Ayukawa's two main series, one can say that the Ryūzō Hoshikage series feature a classic, whodunit/howdunit puzzle style, while the more prolific Onitsura is mostly occupied with breaking down alibis. Due to the latter's larger output, Ayukawa's novels are often categorised as realistic police procedurals, but these stories are actually brimming with original tricks and impressive lines of logic. Onitsura is perhaps best described as "Ellery Queen wearing the face of Inspector French."

But why is Onitsura always busy cracking alibis? As stated previously, in the period post 1960, detective novels in Japan focused on the motive for the crime and the psychology of the criminal and eschewed the brilliant detective, the murder in the country house and fantastic murder schemes. Ayukawa therefore decided to focus on the web of railways that covered the islands of Japan, and the diverse trains that ran along the rails with impeccable timing. Such trains would provide the stage for his tales of mystery and logic. It was far more realistic to portray a clever criminal who, in order to evade the hands of justice, would come up with an iron-clad alibi for themselves, rather than create some kind of locked room. Railway mysteries were thus able to offer a unique experience, by portraying Japanese locales in the second half of the twentieth century and the people who lived there, while at the same time also presenting daring murder schemes.

From 1975 on, Ayukawa started taking up new interests besides his career as a novelist, first by compiling dozens of mystery anthologies. He also started locating forgotten writers through interviews and research. Finally, he gave new writers a hand, helping them make their professional debut. All these achievements can probably be traced back to his own experiences starting out as a writer and to the fact that he had seen how many writers and their work had been forgotten by time.

In 1990, the annual Tetsuya Ayukawa Award was established. Ayukawa passed away in 2002, but even now, this award is still the gateway to success for writers of *honkaku* mystery in Japan and it will be awarded for the thirtieth time this year. The award has indeed become a synonym for *honkaku* mystery. The book you are holding now comprises a selection of short stories featuring the master's two best-known detectives and is the first time they have appeared in the English-speaking world.

To introduce the amateur detective Ryūzō Hoshikage first: this obnoxious merchant with a snobbish moustache and a love for pipes was originally conceived as a caricature of the classic great detective. When Ayukawa was deprived of the opportunity to publish his first novel, he submitted a story to the club magazine of the most famous mystery aficionado society in Japan, SR no Kai (SR stands for 'Sealed Room.') In that story, Hoshikage appeared as a rival to Onitsura. Hoshikage lost the battle horribly then, but Ayukawa decided to use the character when he wanted to write fantastical impossible crime stories which wouldn't fit the character of Onitsura. It is funny how, despite his origins, Hoshikage managed to grow into one of Japan's greatest fictional detectives, to whom Chief Inspector Tadokoro turns in much the same way Inspector Lestrade turned to Sherlock Holmes.

His best novel-length exploit is *The Villa Lilac Case* (*Rira-sō Jiken*). There are few novels, both in and outside Japan, which can come close to this masterpiece about a series of murders in a mountain villa.

As the title *The White Locked Room* (1958) suggests, this story has the problem of 'no footsteps in the snow' as its theme. One victim and one witness are found in a house surrounded by snow. If the witness is innocent, the murder becomes an impossible crime. Both the solution and the true meaning hidden within the eccentric and almost prophetic questions asked by Hoshikage are sure to shock readers. Perhaps they might also think that Ryūzō Hoshikage reminds them of Sir Henry Merrivale or Dr. Gideon Fell after a successful diet.

The Blue Locked Room (1961) may not have some grand-scale idea, but the twisty solution is highly enjoyable. The culprits in the *Red* and *White* locked rooms go through a great deal of trouble to create their locked rooms, but that is not the case here. But what is the meaning behind that? The way the mystery is presented and the skill with which the author plays with logic is impressive.

The Clown in the Tunnel (1958) is about an impossible disappearance. A clown suddenly appears in a house where musicians live and, after attacking people there and killing one person, he disappears equally quickly. He escapes through a narrow passage, basically a tunnel, but nobody sees him leave from the other side. In order to solve the apparent miracle, perhaps one might even be tempted to turn to the author's other detective for help.

The Red Locked Room (1954) is the best-known short story featuring Hoshikage and is undoubtedly one of the greatest impossible crime stories ever written in any language. How could a dismembered body have been introduced into an autopsy room completely locked from the inside save for a small air vent? The crime appears to be utterly impossible, but Hoshikage's deductions slowly unravel the mystery. While the brilliant solution will surely surprise, many a reader will wonder how they missed the many clues dangled in front of them.

Now let me introduce Chief Inspector Onitsura. The rational and cool-headed police detective decided to go to Northeast China due to a broken heart. As an officer of the Japanese police force, he was first posted in Harbin and later Dalian, where he solved several cases. Upon his return to Japan, he was assigned to the Metropolitan Police Department. He had spent much of his younger days abroad, so his intelligent, gentlemanly attitude is more reminiscent of an inspector of Scotland Yard when compared to his Japanese colleagues.

Onitsura has a partner in his subordinate, Detective Tanna. Interestingly, Chief Inspector Tadokoro, who brings Ryūzō Hoshikage most of his cases, is a direct colleague of Onitsura, so perhaps Onitsura has met Hoshikage.

Whose Body? (1957) gives one a miraculous taste of how the impossible becomes possible. One could say this story does not feature any locked rooms or fabricated alibis, but one could also claim that's not exactly correct. The story features a Grand Guignol-worthy tragedy and a relentless stream of mysteries offered by the suspects. With what prop is Tetsuya Ayukawa deceiving the reader? Time? Space? Characters? In any case, this is a story that makes you realise how far an author specialising in illusions and surprise can go.

Death in Early Spring (1958) involves a perfect alibi. A crime which seemed utterly impossible time-wise, suddenly becomes possible simply by changing the viewpoint ever so slightly. In the eyes of Tetsuya Ayukawa, an alibi is basically a "locked room in time." A locked room on the other hand is an "alibi in space." It is therefore only natural he was such a master of both the alibi trick and the locked room mystery.

The Five Clocks (1957) is a masterpiece written at the request of Edogawa Rampo. The manner in which Ayukawa managed to include such an intricate fabricated alibi and the solution to the problem within the restraints of so few pages makes one think of precision machinery. In order to save a person framed for a murder he did not commit, Onitsura has to break down the alibi of the real culprit. An alibi protected completely by five separate clocks. Each step in the solving process is imposing, but the wit of the whole deal when everything is revealed also invites a smile.

I hope you too can now agree with the statement that Tetsuya Ayukawa is the Japanese *honkaku* mystery story. This collection only offers a glimpse of his oeuvre. He has also written for television, radio and YA audiences, and naturally basically all of this output too belongs to the mystery genre. I can only hope that the publication of this short story collection will lead to more of his work being published in English.

Tōkyō, 2020.

Addendum.

The initial selection of stories for this collection was conducted by Alice Arisugawa and Taku Ashibe. Five stories each were chosen from the Onitsura and Hoshikage series, as well as one non-series story. It was decided to not pick stories from the Number 3 series until the final page count of the collection was decided upon. Ashibe wrote summaries for the eleven selected stories, which were translated by Ho-Ling Wong. The final selection of the stories to be included was made by Ashibe and Wong.

The White Locked Room

1

It had been snowing since noon due to a weather front, but nobody had foreseen how high the snow would pile up. At first the snow was powdery, dropping gently from the sky, but by the evening, the flakes had become as large as the feathers of swans. Just as it seemed likely that the snowfall would continue through the night, it suddenly ceased before nine o'clock. As usual, the forecast from the Meteorological Agency had been completely wrong. Although their misreading was understandable, as they lacked sufficient data, the officials at the Agency must have been quite embarrassed by the sheer amount of snow that fell. It was almost sad to hear them being accused of squandering taxpayers' money. Yet it was those very same meteorologists who played a vital role in the incident, subsequently dubbed "The White Locked Room Murder Case," by correctly recording the exact time the snow stopped as 8:40 p.m.

It was the night after a full moon, and after the snow had stopped, its bright face shone from between the clouds as if to laugh at the agency officials. Like a giant spotlight hanging above a children's theatre play, it cast a dreamlike cream colour on the metropolis, making Professor Zama's snow-covered home in Nishi-Ōkubo look like the perfect Christmas picture. He had a fancy cottage-like house, befitting someone who had lived for a long time in Europe, and a garden of over 600 square metres with several Himalayan cedars.

The pale illumination from an 80w light hanging on the porch reached about half the garden.

Kimiko Satō stood on the porch and stamped a few times on the floor to get the snow off her boots. She placed a slender finger on the white button on the wall and pressed it. She could faintly hear the noise of a buzzer inside, but there was no answer. She waited a minute and pressed the button again, but again there was no answer. Only at the third attempt did she hear a reaction from inside.

A man with a long, pale face and protruding teeth answered the door. She had never seen him before. He was wearing a beret and appeared to be about forty years old. He was not the person she had expected to appear, so she reflexively stepped back from the door. Professor Zama had been single his whole life and it had always been he who answered the door, as he had no wife or housekeeper.

'Excuse me, is the professor at home?'

'He's here, but I am afraid he's in no condition to see you,' the man replied bluntly. His unfriendly face betrayed feelings of confusion. Kimiko frowned as she detected the smell of alcohol on the man's breath. There's no smell as unpleasant to those who don't drink as the odour of stale alcohol.

'Why, is there something wrong with him?'

'You could say that. He's dead.'

'When did that happen? Was he ill?'

'No, he was murdered. I only got here just now. It gave me the shock of a lifetime. I was just about to phone the police.'

Kimiko would have cried out, but her lips were dry.

'Are you a student at the Kyōwa Women's Medical University?' the man asked, after noticing the badge on her overall.

'Yes. I attend the professor's seminars.'

'A doctor in training? Perfect. Could you please come inside? We'd better make sure it was murder before phoning the police.'

Without waiting for Kimiko's reply, he turned and went into the study next to the entrance hall.

The night was silent because of the snow. But the silence in the house was different: it was painful. Kimiko could feel it in every hair on her body, affecting all her nerves. A pair of wet shoes had been tossed carelessly on the tiled floor of the entrance hall. Kimiko removed her own boots, placed them next to the shoes, and went into the study. She had visited the house several times previously with her fellow students and was already familiar with its layout.

The thick curtains of the large window facing the garden had been drawn shut. The study was a business-like room devoid of any feminine touch, with three of the walls hiding behind thousands of medical books. A large table and swivel-chair had been placed in front of the window and the gas heater nearby was puffing noisily.

The professor was lying face down in front of a sofa opposite the window. The pool of blood that had coloured his charcoal grey jacket red had also covered the edge of the green carpet, the mosaic floor and the legs of the sofa. Kimiko could feel herself getting tense but, as expected of a medical student, she managed to inspect everything calmly, as if she were accustomed to such a sight.

'There's no weapon, so I think it's probably murder.' The man, who was standing near the wall, had spoken so softly Kimiko could hardly understand him. She didn't answer immediately, first taking a closer look at the wound in the professor's back.

'Yes, it must be murder. Even if there had been a weapon here, no one could have stabbed themselves at such an angle.'

'Very well. We'll have to call the authorities.'

He stepped around the feet of the body and picked up the receiver of the telephone on the table with a handkerchief. Kimiko absently watched the movements of his fingers as he dialed the number.

2

The following is a reprint of an article entitled *The White Locked Room*, originally published in the January issue of the middle-brow magazine *New Century*, and written by its editor-in-chief Nobuo Mine. Due to page constraints, the article has been shortened.

I was the moderator in the discussion between Professor Zama and the spirit mediums published elsewhere in this issue, but only heaven could have foreseen that, on the following night, I would be confronted with the professor's death. I had called the professor that evening because I wanted him to proofread the article I had written based on the aforementioned discussion, and was told that I could come at nine-thirty. If I am allowed to express my personal feelings here, I have to confess that, while the professor had scolded me occasionally, he had really looked after me during these last ten years when we worked together, and I am deeply moved now knowing that the phone call would be the last time I would ever hear the professor's voice. Setting aside his academic achievements, the professor was also a gentleman of strict principles, who did not accept any ambiguities of conduct.

I arrived at the professor's house in Nishi-Ōkubo about three minutes before my nine-thirty appointment. The gate was open, so I made my way through to the garden to the porch, and rang the bell as always. Looking back, I realise that my sixth sense had already noticed something out of the ordinary had occurred. There was no answer despite my constant ringing, and, when I tried turning the door knob, it opened without any trouble. Leaving the door unlocked was unlike the professor, who was cautious by nature. I became more

19

suspicious and called out several times before removing my shoes and entering the study, where I discovered the appalling sight of the deceased professor.

I was absolutely stunned. I had heard the professor's lively voice a mere two hours before, so I could not believe he had committed suicide. But if it was murder, who was the murderer? The outrage welling inside me made me temporarily forget my duty. I was only brought back to my senses by the noise of the doorbell being rung by someone at the porch. I might sound like a coward, but for a moment I felt nothing but fear that the murderer might have returned. Of course, thinking about it calmly, even if the murderer had some reason to return, he would hardly have rung the bell first. To be fair, it was no wonder I could not think clearly, as I was standing in front of a blood-stained corpse.

If the murderer had come back, I had to hide somewhere. I harboured feelings of intense anger against him, but it was up to the authorities to judge him and it was not my place to avenge the professor there and then. I looked for some place to hide in the room, but the doorbell kept on ringing incessantly. When I finally gave up and answered the door, I found, not the killer, but a beautiful young girl. As soon as I noticed the school badge of Kyōwa Women's Medical University, where the professor taught, pinned to her chest, I could feel all the tension ebb away from my body out of relief. I had expected a dangerous killer, so it was quite a surprise to find a beautiful specimen of the fair sex at the door.

I had her examine the body and, after she determined it was indeed murder, I called the police. I was later asked by the police why I had not informed them at once, but I knew of past incidents where a suicide had been reported erroneously as a homicide, and that had acted as a psychological brake.

I made my call at nine thirty-five. The loud sirens of the police car that arrived five minutes later actually calmed me. Almost immediately the patrol officers discovered an overcoat which had been left in the garden. They had only found the coat lying beneath the shrubs by accident, as they walked around my footprints and those of the student as a precaution.

The student, who had been silent up until then, suddenly declared that it was the professor's overcoat. The coat had looked familiar to me too, but what had caught my attention first was the blood on the coat. Unlike the student or the police, I was not used to the sight of blood and so I found the bloodstains intimidating.

The patrol officers quickly grasped what had happened and used the phone on the desk to contact Investigative Division I of the Metropolitan Police Department. The student and I stood anxiously in a corner of the room as things developed.

At about ten minutes past eleven, voices came from behind the house. The police detectives had come in through the rear entrance following the patrol officers' warning about the footprints in front. The hulking plain-clothes detective standing in front of the officers in uniform and the forensic examiners in white coats was Chief Inspector Tadokoro, known to be one of the most impulsive men of Division I. I had met him myself a few times, so even when I was later put in a difficult spot, I was able to handle him relatively calmly.

Even the most routine medical examination would probably look remarkably gruesome to the uninitiated like myself. A portly bearded police surgeon crouched across the body and performed a detailed examination. Then photographs were taken, fingerprints were checked and the professor's remains were taken away. With the master of the house now absent, a sudden air of loneliness came over the study.

Meanwhile, other forensic investigators and the chief inspector appeared to have been busy in the garden. I soon realised they were conducting an extensive examination of every trace left in the snow, including our footprints. Their meticulous examination determined that the only footprints were those of myself and the female student, and nobody else. The case was therefore theoretically an impossible crime. I was surprised to learn, a few days later, that Chief Inspector Tadokoro and forensic officials had actually considered the method used by the murderer in Carter Dickson's novel *The White Priory Murders,* but had determined that the method would not apply to the Zama case.

After the chief inspector concluded his investigation of the garden, he returned to the study to give orders to his detectives. As I watched them work, I realized that their orders were to search the house. As the chief inspector had not found any footprints of the murderer leaving the premises, it was only natural to assume he might still be hiding somewhere in the house. I shuddered to think what might have happened if the murderer had shown himself before the patrol officers arrived. The student and I would most definitely not have been left unscathed. After an hour, the whole house had been searched, even the loft, but not even a mouse was found. While it relieved me to learn that the murderer was not in the house, it also meant that another possible solution to the impossible crime had been eliminated.

3

Questioning commenced around one in the morning. It was only then that I learned that the female student's name was Kimiko Satō, aged twenty-one, and that she lived alone in an apartment in Tozuka. I don't mind the company of a beautiful woman, no matter the occasion. Her large, deep eyes and small red lips, reminiscent of Western dolls, especially made an impression. Beneath her overcoat she wore a midnight-blue sweater and a camel skirt, a cute outfit which looked good on her.

'Miss, what was the reason you went to visit the professor?'

Even Chief Inspector Tadokoro spoke more softly when questioning a woman. He spoke in a coaxing manner, quite unbefitting his appearance.

'I had some questions for the professor regarding my graduation thesis.'

'At that hour?'

'Yes. I was planning a ski trip to Akakura with friends later today, so I wanted to take care of it this evening,' she started to reply, but then she realised what the chief inspector might be implying. She blushed and her large eyes flashed in anger.

'I'll have you know the professor was a gentleman. It's one thing to talk like that about me, but your insinuation is nothing more than an uncouth insult to the poor professor!'

'I'm sorry, I'm sorry,' replied the policeman, with an awkward grin. Afterwards, I learned that that was his way of questioning witnesses. One step back, two steps forward. Provoking his targets emotionally first and noting their true colours when they lost their self-control. That skill was what had got him to his current position. But writing about the man is not the purpose of the article, which is to describe how the incident became an impossible crime.

After the interrogation was over, a detective entered the room and whispered something to the chief inspector, who told us what the man had said, probably in an attempt to get a give-and-take deal with us.

'The medical report is in.'

'That was fast,' I replied.

'It's because the cause of death was relatively clear. The professor had only one wound, which proved fatal. His right lung was pierced from behind and the murder weapon was probably a knife with a blade eight centimetres long. There was internal bleeding in one lung, which led to pressure on the organ.'

The medical student Kimiko Satō listened with interest to the report, but I could only feel a shudder run down my spine.

'The time of death is estimated to be around nine o'clock. But, judging by the internal bleeding, the murderer must have kept the professor alive for quite some time by leaving the weapon in the wound. For some reason, he only pulled it out later when, not unexpectedly, he took it with him.'

He spoke quite freely, and while it may have been my imagination, it seemed to me his eyes were carefully following our reactions, especially mine. I had my own ideas about why the murderer would have left the weapon in the wound for a while to keep the professor alive, but I didn't like the way the chief inspector looked at me, so I decided to keep my mouth shut.

'The knife acted like a kind of plug, so the moment it was pulled out, the professor started to bleed profusely. According to the report, the victim must have died almost instantaneously. As for the overcoat found in the garden, it appears to have been used to cover the wound when the knife was pulled out, which is how the murderer avoided being covered by the blood spraying out of the wound.'

He stopped and stared at me again.

The murder weapon had been discovered that morning in the snow. It was a fruit knife with a blade eight centimetres long, exactly as the chief inspector had told us. We were shown it later. It was made of stainless steel, but instead of a normal blade it had a triangular tip to cut out fruit cores. Even the chief inspector seemed to have trouble explaining why the culprit had left the weapon just outside the crime scene.

'Mine, you say you arrived here at the house just before Ms. Satō, but didn't you actually get here much earlier? The Meteorological Agency reported to us that the snow stopped falling at eight-forty, and as your footprints were found in the snow, we know you didn't arrive before that. But, supposing you did arrive at eight-forty, you'd still have plenty of time to get into a fight with the professor and commit the crime. What do you say to that?'

'Wha—what are you saying! That's nonsense. I arrived here only two or three minutes before Ms. Satō. That was at nine twenty-six or twenty-seven. You may think everyone you meet is a crook, but I don't take lightly to being accused of murder. I've known Professor Zama since just after the war. How could I ever kill a man I respected so much? Try someone else.'

I don't remember my precise words, but it was something like that. A grin appeared on Chief Inspector Tadokoro's ugly face.

'Mine, do you have an alibi between eight-forty and nine o'clock?' he asked as he patted his shoulder with a large fist. I had felt really cold after getting off the train at Takadanobaba, so I decided to have something to warm myself up at one of the *oden* food stalls lined up outside the station. That was probably within the time frame, but who was going to remember the name of a random food stall?

'Now you mention it, I do remember your breath smelled of alcohol when I got here.' Kimiko collaborated my story.

'I see. While we're at it, would you mind telling me your own alibi then?'

'I was in my room all the time.'

'Well, that's a clear-cut answer.'

The chief inspector called for two detectives to check out the food stall and the girl's lodgings. I pitied them having to go out into the snow. They, as well as the two of us who had stumbled into the crime scene by accident, were having a very rough night.

'Mine, you never know whether something like tonight will happen again, so the next time you're out eating *yakitori*, you'd better take a good look at the name of the stand.'

The chief inspector grinned as he spoke to me, but I looked the other way and pretended I hadn't heard him.

Ms. Satō's alibi was soon confirmed, but mine could not be proved. The detectives had asked around the food stalls there, but bad luck always has company, and none of the servers at the oden food stalls remembered me as a customer. Subsequent investigation made it clear I had no motive to murder the professor, however, so the matter was not pursued further.

With the Mine Hypothesis on hold for the moment, the chief inspector looked at both of us and that awkward smile appeared on his face again.

'You two must be familiar with the people around the professor. Are you aware of anyone who may have had a motive? Don't worry, we're not going to arrest someone just because you've named them. It's just normal procedure.'

As a reflex I pointed to my manuscript about the discussion, which I had brought along.

'Chief Inspector, you might want to take a look at this article. It may interest you.'

4

Having got nowhere on the case, Tadokoro asked Ryūzō Hoshikage for help, as usual. The latter was in the international trading business and had only returned the evening of the day before from a business trip to South-East Asia. It almost appeared that his white forehead had acquired a tan.

'Well, what did the manuscript say?' asked Hoshikage. He was blunt by nature and his tone was very arrogant, which invariably rubbed the police the wrong way. As a result, he wasn't much liked.

'I'll bring you the magazine with the article later, but it was basically a round-table talk with a psychic and a spirit medium. Well, perhaps round-table talk isn't the right way to describe it. Professor Zama was a very straightforward individual, so he began calling all spiritual experiments fakes, frauds and more. But a doctor specialising in ectoplasm wouldn't have any of that, so the conversation became quite heated.'

As the events had occurred while Mr. Hoshikage was abroad, he was completely unaware of the case, so the chief inspector had to explain all the details to him.

'The psychic is Donryū Ōta, fifty years old, who owns a laboratory in Honjo. He has large eyes, thick eyebrows and a moustache. The spirit medium is Shikibu Takemoto, who behaves almost like an aristocrat. She's approaching thirty and is very attractive, with fair skin. What's odd about her is that she never seems to blink. She stares at you fixedly with her narrow eyes, like a snake eyeing its prey. She can make you feel as though you're drowning in her eyes.'

With no meaningful developments in the investigation, Tadokoro must have felt under pressure, which made him a lot more talkative. Hoshikage had a pipe in his mouth, but had not lit it and urged the chief inspector to continue.

'You'll see it for yourself when you read the article, but that Shikibu Takemoto was like still water, and hardly spoke during the talk. Donryū, on the other hand, was reportedly red in the face and ready to explode. The professor maintained that simply mentioning thousands of experiments which had not provided real data was scarcely convincing, scientifically speaking. He started out with some harsh critiques, but then he simply sneered and laughed at them, so that Donryū became quieter and quieter as the talk continued. Being treated like that, I wouldn't be surprised if either of them thought about killing the professor.'

Tadokoro paused and took a swig of whisky. Hoshikage lit his pipe.

'At the round-table talk, Donryū claimed that the spirit medium could manifest herself as ectoplasm outside her physical body and that he could control that ectoplasm, so he threatened the professor, saying that if they wanted, they could send an apparition to kill him. The talk ended with the professor laughing at the threat. I don't believe in that spiritual mumbo-jumbo, but considering I have a real murder where the culprit left no footprints before me now, I'm starting to ask myself whether it really wasn't ectoplasm that killed the man.'

Hoshikage puffed calmly on his pipe and merely asked:

'How are their alibis?'

'Both have an alibi, being at the laboratory in Honjo at the time of the murder. At least, they should have an alibi, but...'

'Yes?'

'It's very unfortunate, but Donryū is proclaiming proudly that he's the murderer. He claims to have controlled Shikibu's ectoplasm and killed the professor. He couldn't do nothing, having had his psychic powers insulted like that, so this was revenge. The professor himself had laughed and said that if their powers were real, they should try to kill him. So they showed him exactly what the true powers of the spirit were—at least, that's his story. But suppose he really committed the murder with his spiritual powers, we can hardly go out and arrest a ghost, and I don't think that it would be legally possible to punish the mastermind Donryū either.'

'He knows that too, which is why he's boasting about it.'

'Indeed.'

'Meanwhile, Mine, the editor-in-chief of the magazine *New Century*, had an idea that could explain why the murderer let the professor live a bit longer by leaving the knife in the wound. If

Donryū really was the murderer, he might have used the extra time to communicate to the professor through the ectoplasm that it was revenge for his sneering remarks.'

As a plain man, Tadokoro found dealing with such a strange case very difficult. But after taking another swig of whisky, he changed his manner.

'There are theoretically two ways in which the murderer could have left the house without leaving footprints. I could recite them, but they've been examined already and don't seem to withstand scrutiny.'

The two men were not in Hoshikage's office, located in the Maru Building, but in Hoshikage's residence in Meguro. Just as in Professor Zama's study, a gas heater was on, and its warmth seemed to soothe the chief inspector's mind.

'You see, the time of death of the victim hasn't been determined precisely, so one theory is that the murder may have been committed while the snow was still falling.'

'Hm.'

'In which case the culprit's footprints leaving the house would naturally be covered by the falling snow.'

'But who pulled the knife out and threw it into the garden?'

'That's the problem. It seemed like a promising explanation, but it only led us to a dead end. If that had been the case, it must have been Nobuo Mine who pulled the knife out of the victim and threw it into the garden, because he arrived just before Kimiko Satō. But he has no reason for helping the murderer and hiding the weapon. Even if we suppose he did pull the knife from the back of the mortally wounded professor, the question remains why? That act on its own is completely meaningless. So the first idea seems to be a dud.'

'I agree. And the other theory?'

'If the murderer were someone with small feet—a woman like Shikibu Takemoto or Kimiko Satō, for example—that person could escape by simply walking across the snow. Then Mine, who arrived later, could erase their tracks by stepping on top of them one by one. But there again, there's no motive for Mine to become an accomplice to the crime. So that idea doesn't work either. And, in any case, Shikibu Takemoto has an alibi, since she didn't set foot outside the whole night,' Tadokoro concluded in some desperation.

'So what are your thoughts about the case, Mr. Hoshikage?'

'Well, there's one thing I want to ask you first: has it been confirmed that the footprints left in the snow belong to Mine and the female student?'

'Yes. To be precise, there were two sets of prints going from the gate to the house entrance. The forensics people examined them closely and there was no trickery like walking backwards from the porch in their own footprints, or anything like that. Both sets of footprints were made by them walking forwards,' the chief inspector declared confidently.

'And there were no footprints of dogs, cats or other animals, or imprints left by some implement?'

The policeman looked puzzled and shook his head.

'Nothing at all like that,' he replied. He had examined the garden himself, so he was absolutely sure.

'Hmm.'

Hoshikage turned his chiselled features towards the beautiful orchids outside as he contemplated the matter at hand. Lost in thought, his well-manicured slim fingers caressed his pencil moustache. Not wishing to disturb the amateur detective, Tadokoro remained seated, not making a sound or moving a muscle.

'You said Mine has no motive, but that's not strictly correct,' said Hoshikage suddenly, after ten minutes of complete silence. 'I've heard that his magazine *New Century* has been in the red for the last two or three years. According to news reports, as a result of the commotion he's been making about the Zama murder, the first issue of this year has been selling extremely well. To put it another way, this case has been a genuine lifesaver for *New Century*.'

'Well…'

'What I'm asking is whether Mine is really so patient as to wait for the heavens to provide him with such an opportunity? With those business results he might have been motivated not to wait.'

'But…'

'I know what you're thinking, and it's probably true that he respected the professor. But you shouldn't forget he's also feared as an editor-in-chief who's willing to do anything.'

Tadokoro was still not convinced. Would anyone commit murder for such a reason? But then Hoshikage grinned mischievously and he suddenly declared: 'I've solved the mystery.'

'You mean, Mine is really our man?'

'Mine? Who ever said such a thing? I only told you he had a motive,' he replied solemnly, but then loosened up again. 'By the way, I have another question. Did Mine happen to have hurt his foot?'

The chief inspector was a man who was not easily surprised, but he was taken aback by this question out of nowhere. His boorish face contorted and the Lucky Strike cigarette in his mouth fell to the floor.

'Well, why are you staring at me? Answer the question.'

'Yes, he did, he did!' gasped the chief inspector in astonishment. 'Bu—but how did you know? The night of the murder, when he was allowed to leave, he said he had slipped in front of his house and sprained his ankle.'

Hoshikage did not answer his question, however.

'And another question. On the night of the murder, was there any talk about a cat or dog being burnt in the neighbourhood?'

'Yes, yes!' replied the chief inspector, with his eyes wide open. But now that Hoshikage was using his exceptional talents for making deductions, he could feel his spirits rising again.

'But how could you possibly know that? It hasn't even been mentioned in the newspapers or on the radio. A letter was sent to the Animal Protection League claiming that the writer had seen a cook throwing a live cat into a furnace and killing it. You know about the group, of course. A bunch of kooky ladies there who once sent a telegram to Khrushchev to protest sending a dog into space. They were not about to ignore such a letter, so they went to the Tozuka Police Station and demanded the cook be apprehended immediately. Of course, we couldn't assign a detective to a cat case while we had our hands full with the Zama case. But to those ladies, the death of a stray cat was far more important than any professor being murdered. They looked like the *bakeneko* in ghost stories, the cat-like ghouls who lick the oil from oriental lamps.'

The chief inspector didn't seem to think highly of the Animal Protection League. He seemed relieved to have poured his heart out on the subject.

'But how did you know about that?'

'Oh, it spoke for itself. But how did it end up?'

29

'Nothing much came out of it. The letter was sent anonymously, so we couldn't learn more. But it doesn't appear to have been a hoax. Several people did complain about an awful smell that evening. But how did you know about it?'

'Just a hunch. The sprained ankle was also a one-in-three chance.'

Hoshikage still spoke in riddles, but he wasn't likely to talk even if Tadokoro pursued the matter, so he decided to change the subject.

'You just said you solved the mystery. Do you mean the mystery of the footprints?'

'Yes.'

'Did the murderer set up a tightrope and—.'

'No, no,' Hoshikage immediately shot down the suggestion. 'It was nothing so mechanical.'

The chief inspector cocked his head in wonder. He simply couldn't see it. The murderer had not used any mechanical trickery, but as no footprints had been left in the snow, it seemed as if the only solution left was that the murderer had been hiding inside the house. But he himself had led the investigation of the house, and not even a mouse had been found inside. So what had Hoshikage thought of?

'But we searched the house extensively. There was no way we could have overlooked the murderer.'

'Of course. I don't remember ever saying he was inside the house,' said Hoshikage nonchalantly.

'But then I simply can't comprehend what you are saying. If no mechanical trick was utilized, then the murderer must have walked across the snow, but as no footprints were left in the snow, then the only explanation is that the murderer must have been inside the house.'

'You don't comprehend? You really don't comprehend?'

Hoshikage grinned, as if he was having the time of his life because of the expression on Tadokoro's face.

It was as if he were hinting at the truth while laughing at the chief inspector. Yes, Hoshikage must mean that Mine was in fact the culprit. Mine had no alibi, but did have a motive. Didn't it all fit if Mine was the murderer? Everything would be solved.

Hoshikage, however, seemed to have guessed what was on the chief inspector's mind and let out a cynical laugh. He then proceeded to add further to the chief inspector's confusion.

'My dear Tadokoro, the murderer simply left the Zama residence and walked across the snow. There was never any trick. Only you didn't see those footprints. They were invisible to you!'

'Invisible! Invisible footprints!?'

The chief inspector muttered those same words over and over again. The murder simply walked across the snow. But his footprints weren't visible. And Hoshikage had even declared the murderer used no tricks at all. Who was the murderer? And how they did manage to walk out of the house?'

'Hahahaha.' Hoshikage cackled joyfully as he observed the confusion on Tadokoro's face. 'Tadokoro, I have now solved the whole mystery, but further investigation is required before I can tell you whether my solution is correct. May I borrow your man Mizuhara, so he can conduct those investigations on my behalf?'

'Of course. I'll give him his orders at once.' Mizuhara was one of the very few detectives who could get along with Hoshikage. They had worked together a couple of times before.

'It's nothing much. It should only take two or three days.'

The trader grinned once more as he looked at the chief inspector, who could only blink his eyes in wonder.

6

Who is the murderer? How did they escape without leaving footprints? What are invisible footprints anyway? While it was unlikely he could ever solve those three questions no matter how long he thought about them, the chief inspector kept repeating them to himself from the moment he woke up until he went to bed. He even thought about them in his dreams. He saw Mizuhara in the mornings and evenings, but the latter only smiled and never said a word. Nevertheless, he imagined the investigation was going as expected.

On the third evening, the chief inspector visited Hoshikage in his house in Meguro once again. The only difference from the previous visits was that a cheerful Mizuhara was sitting in the corner of the sofa with a gin fizz in his hands. Hoshikage was puffing smoke out of his virgin briar pipe. Tadokoro lit his American cigarette and waited for the discussion to start. The gas heater warmed the winter air inside the room to a pleasant temperature. Outside, the sky was starlit.

'Well, where shall I begin?'

Hoshikage, his eyes fixed on his beloved lustrous pipe, seemed not to have up his mind how to start.

'The keys to solving the mystery were all present in your account of the incident the other day.'

'But what were they?'

'For example, that Mine is an editor-in-chief who is willing to do anything for a story, or that the weapon was thrown into the garden.'

That was still not enough to explain the case. The chief inspector frowned as he stared at Hoshikage's splendid forehead. Was he imagining things, or was Mizuhara trying his best to suppress a laugh?

'The first thing you need to understand is that not everything Mine told you or wrote in his article was the truth. To give an example, he did not arrive at the Zama residence at nine-thirty.'

The chief inspector raised his eyebrows. So he was the one!

'At what time did he arrive, then?'

'While the snow was still falling. Around eight o'clock.'

Tadokoro's eyebrows shot up again. So his tale about having a drink at a food stall in Takadonobaba had been a lie. No wonder nobody at any of the food stalls remembered him.

But then Hoshikage added another comment that flabbergasted Tadokoro.

'I think you're misunderstanding me. Mine is not the murderer.'

'What! He isn't?'

'No. I told you the last time he wasn't the culprit.'

'Then who is?'

'Who do you think it is?'

Hoshikage grinned mischievously.

'But that means the murderer must have entered the house while the professor and Mine were together inside. Was Mine a witness to the murder?'

'Surely even you can't believe that. He might be an easy-going person, but even he wouldn't just look on while someone was being killed in front of him. That tells us Mine wasn't present when the murder was committed.'

Tadokoro nodded silently. So Mine had gone out for some reason, and according to the footprints left in the garden, the snow had already stopped falling by the time he returned to the Zama residence. Or so he thought.

32

But when he voiced his thoughts, they were once again greeted by a sneering laugh from the sofa. He turned around to glare at Mizuhara, then looked back at Hoshikage.

'Wrong?'

'Wrong. Mine was in the professor's study all the time. He was enjoying himself with the books and the whisky offered to him by his host. The bathtub had also been prepared, so if he'd wanted he could have taken a nice warm bath as well.'

'But that means…'

'Exactly. It was the professor who went out. He probably told Mine that something had suddenly come up and he had to leave right away, but he would be back in forty or fifty minutes. He told his guest to help himself and even take a bath if he felt cold. Being on close terms with the professor, Mine agreed without giving it much thought, and waited for his friend's return while having some biscuits. The reason the female student noticed the smell of alcohol on his breath was because he'd been drinking in the study.'

Well, that would explain everything. But then where had the professor gone?

'I'll tell you his destination and his purpose later. First, I want to point out that the professor's own footprints when he left the house would be covered by the snow, which was still falling and wouldn't stop until thirty minutes later. And he did step into the packed snow in the garden when he returned around nine o'clock, leaving clear footprints.'

Hoshikage had finally arrived at the core of the mystery. Tadokoro waited silently for him to continue, while Mizuhara sipped his gin fizz contentedly in the warmth afforded by the gas heater.

'Professor, what happened?'

'Urgh,' came the answer. It wasn't much of an answer, more like a groan. The professor staggered and tried to get his shoes off as he supported himself against a wall. Snow covered the shoulders and sleeves of his overcoat. His breathing was shallow and came in short bursts.

Mine supported him by the shoulders and led him to the sofa in the study. It was only then that he noticed a blueish discolouration, cyanosis, on the lips of the professor, which gave him great concern.

'Professor, what happened? Shall I call the doctor?'

'No, there's no need. Don't bother,' said the professor, obviously in extreme pain. His breathing was in shorter bursts than before. 'I'm a medical man myself. I know it's already too late.'

'But professor!'

'Listen to me. Look at my back.'

Mine saw there was a bulge at the back of the overcoat.

'What is that?'

'Take my coat off and you'll see.'

Mine gently took the overcoat off. The professor's shallow breathing was sounding more agonised by the minute.

'But it's a knife!'

'Yes. We had a disagreement and I was stabbed. The knife is now acting as a sort of plug, which is why I managed to walk back here without dying, but I expect I'll die immediately the knife is removed.'

Mine was speechless.

'But I don't resent him. I forgive the man who stabbed me.'

'But professor…'

'Don't talk. Let me speak while I still can. Mine, I'm going to forgive him. I want to make it seem as if I was attacked right here in the study. That will provide him… with an alibi…'

Mine assumed the professor meant Donryū, but how could he forgive that man? But now was not the time to question anything.

'Listen, you must pretend you arrived here after I died, and that you discovered my body. Do you understand?'

'Ye—yes,' Mine answered obediently. He was determined to fulfil the dying wishes of a man he respected so much.

'You know nothing at all. Forget about coming here at eight, forget about me leaving the house.'

'I've already forgotten.'

But, even as he was answering the professor, Mine was doing some calculating of his own. He realised that if they featured the professor's demise in the promotion campaign for the upcoming issue, it would be a tremendous boost for sales, especially if they insinuated that the murderer was Donryū Ōta… The last round-table talk with Professor Zama! A killer psychic! How wonderful, what a fantastic idea!

'Mine, did you get all that? Now wipe the fingerprints off the handle of the knife.'

As Mine wiped the handle clean with his handkerchief, the professor closed his eyes with a satisfied look.

'Once you're done, you can help me lie down on the floor.'

The editor-in-chief did as the professor requested, but the simple action seemed to have quite an effect on the professor, who coughed painfully.

'Mine,' he called out between coughs, 'this will be the last thing I ask of you. Please pull the knife out of my back and throw it away in the garden. Nobody must know I returned home with a knife in my back.'

'Ye—yes...'

'We can't have any bloodstains on your clothes, so place my overcoat over the knife as you pull it out, to contain the blood. Don't forget to leave the overcoat outside as well.'

'Yes.'

'Do it now!'

Mine crouched down on the floor. He may have been known as a heartless editor, but even he hesitated to condemn a person he respected to an instant death.

He called out to the professor, but the latter did not respond. Signs of discolouration were starting to show in his nails. Mine trembled as he grasped the handle of the knife.

'I'm sorry!'

As instructed, Mine covered the knife with the overcoat as he pulled it out in one go. There was a moment of resistance, but then the knife slid out easily. Fresh blood squirted from the wound. For a moment, the professor's eyelids seem to quiver, but then the life drained visibly out of him.

By the time Mine returned to his senses, the professor had become a corpse. Emotions of pain and sadness raged like a storm within him.

When he finally got a grip on himself, he remembered he had to get rid of the murder weapon. But his own fingerprints were now on it, so he wiped the knife clean again. He switched off the study light and drew the curtains open. He opened the window and threw the knife into the middle of the garden. He made a bundle of the overcoat and threw it into the garden as well. Once he had finished, he could feel the tension ebbing from his body as he sat down in the swivel chair.

He stared vacantly at the garden outside, illuminated by the porch light and the moon. As he sat there in his chair, he reflected on the tremendous willpower the professor had shown by walking back home while fatally wounded. What an impressive mind the professor had under the circumstances, to be able to think of what had to be done after his death. Mine took another look at the dark silhouette of the rolled-up overcoat beneath the moonlight. But as he stood up to close the window, he noticed the professor's footprints leading from the front gate to the porch.

He turned pale at the sight. Damn! The professor had left him a huge problem. With those footprints there, it would be obvious to anyone that the professor had gone out. What should he do, what should he do!? His flustered mind drew a blank.

He stayed in a state of panic for a while, but eventually calmed down. In fact, he had thought of a great idea. That was it! He could just claim that the footprints in the garden were his.

The editor inside him started to do a small victory dance. It was a murder where the culprit had left no footprints at the scene of the crime: an impossible murder! Didn't such a situation fit perfectly with psychics and spirit mediums?

Perhaps he should write a spectacular article himself for the next issue. He would follow the professor's wishes, and make it a story about him being killed in his own study. What should the title be? A murder in a room inside a house surrounded by snow. That was it! The white locked room sounded good. The white locked room!

Once the idea took hold, Mine became like a sleepwalker. With unsteady steps, he started cleaning up the biscuits and whisky he had consumed. He was only awakened from his trance-like state when Kimiko Satō rang the doorbell.

7

'I have to ask again, where had the professor gone, and for what reason?'

'What do you think?'

'I wouldn't be asking if I had any ideas,' snapped the chief inspector irritably. He was angry now he realised that the editor had played him for a fool. He'd get him the next time they met in person.

'Let me put the question differently,' said Hoshikage. 'The professor said he would forgive the man who killed him, but would he really have felt like that if his killer had been Donryū Ōta?'

'Given they had that big row, I doubt it.'

'I agree. Which means that the professor wasn't being honest when he said that. I concluded that his real purpose in making that statement was to divert suspicion from the real culprit.'

36

'What do you mean?'

'The very first thought that occurred to me was that the killer was someone of the opposite sex. Envision if you will a man who is respected by all as a gentleman, and who prides himself on such a reputation, being stabbed by a woman. I can readily imagine such a man chivalrously concealing the truth. Mizuhara, present your results.'

The detective gulped down his drink and pulled a small notebook from his pocket.

'Following Mr. Hoshikage's instructions, I visited the boarding house in Tozuka where the student Kimiko Satō lives. There I learned that the relationship between her and the professor was not only that of student and teacher, but was also financial. As you know, Ms. Satō is quite attractive and, to put it bluntly, the professor became infatuated with her. The gossips there didn't know that the gentleman with greying hair who visited her was Professor Zama. Kimiko claimed he was her uncle. But recently Kimiko found herself a younger boyfriend and they found themselves in a love triangle. Even a grand professor of medicine is just like one of us when it comes to such matters, and the two had fights about it.'

'So that evening, the professor went to her room in Tozuka?' the chief inspector asked.

'The professor must have had enough, so he'd stopped making payments to her. I checked with the bank. I believe that Kimiko threatened to go public unless the professor continued to pay. That's why the professor went out while it was still snowing. But their discussion went badly and, in the heat of the moment, Kimiko must have stabbed the professor in the back with her fruit knife. It was one of a set of six, and the remaining five were in her cupboard.'

Mizuhara had waited for Kimiko to leave before taking a look. The professor had been intensely fearful of his relationship going public, so the chief inspector could understand why he had chosen to go out on a cold night while the snow was still falling.

'The incident only occurred because the professor insisted on guarding his bachelorhood. Everything in the universe consists of connections between positive and negative phenomena. To go against the will of nature and remain single is like defying the gods,' said Ryūzō Hoshikage, who was single himself. He seemed to be serious and joking at the same time. The chief inspector didn't know how to react, so he smiled back vaguely.

'When you told me the professor had bled internally, it occurred to me that he might have walked home himself. That was my first step towards the solution.'

'So I was on the wrong trail entirely,' said the policeman, rubbing his nose. 'But could you explain about the cat being incinerated?'

'Isn't that obvious now all the rest has been explained? If Mine's shoes were found at the entrance, the whole game would be up. So he had to get rid of them. And the most effective way to get rid of something is to incinerate it. When you mentioned that a warm bath had been prepared, it should have been obvious that he'd burnt his shoes in the furnace.'

It all made sense. The chief inspector rubbed his nose again.

'But one has to remember that the smell of burnt leather will go up the chimney and irritate the noses of people outside. That is why it was necessary to point the finger at something else before other rumours spread. Which was the purpose of the anonymous letter sent to the Animal Protection League. Mine confessed he thought of it after he finally returned home that night.'

'With hindsight it all seems so logical. But how did you deduce that Mine had sprained his ankle?'

Tadokoro recalled the proverb "Better to ask the way than go astray." He was sure the explanation would be simple, but he himself couldn't think of it. Hoshikage had previously said it was just a hunch, with one chance in three of success. But how?

'From what you told me I realised that Mine must have switched shoes, in which case there were only three possibilities: the professor's shoes would fit him perfectly, they'd be too big, or they'd be too small for him. In the first two instances, there wouldn't be a problem, but if they were too small, he'd get blisters on his feet. But he couldn't take the professor's shoes off, as that would attract your attention, so he had to cope with the pain. He could hardly confess that he got blisters because the shoes were too small for him, so what better excuse for his limping than to say he sprained his ankle?'

Having explained, Hoshikage started stuffing tobacco in his pipe.

'So the reason Kimiko came to the house was...'

'To see how the professor was doing. She must have been worried about him. But she probably saw through Mine's lies the moment she saw the professor's shoes in the entrance hall. Lies that protected her.'

Tadokoro remained silent. He was thinking of something completely different at that moment. He had finally understood the mysterious comment Hoshikage had made the previous night. After they had finished the questioning at the Zama residence, Tadokoro had ordered a detective to take Kimiko Satō back home by jeep and had watched her as she left the house. He recalled what he had seen at that precise moment. The murderer had indeed left the Zama residence simply by walking across the snow, just as Hoshikage had told him. There never was any trickery!

The culprit was arrested the following day and made a full confession. Her account of events proved Hoshikage's deductions and Mizuhara's investigation correct in every way.

Whose Body?

1

It is commonly said that those with a fondness for liquor do not like sweets, but Atsushi Akutagawa, an art merchant in Ginza, was someone who was able to enjoy the best of both worlds. He loved Curaçao and mint cocktails, but also the sweet azuki bean porridge *shiruko,* and every New Year, he would put away two bottles of sweet *toso* spiced sake.

It was the third of March, the Peach Festival, also known as *Hinamatsuri,* Doll's Day or Girls' Day, one of five seasonal festivals when mothers and daughters set out displays of ornamental dolls representing the Emperor, Empress and court staff from the Heian period.

That year, the third of March fell on a Sunday, so Akutagawa let his employees run the shop. After breakfast, he started on the sake while admiring the *hina* doll display. One bottle was already empty, and he was working on the second, when his phone started to ring. He could sense his wife talking far away, but he dozed off and started to snore gently.

'Wake up, dear.'

It was his wife, who appeared agitated.

'It's a phone call.'

'Who is it?'

'Mr. Ikeda from the Shūyō Group?'

As the wife of an art merchant, she was quite knowledgeable about the various artists' groups. Inosuke Ikeda had been in the same year as Akutagawa at art school. He had once specialised in Western-style paintings, but had recently gone through formalist, cubist and expressionist phases to arrive at a new style of his own. He had been a mainstay of the art scene for several years.

'What does he want? An advance?'

'Just answer the phone!' urged his wife.

Akutagawa was suddenly wide awake as he took the phone.

'It's me. What's the matter?'

'That's what I wanted to ask you. What is this parcel all about?'

The strange reply rendered Akutagawa speechless for a moment.

'Wha—what parcel?'

'Hey, no jokes now. You even sent it registered.'

'Registered? I have no idea what you're babbling about. Calm down and tell me what's the matter.'

'Have you been drinking? I can smell it even on this end of the line.'

'Just had a small sip of sake. I'm not drunk at all. Describe the parcel to me.'

From Akutagawa's tone, the painter finally realised that he really wasn't joking. The voice on the receiver suddenly turned serious.

'You really don't know anything?'

'I don't even know what I don't know. You call me out of the blue with questions.'

'Really? Then it must be a prank, but who did it?'

'You tell me.'

Ikeda seemed to be thinking hard as he answered.

'A registered parcel was just delivered, with your name as the sender. I assumed you'd sent me a present, so I opened it... What do you think I found inside?'

'Stop teasing and tell me!' Akutagawa raised his voice.

'An empty medicine bottle.'

'An empty bottle?'

'Yes. The label says H_2SO_4. I seem to remember that's sulphuric acid?'

'Beats me. I'm no good at chemistry. I only know that H_2O is carbon monoxide.'

'Don't be stupid. H_2O isn't carbon monoxide, it's water.'

The artist was probably grinning on the other end of the line.

'So you really have nothing to do with this?'

'I swear it wasn't me.'

'But who did it then?'

'We'll find out sooner or later. All our friends have a childish side to them.'

The two discussed other matters before hanging up. At that point, Akutagawa could not have imagined the sinister meaning behind the curious parcel.

But things repeated themselves shortly afterwards.

'Dear, it's another phone call.'

'Again? Who is it this time?'

42

'I don't know. It's a woman.' His wife articulated each word loudly and clearly. She seemed suspicious.

Akutagawa picked up the receiver under his wife's watchful eye.

'Sorry to have kept you waiting. Akutagawa speaking.'

'Hello? Is that Atsushi Akutagawa? Why did you do it? I was all set to start on my new creation, but now I'm distracted. You knew that would happen. Why did you play this prank on me!'

The woman sounded hysterical and his wife was listening in from the parlour. He felt surrounded by enemies.

'E—excuse me, who are you!'

'Utako Ui.'

Utako Ui? Wasn't there a sculptress among the members of the Independent Artists Association by that name? She had focused on terracotta for a period, making creations very similar to Tanagra figurines, but lately she had returned to her first passion and her torso sculpture had won an award at an exhibition last autumn.

'What are you calling me about?'

'The parcel you sent me. I'll set the police on you!'

'Just hold on. I know your name, but the two of us haven't even met, so why would I be sending you a parcel?'

Utako Ui didn't sound convinced.

'But you did do it? Denying it would be cowardly.'

'Someone must have used my name. The same thing happened this morning. A friend called me, but fortunately the misunderstanding was soon cleared up.'

'It happened to someone else too?'

'Yes. Did you get an empty bottle with H_2SO_4 on the label?'

'No.' The sculptress raised her voice in a shriek. 'It was a revolver!'

2

More than a whole day had passed. On the afternoon of the fifth of March, the section chief of the Investigative Division sat at his desk, examining two objects. One was a common Browning. It was not loaded, but a look inside the barrel showed that it had been fired recently. There was a smell of burnt metal and gunpowder. Utako Ui had filed a report with her local police box the day before, saying it had arrived in a parcel.

43

The other object was a transparent, colourless 500cc glass bottle for strong poison, with a glass stopper and a yellow-stained label bearing the scientific formula for sulphuric acid. There was a thick colourless liquid at the bottom of the bottle, which the forensic report had confirmed as concentrated sulphuric acid. Inosuke Ikeda had brought the bottle to his local police box two nights ago, on the evening of the third.

Once reported, both items had been transported to the Metropolitan Police Department at Sakuradamon.

Later that afternoon a detective from the department visited the Akutagawa Gallery. After making his way through a crowd of people, he found Akutagawa sitting in a chair, talking to a man wearing a beret, probably an artist. The man left and the detective presented his business card to Akutagawa. The master of the gallery was in his mid-forties and looked like a Zen monk, with a double chin reminiscent of a Daruma doll (1).

'Mr. Detective, you can't believe how frustrated I am,' he said, offering the man a chair. 'Ikeda comes here often, and is quite an understanding man, but Utako Ui is someone I basically don't know at all. Why would I send someone I don't know a gun? And if I did, I'd use former Prime Minister Shigeru Yoshida's name. Hahaha!'

The art dealer laughed heartily at his own joke.

'Anyway, someone used my name to hide their own, and caused me a lot of trouble. You need to find out from the post office who sent the parcels before their memories fade. My face is easy enough to remember!'

'Do you know anyone who might do such a thing?'

'My wife asked me the same thing. I have some strange friends, but no one who would mail a revolver.'

The detective left the gallery with little to show for his visit. He took a bus to the Central Post Office, where the mysterious sender had mailed his parcels. Looking at the sea of people waiting, he felt it quite unlikely that the clerks would have remembered the sender, but he went to the parcel counter and asked to see the clerk on duty. After asking some questions, he left the building twenty minutes later and took a bus to Ogikubo.

(1) A traditional round hollow doll modelled after Bodhidharma, founder of the Zen tradition of Buddhism.

His next stop was Kugayama, to visit the atelier of the painter Shunsuke Egi of the Kōyō Group. He calmly explained the case he was working on to the well-dressed artist, who seemed younger than his forty-four years.

'I visited the Central Post Office, hoping they would know who sent the parcels. Fortunately they had been sent by registered mail, so there were copies of the forms. We thought that only two parcels had been sent, but to my surprise there were three, and the third parcel was addressed to you.'

'Yes, I did receive a parcel on the afternoon of the third. I'd met Mr. Akutagawa once or twice, but we hardly knew each other well enough to be sending presents, so I thought that was strange. I opened the parcel and I must say I was quite disappointed.'

The detective asked him what was inside. The artist stepped out of the room and returned with the parcel in question. 'I guessed he would send me a letter explaining everything later, so I kept it in storage.'

He unwrapped the paper to reveal a small wooden box, inside which was a white vinyl rope, curled around like a snake. He had only been sent a rope!

A gun, sulphuric acid and a rope. They were like the three topics for a rakugo improvisation act (2). The rope looked quite clean, perhaps newly purchased. The detective held it in his hands. It was about six or seven millimetres thick and two metres long.

'You mentioned there were also a gun and a bottle with sulphuric acid. Given that the gun had been fired, was anyone shot?'

'That's definitely a possibility.'

'And the sulphuric acid?'

'It's not a pretty thought. It could be used to make someone's face unrecognizable, and the same for fingerprints.'

'How horrible. Then this rope...'

'There's only one way to use such a rope.'

'This is truly frightening. Just imagining someone was strangled with this makes my blood run cold.'

The spring sun had already started setting in the west, and a cold darkness had begun to creep into the atelier.

(2) Rakugo is a traditional verbal entertainment act, where one storyteller (the rakugoka) tells a long, comical story, using only a sitting cushion and a paper fan as props.

'At this point, I can't tell you whether such a murder has already occurred, or whether this is all just a prank. Can you think of anyone who might have done this?'

'Nobody comes to mind. No one at all.'

The artist's gentle eyes had clouded over. He was like a child in fear. When the detective asked to take the rope away, he immediately gave permission, as if he were getting rid of a cursed item.

3

Utako Ui's atelier was located in Komagome Hayashichō, near the old residence of the poet Kōtarō Takamura, which had sadly been destroyed in the war.

The sculptress was wearing a bright red sweater and black slacks, and the large golden rings hanging from her ears would sway and flicker each time she spoke. She was a not unattractive woman in her mid-thirties, heavily built and with distinctive facial features. On a stand near one wall were the abstract plaster sculptures the detective had seen earlier in an art magazine. She was said to have been influenced by Mondrian.

Her face turned grim when the detective asked about the parcel, and it was clearly not a happy memory.

'It was really creepy,' said Utako as she turned to the young man sitting next to her. 'It was Doll's Day. My disciples and I were having tea. When the parcel arrived, I assumed it was a present because of Doll's Day, but when I opened it there was a revolver lying there, its cold metal bare to the eye. Everyone gasped and the whole room turned silent.'

Each time the woman looked at the young man, he nodded. He wasn't much of a speaker.

'My disciple here used to be in the Self Defence Force and has experience with guns. He took a look at the revolver, and scared us all when he told us it had been fired recently. We all could all feel our legs trembling.'

'I wasn't trying to scare you. It was clear to the eye,' the young man observed.

'It was very upsetting, and I was under the impression it was the work of Mr. Akutagawa. I was furious, so I got him on the phone and gave him a piece of my mind. He denied it, of course.'

The detective asked her whether she had any idea who else might have sent it, but she shook her head.

'Would you happen to know Inosuke Ikeda?'

'I've heard the name. Of the Shūyō Group, I believe?'

'And Shunsuke Egi?'

'No. Have you?' she asked the young man sitting next to her, but the art-loving boy shook his head silently.

When the detective left the Ui residence he found it was already dark outside. The evening had brought silence to the high-class residential area, and the streets were empty.

His final stop was Inosuke Ikeda's home in Kamimeguro, 6-chōme. He took the bus from Shibuya, got off at the top of a hill and found the place in a silent spot between two temples.

Inosuke Ikeda was the same age as the owner of the Akutagawa Gallery, but he looked far younger, probably due to his slender build. He had a long face and small eyes, which gave him a sleepy look, and he always appeared to be grinning sardonically.

'As I told you earlier when you called, I don't know anything that could help you,' he stated firmly.

'I often swing by Akutagawa's gallery, so I thought he was playing a prank on me. But when I called him, he said he knew nothing about it, so I tried every single one of my close friends. Nobody admitted to it. That's when I heard that Ms. Ui had also received such a parcel. When I learned she had been sent a revolver, I thought the whole business was a bit too creepy, so that evening, I went to the closest police box to report it.'

'Has anything out of the ordinary happened since then?'

'No, nothing I can think of. But not knowing who sent the parcels and why is really eerie. So I try not to think about it.'

'Do you know Shunsuke Egi?'

'I've seen him at various events, but I am not interested in his style, so I've never talked to him.' He paused and he gazed at his visitor. 'Does Mr. Egi have anything to do with this?'

'No, no. By the way, what about Ms. Ui?'

'I don't know her at all. I am only slightly interested by the fact she is a female artist. Not as a fellow artist, but as a man of course, hahaha.'

His eyes looked even smaller when he laughed.

Once again, the detective had failed to make a discovery. He assumed some incident must have happened, but until he could find out what it was, there was not much more that he could do. He was therefore not particularly disappointed when he left the artist's home.

4

The incident finally occurred shortly after ten o'clock on the evening of the tenth of March. An emergency call came in, reporting the discovery of a corpse in a cellar room in a burnt-down building in Kanda Sarugakuchō. When the operator had asked for details, the caller had hung up. Fortunately, MPD Patrol Car 35 was near the Kasugachō crossing, so it was dispatched to the scene at once.

Sarugakuchō was an extended block located below the elevated Surugadai neighbourhood. It was something between a residential and a shopping area. The patrol car passed beneath Suidō Bridge and turned left from the main road with the train tracks. It was an unusually foggy night, and the fog had only turned thicker with each hour. The patrol car slowed down once it entered Sarugakuchō and started searching for its destination beneath the grey veil.

'Isn't the Kōryō Building the only one around here that's been burnt down?' asked one of the nervous young police officers.

'I've never been here before. Where is it?' replied the other.

'I think it's about a hundred metres down this road, to the right.'

After the brief exchange they stopped talking and kept their eyes open.

The Kōryō Building was a small, four-storey construction that had indeed been burnt down in the war, after which the New Kōryō Building had been built on the main street near the train tracks. The rent for the defunct plot had proved to be too high, so the remnants of the burnt-out building were still standing.

'This is it, stop!'

The two parked the car and stood on the cold, wet pavement. The houses in the neighbourhood were all dark, either because they were empty, or because the residents were asleep, the officers did not know which. There was total silence and the fog seemed even thicker.

Like the antennae of an insect, the lights from the policemen's torches illuminated the wet concrete remains, searching for the cellar.

'There it is. I'll go down, you stay up here,' said one of them, as he made his way around a pile of bricks and descended the stairs into the abyss. He counted them as he went down, all twenty-three of them. A grey wall stood in front of him at the bottom, with a door to his right.

48

It had apparently not been oiled, as it made the noise of a longhorn beetle when he pushed it open, releasing a cloud of stuffy, mouldy air. There was a corridor straight in front of him, with a door on the left leading to a large dimly-lit room about fifty square metres in size. A large wooden screen stood against the right-hand wall. There was also a broken chair, but no corpse.

The young officer continued down the corridor. He found another door to his left, unlocked. He peered inside and saw a storage room, filled with various objects: a pile of tables, a broken portable heater, apple boxes, two loose doors. Eventually, the circle of light from his torch illuminated a sofa and he gasped.

The dark leather sofa was torn and stuffing material had come out. On top of it lay a man, his face covered by a newspaper. He was wearing black shoes, charcoal grey trousers and a gaudy green spring jacket, but the blood coming from his chest had stained his clothes dark.

The man's left hand was resting on the sofa, while his right arm was dangling above the floor. Both his hands had been horribly burned, and the parts of the sofa beneath ruined, probably by acid. The officer had seen dead bodies before and usually remained calm, but when he removed the newspaper to take a look at the face of the corpse, he dropped his torch on the floor due to the sheer shock. Although it only lasted a moment, he would never forget the sight as long as he lived. The corpse had no head, and the sight of the horrendous wound would forever haunt him in his nightmares.

Later, the young officer couldn't recall how he had managed to make his way out of the storage room and back up the stairs. He only remembered shouting to his colleague waiting above, who had then run to the police car.

'This is MPD 35. We've found a headless corpse in the ruins of a building. Both hands have been burnt by chemicals, and he's been shot in the chest, over.'

Thirty minutes later, uniformed and plainclothes police officers were crawling around the cellar floor.

For some time they had been expecting to discover a body and had been patiently waiting, so they were eager to get started.

Once the forensic investigators had put away their cameras, the police surgeon started to examine the body and the unit commander ordered his men out. It was vital to retrieve the bullets from the victim's chest and determine whether they had been fired from the revolver in the parcel. It was also necessary to determine whether the fingerprints had been burnt off with sulphuric acid, hydrochloric acid or nitric acid. It was assumed the man had been strangled with the vinyl rope, but it was necessary to check whether there was blood congestion in his lungs. And, of course, the time of death had to be established.

The police surgeon examined the victim's back, speaking without looking up, as if he were addressing the corpse.

'Two shots in the back. One through the waist, bullet stuck there. The other penetrated the upper part of the stomach.'

Once the preliminary examination of the body was finished, they went through his clothes and possessions. The fabric of his spring jacket and his clothes were of good material and well-made. They seemed to come from well-known stores, which suggested the victim was someone who dressed smartly. The name Okabe was found inside the jacket, as well as on his shirt.

'Okabe, Okabe. Do you know of an artist named Okabe?'

'I know my criminals, but artists I don't know. How do you know he's an artist anyway?'

'I'm not completely sure, of course, but don't you think this murder stinks of paint? It's almost certainly connected to that business with the parcels, and considering this guy's clothes, I bet you he's an artist,' said the unit chief as he checked each pocket. A pipe, a wallet with about five thousand yen, a hand mirror and a comb. All the items looked expensive. When the pipe-loving detective noticed the white mark on the briar pipe, he couldn't help but feel jealous because of the Dunhill pipe.

Once the victim's body had been removed, the hunt for the bullet that had gone through him began. Hunting for a bullet in all the trash was like looking for a pearl floating in the ocean, but they couldn't give up. An officer was dispatched to buy a 100-watt bulb to light the room.

About ten detectives were now clearing the room in an organised manner, moving the apple boxes and the tables out of the way. After an hour all the corners of the room had been searched, but the bullet had still not been found.

'Perhaps the killer took the bullet with him,' someone suggested.

Now the room was illuminated, the unit chief could see that there was a window in one wall, allowing a view of the adjoining storage room. He thought the bullet might have passed into the second room and decided to search it himself.

The room didn't only look cold because of the dim light in the ceiling, but also because it was mostly empty. There was a chair with a broken leg and a high, sturdy wooden screen nearly two metres wide standing against the wall dividing this room from the other.

'Look at this,' he said to a detective who had followed him in, pointing to bullet hole in the chocolate-coloured screen. There was indeed a small hole in the screen and, looking through it, they could see into the brightly-lit room next door.

'Here's the bullet!' shouted another detective standing near the opposite wall.

Obviously, the bullet had passed through the screen to hit the wall, but had then lost much of its power and had merely left a small indent there before falling to the floor. There were white stucco fragments on the tip of the slightly flattened bullet, which the detective put into a plastic bag and carefully placed in the evidence box.

The investigation of the crime scene being over for the night, everyone left, save for some officers on guard from the local police station. Once they were outside, they found the fog to be as thick as ever. To the unit chief, the fog seemed to be covering the whole case.

Everyone present at the crime scene had been troubled by the contradictions discovered there. It could be assumed that the culprit had decapitated the victim and burnt his fingers off in order to hide his identity. But in that case, why hadn't the murderer ripped the name tags in the clothes out and taken the victim's possessions with him? It might well be that the killer had dressed the victim in someone else's clothes, to make the police think the victim was someone called Okabe. If so, pursuing that line of reasoning could eventually lead to solving the case.

5

It was now imperative to learn who Okabe was. From a newspaper the police learned details about him.

Otsugorō Okabe was a member of the Independent Artists Association who wrote sharply critical reviews for art magazines under the pen name Hankotsu. For that he was unpopular, and most people tried to keep their distance from him. There had been rumours he might return to Paris. His colleagues all agreed that, although his critiques were well-written, Okabe's own painting skills were not worthy of much praise. The police were surprised to learn that he had been living with Utako Ui in her home in Hayashichō, but they had broken up near the end of the previous year.

That fact greatly surprised Chief Inspector Onitsura, now heading the investigation, who immediately decided to call on the female artist again.

After receiving the autopsy report and the results from forensics, he headed the same afternoon for Hayashichō. The fog of the day before had cleared completely, resulting in a bright spring day. The artist's hands were covered in clay and she was wearing working clothes, which she quickly changed for the red sweater and slacks she had worn before.

'When I saw the name Okabe in the newspapers, I assumed it was someone else with the same name. But then on the radio they mentioned his full name, Otsugorō Okabe. You can't imagine how shocked I was. I knew you would visit me again. I still can't believe he was murdered.'

After washing her hands, she sat down and offered Onitsura Pall Mall cigarettes, lighting one for herself. He told her about the discovery the previous night.

'When was he killed?'

'He died somewhere between a week and ten days ago. That would put it between the first and third of the month.'

'How did he die?'

'He was strangled.'

'Oh, on the radio they said he was shot…'

'He was shot twice in the back, but that only disabled him, so he was then strangled.'

'How horrible! Why didn't the murderer simply shoot him again?'

'We don't know. Perhaps there were only two bullets, or perhaps the killer was afraid someone outside might hear. But that's not all. The fingerprints of the body were burnt off with sulphuric acid.'

'Oh!' Utako cried out. The Pall Mall fell from her fingers and onto the table.

'There is still a lot we don't know at this point,' said Onitsura, picking the cigarette up. 'We suspect the culprit used a vinyl rope to strangle the victim. It's still a mystery whether the culprit had prepared that item, or simply happened to have it to hand.'

Utako didn't seem to grasp the full extent of what Onitsura was saying. She seemed reluctant to interrupt and limited herself to the occasional gasp.

'Did you want to say something?'

'Well, yes, what about the vinyl rope?'

'Further explanation is needed. On the same day you received your parcel, Inosuke Ikeda and Shunsuke Egi each received one as well. Mr. Ikeda was sent an empty bottle of sulphuric acid, and Mr. Egi was sent a vinyl rope.'

'Oh, how bizarre!'

'It appears the murderer sent the objects he used to the three of you, for some reason. This morning I received a report confirming that the revolver you were sent was the one used to shoot the victim.'

Her face turned pale and her large physique appeared to shrink. She wrapped her arms around herself. Not knowing why the killer had sent those horrible tools of death was what made the whole business so eerie.

'We haven't shared the information with the public yet, but the victim might not actually be Mr. Okabe.'

'Oh!' cried Utako in surprise. She didn't seem quite sure whether she should be pleased with the news or not, and waited for the chief inspector to continue.

'I need to explain this carefully. The mysterious sender posted the parcels on the morning of the second of March, so we can assume the murder occurred in the early hours of the second, or the night of the first, because it's unlikely the victim was murdered during the day. However, Mr. Okabe was seen alive after the parcels were posted, in the afternoon of the second of March, to be precise.'

Utako Ui's eyes opened wide. If the victim assumed to be Okabe was actually someone else, why were they wearing Okabe's clothes? After a moment, she asked in an emotionally restrained tone: 'Couldn't someone have been mistaken for him?'

'Do you know the art supply shop Deidosha in Kanda? The owner there called us. A person believed to be Mr. Okabe bought ten picture frames there.'

'And he is sure about the day?'

'Yes, and there's a receipt, so there's no doubt about the date. The boy who worked at the shop that day still remembered, and was sure it was Mr. Okabe. The owner was in a room in the back, but he saw him as well and confirms it was Mr. Okabe. They say he was wearing flannel trousers and a gabardine jacket.'

'Perhaps they're mistaken? He usually bought his materials from a shop in Kyōbashi.'

She looked as if she would have preferred it to be a case of mistaken identity.

'Yes, that point bothers us too. But the people at Deidosha say they are sure, as they knew his face from photographs. That's why I believe that the only person who can determine whether the body belongs to Mr. Okabe is you. Would you be willing to take a look?'

It took a while, because artists are sensitive people, but she finally made up her mind to comply with the request and put on a gorgeous green duffle coat and red beret wholly unsuitable for the task ahead. In the police car on the way to Ōtsuka, Onitsura made use of the time to learn more about Okabe.

'Would Mr. Okabe have anything particular in his medical history, such as pleurisy?'

'He never mentioned anything like that. In fact, he was always boasting how nothing could hurt him, so I don't think he ever suffered from any serious medical condition.'

'The corpse also lacks any distinctive characteristics, which is what makes it so difficult to identify him. Suppose Mr. Okabe himself is the culprit and is on the run, do you have any idea where he might have fled?'

'Well, he was born in Hokkaidō, so I would imagine he'd go there. Of course, I don't know how a murderer's mind works. Have you searched his home?'

'Yes. But he left in the afternoon of the first of March, and never returned. We searched his rooms, but we found nothing that could shed a light on his whereabouts. Forgive me for intruding, but could you tell us about what kind of person Mr. Okabe was, and how you broke up?'

The chief inspector purposely did not look at the sculptress as he asked the question. Experience had taught him that this was the most effective method to induce people to talk. The car passed through Hikawashitamachi and started climbing the sloping road again.

'Is it necessary?'

'I wouldn't ask if it wasn't. It's possible that when I learn what kind of person he was and why you broke up, we could discover why he might have sent those strange parcels.'

'What did Mr. Ikeda and Mr. Egi tell you about him?'

'They said that they could well imagine Mr. Okabe having done it, as a form of pestering. The two of them were often the target of Mr. Okabe's criticisms and they often argued with him about that.'

'Yes, he never minced his words and always spoke his mind. If anyone tried to retaliate, he would become even more determined to attack them,' replied Utako, who had finally decided to talk.

'He was always so stubborn, which often led to trouble. But deep down, he was a gentle person, just a bit self-centred and spoilt. He was definitely not the kind of person who would murder someone else for any reason, and I can't imagine him being hated so much someone would want to kill him, either. So if he has indeed been murdered, I have no idea who would have done it. To put it fancifully, you could say we broke up because our visions as artists were incompatible. But I must admit I'd had enough of his self-centred, stubborn personality.'

'So what is your opinion about the parcels?'

'I tend to agree with Mr. Ikeda and Mr. Egi.'

'Harassment?'

'Yes.'

Utako Ui uttered that word with such determination that no other interpretation was possible. The car swayed wildly as it passed the large, metal gates of the Medical Examiner's Office and, between the trees, the two caught glimpses of the dark, stately building.

6

The woman was small, barely over 1.5 metres. Her nimble movements suggested she had done sports in her college years. She was wearing a plain grey collarless two-piece dress that made her look more mature, but the manner in which she spoke and the expression on her face still had something childish about them, and she appeared to be twenty-two at most.

She opened her enamel handbag and out came a fittingly small business card. As she looked up at Shunsuke Egi, she smiled in a natural manner. Dimples appeared on her face as she smiled, which caused a moment of temptation, but when Shunsuke saw the name on her business card, he changed his mind. On it was written: Kimiko Kiriyama, Washizu Detective Agency – Investigative Section.

'Oh, so you're a detective? Well, that's a surprise. But I can't remember having done anything wrong. What do you want with me?'

Kiriyama smiled again before she answered his question. Her red lips parted to reveal white buck teeth, which only made her look even cuter. Shunsuke was much taken by her and felt he wanted to answer any questions she might fire at him.

'I've been hired to investigate the incident of the decapitated body found in the cellar of the Kōryō Building in Kanda,' said Kiriyama, taking out a small notebook and looking at Shunsuke with a pencil in her hand. The business-like gesture was definitely not that of someone who had only become a detective recently.

Shunsuke Egi began to recall the incident, which had started to fade from his mind. The identity of the decapitated corpse was still unknown and, despite an extensive manhunt, the whereabouts of the disappeared Otsugorō Okabe remained unknown. Given what had happened with the culprits Shōda of the Mekka murder case and Ōtani of the trunk incident, the authorities were preparing for a long battle of endurance. Okabe's picture had been printed 500,000 times and his face spread across the country. Although there were dozens of artists with whom Okabe had argued, whenever Egi found himself working alone in his spacious atelier, he couldn't help imagining Okabe hiding behind the shrubs in the garden and trembled at the thought. But after a month had gone by uneventfully, the feeling of fear had dissipated.

'The client who asked me investigate the case has a different theory from that of the police, and has retained me to gather any information in support of their theory. For example...'

The woman probed deeply with her questions, never getting distracted. After a while she apologised for the intrusion and flew off like a little bird. Later, when Shunsuke Egi thought back to the interview, he had no idea who her client was, nor could he imagine in what manner their ideas on the case differed from those of the police.

The beautiful female detective appeared at various places and each time, falling for her charm, everyone she talked to would pause in their work and go over the case with her.

At Deidosha, she fired questions at the owner and the clerk, which finally dispelled the doubts she had about their testimony.

'You know how *ezōshi* artists needed to be able to know to recall the stage name of any kabuki actor just by seeing his face? It's the same for us. Doesn't matter whether their style is Western or Japanese, or they're in paintings or sculptures. We know all artists. Even with first-time customers, we know they're this-or-that from

Nika or the Seiryū Group. And we're not only talking about the *Grand maîtres* here. So I am absolutely sure that the person who bought those frames from us was Mr. Okabe.'

The exceptionally tall elderly owner had emphasised the word "absolutely" as he spoke.

The female detective also paid a visit to the buildings near the crime scene, a shop selling decorative tiles, a publisher specialising in transcripts of high school lectures and a trading company on the verge of shutting down, but unfortunately she learned nothing of interest because they all shut at dusk and everyone had already gone home. Kiriyama wouldn't give up however, so she went to the Kōryō Building itself to speak with the concierges. There were two, one of them an elderly man with a beard, and the other a slow, androgynous individual.

'So they still haven't caught him? He's probably laying low somewhere.'

'I was really shocked when I first heard the news. Never in my dreams could I imagine something like that would happen. The two of us had carried something down to the other storage room, you see,' said the elderly man.

'Little did we know there was a headless body lying in the room next door.'

'Haven't set foot in the cellar since. It's lucky we seldom need to go down there, but I wouldn't dare go alone now.'

'Haha, it's kind of pathetic, but I wouldn't go alone either.'

One of them was smoking a traditional *kiseru* pipe, the other a Bat cigarette, but both were speaking freely as they eyed the attractive detective. She, however, had learnt nothing interesting and looked very depressed as she left their office. Despite her meticulous investigation over the last few days, she had obtained zero results.

Weeks passed. Okabe's whereabouts were still unknown. Occasionally there were reports of people claiming to have seen him in Hokkaidō, but they were either cases of mistaken identity or impossible to confirm. And so it went on, until June.

If one rides the bus from Ōme City in the direction of Hannō, Saitama for about twenty minutes one arrives at a place called Iwakura. It is there that the Musashino Terrace starts, south of the mountains of Okutama. It is a very peaceful place, with several traditional inns clustered around the mineral springs there. If one were to head west from the bus road and climb the slope, one would find fields to one's left and, to one's right, a cliff six or seven metres high. About halfway up the slope is a large hole sealed by *shimenawa*, hemp ropes used for ritual purification.

In ancient times, Yamato Takeru-no-Mikoto passed by there after conquering Ezo (modern-day Hokkaidō) and placed his weapons in the hole. Because of that, the place was given the name of Musashi, written with the characters for "weapon" and "storage."

On one bright morning in June, a local farmer climbed the slope to dig up and replant his sweet potatoes. Rover, his crossbreed dog, for which he didn't even have a license, had been walking in front of him, but the dog had suddenly stopped and started to howl horribly. The farmer thought Rover had found a toad and yelled back at him, but the dog would not stop, and only seemed to howl even louder in an attempt to attract its master's attention. The farmer finally walked over to his dog to see what was wrong.

About a hundred metres from the hole used as a weapon storage, there had been a miniature landslide due to the extremely heavy rainfall a few days earlier. Black earth covered the area, but something odd was sticking out from the dirt. The farmer's suspicions were aroused, so he dug around until he made an unexpected discovery, at which he cried out and fell on his backside. Rover wagged his tail as he looked at the pathetic sight of his master trying to get up, and at the skull of a human which he had dug up.

The skull still had flesh, so the officers at the Ōme Police Station immediately thought of the case of the decapitated corpse. They reported the incident to the Metropolitan Police Department and forensic investigators were sent to Ōme. The conclusion of their investigation was that the skull belonged to a male around forty-five, the same age as the headless body found in the cellar. Furthermore, the lower left first molar had a relatively new crown, so if they could find the dental surgeon who put it on, they could identify the victim. Two days later, the skull's dental characteristics were shared with dentists in the Greater Tōkyō Area.

The authorities had planned to wait for five days if necessary, and then ask dentists from the whole Kantō region, but fortunately there was no need for that, for Doctor Minai from Hanayama Dentists, located in the ground floor of the Hōrai Building in Shinbashi Tamurachō, called the police, confirming that the skull belonged to one of his patients.

The more talented a dentist is, the more creative their medical treatment becomes, almost like art. They will look at the crowns placed by colleague dentists and admire or criticise the results. And it was normal that someone would recognize a crown he himself had set. Fortunately, Hanayama Dentists still had an impression of the teeth of the victim. Minai examined the skull meticulously and confirmed his conclusions with Onitsura. He presented his notebook, where he had copied the name and address of the victim copied from his medical files.

Kanichi Karasuda - Age 47.
Chigasaki City - Nango 19983

7

The police soon learned about Kanichi Karasuda. Like Okabe, Karasuda was a painter and member of the Independent Artists Association. He detested the company of other people, however, and had of late hardly interacted with other people, nor presented any new work. When it came to the art world, he had already become a person from the past. But why was he murdered? All those who knew him were puzzled. The fact that he was murdered at such an odd location, the cellar of a burnt-out building in Kanda, was curious enough on its own, but then the corpse was mutilated, and the head buried near some farms at the border of the Saitama Prefecture. Why had Okabe gone so far? It was impossible to even guess. Furthermore, Okabe had been the only artist to remain in contact with Karasuda, and although nobody could guess what lay beneath the surface, to the outside world they seemed to get along perfectly well. Everyone had thought the two were sworn friends, which was why the whole art world was in shock.

It was necessary to search the home of the victim, so Onitsura drove down the Tōkaidō road to Chigasaki, together with his detectives and forensic investigators. A trip on a bright afternoon late in spring should have been pleasant, but nobody said a word during the ride, as they all had the case on their mind. At the Chigasaki Police Station an officer was assigned to them as their local guide and they eventually arrived in a peaceful town with cramped roads. Turning left, they used the railway crossing over the Tōkaidō road.

Onitsura was reminded of Katai Tayama's essay *The Death of Doppo*. In the early spring of the year of Meiji 42 (1909), the famed author Doppo Kunikida stayed at the Nankoin Sanatorium located in this region to recuperate, and Katai would often visit him there.

"I got off at the station and passed through a block still reminiscent of its old post town history. On the other side of the railroad crossing stood an elementary school surrounded by poplars."

Half a century had since passed, and the elementary school was still standing on the right side of the road. Back then, it was still possible to see Mt. Fuji through the pines covering the area, but now it was covered with houses and stores, and those memories had been expunged. As a young woman wearing fancy shorts sped by on her bicycle, Onitsura thought how difficult it was to imagine Katai walking down that very street with heavy steps, while worrying about his friend's condition.

The car continued out of the shopping area and through the residential area, to reach the coast, where children were already playing in the water. They made their way west along the promenade, past the Nankoin Sanatorium where Doppo had stayed, and eventually stopped at a spot where the dunes were covered by pines. Far beyond stood the magnificent Mt. Fuji.

'Nango 19983 should be around here somewhere,' said the local officer, shading his eyes and scanning the surroundings. Chigasaki was the only place in Japan with a postal code of five digits. After a while, he noticed a small cottage beneath the pine-covered cliffs and told the driver to go there. It was the perfect home for someone who didn't like people, hidden as it was within a pine grove. The whole building had been painted the colour of pine leaves, as if to mimic the camouflage of insects. A little sand path lay on the other side of the white wooden fence, leading to the green front door. An officer turned the knob, but the door was locked. He tried knocking and calling, but there was no answer. The eccentric artist had never been married, nor even hired a maid, and had spent his life cooped up in his own shell.

The party went around to the back door, which was easily opened by putting a nail inside the keyhole and twisting it. A thick layer of blown sand covered the floor of the hallway, confirming that nobody had been inside for a long time.

The house was very simple, with barely 30 square metres of surface area and cramped rooms: a bed room with a built-in bed, a small Western-style living room and a kitchen-cum-dining room. On the sink stood an empty can of sardines in tomato sauce and in the cupboard were ten more cans.

'I guess he likes Western-style meals,' said Onitsura as he searched the house, but he did find about 15 kilograms of white rice in the storage, so Karasuda probably ate Japanese style as well.

The living room contained only one table and one chair. If Karasuda ever had a guest over, one of them would have had to stand. Given his personality, guests were unlikely, and if he'd had uninvited guests, it was likely he would have taken the chair and let the other stand.

Onitsura and his men started a thorough investigation of the little house in the hopes of finding something that would indicate a motive for the murder. But not only were his diaries for the current and previous year missing, his letters were also gone. It was assumed the murderer had destroyed them, and when they checked the stove in the kitchen, they found ashes which appeared to have come from paper.

The people from forensics sprayed aluminium powder at suspicious spots and carefully checked them with their magnifying glasses, hoping to find the fingerprints of the culprit. However, only Karasuda's fingerprints were found, and none of their efforts paid off. In the end, the chief inspector and his party had to leave with no results. The only thing they could do now was to pour more effort into determining Okabe's whereabouts.

Another eight days had passed. It was an unpleasant, clammy day, as it had been raining since the morning. It was in the afternoon when a young woman called upon Onitsura. She looked cute with her small face and short physique, and her small red boots only emphasised the impression. She presented her business card, which said Kimiko Kiriyama.

'I believe you have something to tell me about the case of the decapitated body?'

'Yes, I've been hired to work on it. There is something I want to ask of you,' she said firmly as she pulled out a silver, cylindrical object wrapped in plastic from her bag and carefully placed it on the desk in front of the chief inspector.

'I want you to check the fingerprints on this. If my suspicions are confirmed, I will tell you what I know about the case.'

Before replying, Onitsura took a look at the empty can on his desk. The red label on the side said sardines in tomato sauce. Sardines in tomato sauce, sardines in tomato sauce, hadn't he seen that before? Yes, in Kanichi Karasuda's kitchen, of course.

Had the woman sneaked into his house and "borrowed" the can? If so, she was a surprisingly proactive young lady. The policeman took another good look at the woman as he accepted her condition. She left his office with a smile on her face, leaving only the scent of her perfume behind.

Onitsura could not fathom her intent. The police had already made a thorough examination of the fingerprints in the house when they were there eight days ago, so it was unlikely they would find any on this can. He had accepted her condition because she seemed very sure about it, but it seemed clear to him that she would not get the results she was hoping for.

It had been raining on and off, but the following day the weather cleared. A cobalt blue sky peeked out from behind the clouds. Dazzling sunlight had begun to cast its glimmer on the streets, the trees and the walls of the buildings, when she appeared again wearing her red boots. Expectation made her eyes twinkle.

'What did you learn?' she asked with a coaxing voice. She was obviously someone with a natural talent to attract men.

'I am afraid the results won't be to your liking,' said Onitsura apologetically. 'There were a few smeared and indiscernible fingerprints, but the rest were all of Mr. Karasuda himself. There were no clear prints of anyone else.'

The woman appeared to be struggling not to show any signs of desperation.

'Now it's my turn to ask questions. I trust you will answer them?'

Onitsura looked at her in a friendly manner. He had a pleasant and inviting smile.

'Of course, please ask away. But please understand that there are still some things I can't discuss with you yet.'

'Aha. I hope this question belongs in the other category. Where did you find this empty can?'

'In Mr. Karasuda's kitchen. I suppose I'm guilty of trespassing.'

'Well, that's something you really shouldn't say here. Anyway, why did you break in?'

'Hmm, I suppose I can tell you. I don't believe Mr. Okabe is the murderer. So I'm trying to prove his innocence. That was my reason.'

'You think he's innocent? That's the complete opposite of what we think. Why do you believe that? What grounds do you have?'

She bit her lip and seemed about to answer, then controlled herself, shook her head, and said she could not explain. Onitsura knew that she was desperately trying not to betray what was going inside her.

8

Kimiko Kiriyama was indeed a woman strongly moved by her emotions. She had gone all the way to Chigasaki and sneaked into the abandoned house, and her efforts had borne fruit, because she had gathered data that would prove that Okabe hadn't killed Kanichi Karasuda. It was almost farcical how slow-witted the chief inspector had been for not recognising the piece of evidence sitting in front of him, but when he asked those questions, she could not help but be overwhelmed by her thoughts of her lover Okabe, and she almost burst into tears. She barely managed to contain the emotions welling up inside her as she left the Metropolitan Police Department.

She crossed over the railroad and walked along the embankment, looking at the couples chatting and admiring the swans. The sight made her think of Okabe, and tears came into her eyes. Okabe had not been young, but his experience with women allowed him to love her in a way no young man could ever do. They had been due to marry that spring, but it had been three months since his disappearance. Although he had loved her so much, he had not told her anything before he vanished and had not sent her a single letter in the nearly one hundred days that had passed. Her woman's instinct told her that Okabe was no longer alive. That body left in those vile, horrid conditions in that cellar storage had to be Okabe's, and so did the head found in Iwakura. Karasuda had to be the murderer! It was pathetic and vexing to see how stupid the police were, still fixated on finding Okabe. She knew the case would never be solved if it were left up to them. She had to do it herself!

Kimiko turned the corner at Hibiya Park and decided to pay a visit to Hanayama Dentists in the Hōrai Building in Tamurachō. She needed to meet with Dr. Minai, who had identified Okabe's skull as that of Karasuda. She had to know why he had made such a mistake.

There had to be some trick behind all of this. Perhaps the dentist had been bribed to make a false testimony.

Turning left from the street in front of the NHK Broadcasting Station, passing by a few smaller streets and taking a right turn brought her to the Hōrai Building. It was small, only five storeys high. It was just after noon, and there was a rush of office workers all trying to get their teeth fixed. It was obvious she'd be turned away for an interview, so she pretended to be a patient and registered for an examination. Her name was called twenty minutes later.

The dentist Minai was slender and about 1.7 metres tall. He was dark-haired, clean-shaven and wore gold-rimmed glasses, a rare sight in those days. The moment she saw him, any suspicions she had about Karasuda bribing him disappeared.

'Yes, open your mouth please. Hm, hm.'

When the examination was over, he told Kimiko her teeth were all fine, and it was at this moment that Kimiko fired her question.

'I want to ask you something about the head of Mr. Karasuda.'

Minai's eyes widened in surprise. He had not expected such a cute woman to bring up such a horrible topic.

'I have spoken to Chief Inspector Onitsura, but I also have questions for you. Do you mind?'

She flashed a smile at the dentist, making sure to show her dimples and her buck teeth. She tried to look as charming as possible. Her smile had been very effective on Egi, Ikeda, the owner of Deidosha and the concierges at the Kōryō Building, so she felt it was bound to work on the handsome dentist as well.

He considered the matter for a while, peered into the waiting room, and said he could give her three minutes.

'Thank you so much. What kind of person was this Mr. Karasuda?' she asked as she took out her notebook. Kimiko's occupation had taught her how to hold a pencil and a notebook so she could pretend to be a reporter or writer. She had not introduced herself, but it was clear the dentist had mistaken her for a reporter for some magazine.

'Well, the chief inspector asked me the same question, but I don't really remember. As you can see, this is a rather busy place.'

'Oh, how unfortunate. Was there anything distinctive in his walk or the way he spoke?'

'As I said, I really don't remember.'

'Was there nothing that left an impression on you? For example, perhaps he cried when you pulled his teeth?'

The dentist did not seem to mind the persistent line of questioning.

'He wasn't a child anymore, and we have effective anaesthetics, so teeth are pulled while the patient's asleep.'

The dentist then seemed to recall something. He frowned and stared at the turntable with chemical bottles and then looked up again.

'There's one thing I do remember. After I pulled his teeth, he had a light fainting spell, so I loosened his tie and had him rest on the bed in the back there. After a sip of cognac, he redid his necktie and got up again. I think I saw a small blue spot on his neck then, like a bruise.'

'A bruise, that sounds interesting. Do you remember the shape?'

The dentist looked at the clock.

'Your three minutes are up. To tell you the truth, I didn't take a good look at it, because I thought it was not done to take advantage of someone who had fainted. Perhaps the nurse who helped him did.'

He picked up some absorbent cotton with his tweezers. Kimiko prepared to take her leave, but still couldn't help asking further.

'Could I have a talk with her?'

'She's married now, living in Funabashi.'

'Could you tell me her address?'

Kimiko was still wearing her charming smile. The dentist took out his address book and told her the address of the nurse as well as her new, married name.

It would be necessary for her to visit the nurse in Kaijinchō, Funabashi in order to clear up the matter of whether the patient had been Karasuda, as the dentist believed, or Okabe, as Kimiko believed.

9

The following day, Onitsura was paid a third visit by Kimiko. There had always been a sparkle in her eyes, but now they were shining even more brilliantly, accentuating her feminine charm. He offered a seat and waited patiently for what she had to tell him. He could make out the fire of victory in her eyes. The chief inspector could only listen humbly to how this young woman had unravelled a mystery which had baffled the authorities.

Kimiko pulled out a yellow pearl container and offered him a cigarette, which he declined, but lit her cigarette for her. He realised that she was an inexperienced smoker, who was only smoking now to help calm her nerves. She coughed once to clear her throat and began in the same calm manner as always.

'I'll tell you everything today. I've discovered something you don't know about yet. I believed Mr. Okabe was innocent of the murder, so I wanted to find evidence of that, no matter what. That's why I went to Chigasaki on my own and sneaked inside Mr. Karasuda's house to take a look around. My efforts were rewarded, and I found something of interest. What do you think it was?'

'I've no idea.'

'It was the empty can I had you test the day before yesterday.'

Kimiko snapped the cover of her handbag open, took the can out and placed it on Onitsura's desk.

'You determined that Mr. Karasuda's fingerprints were on this can, if you remember. When I found it in the kitchen, it was like the sun breaking through the clouds. Take a look at this.'

She pointed at the printing on the cover of the can. It said 7305.

'This code indicates that the can was produced on March 5th, 1957. If the body found in the cellar storage is Mr. Karasuda, don't you find it strange that his fingerprints are found on a tin of sardines in tomato sauce produced after he died?'

Kimiko spoke casually, but she was absolutely right. If Karasuda's fingerprints were on this can, then that meant the body found in the cellar room was not that of Karasuda. Onitsura felt deeply embarrassed. When the skull had been determined to have been Karasuda's, the authorities had become convinced the murderer was Okabe, and had focused on finding his fingerprints to the exclusion of everything else. It was an inexcusable mistake. It would have taken several days for the can to arrive at the local shops after production, so Karasuda had to have been in that house for a while after the murder occurred, after which he vanished.

'I see your point, but what if the culprit had taken inspiration from detective novels and secured Mr. Karasuda's fingerprint in advance before making a stamp of it? That way, he could place Karasuda's fingerprint on the can after killing him, and leave it the kitchen for others to find. What do you think of that?'

Kimiko's lips contorted. She was probably sneering in her mind at the uninspired possibility Onitsura had just proposed.

'I paid a visit to Hanayama Dentists in Shinbashi, in order to question the dentist who claimed it was Mr. Karasuda's skull, but he couldn't remember the patient's face. I kept pressing, and he finally remembered seeing something like a bruise on the patient's neck. He gave me the address of the nurse that had seen him, and she told me it wasn't a bruise. On his neck, right below the knot of his necktie, was a small tattoo of a blue rose. That was when I finally had confirmation that the patient had in fact been Mr. Okabe. He has a blue tattoo on his neck, which he got in Marseille long ago. I had brought a photograph of him from home and showed it to the nurse. She identified the patient as Mr. Okabe and said she would gladly testify when needed.'

When she had finished, Kimiko looked Onitsura straight in the eye. The joy of victory, the feeling of pride and her contempt for the authorities had all come together, and her eyes shone even more brightly.

Onitsura accepted his defeat, and started to think. If the patient had been Okabe, why had he used someone else's name to get treated? As long as that remained unexplained, it was natural to assume that the person who got treated was the one registered: Kanichi Karasuda. It could simply be said that the nurse had been mistaken. Okabe had a tattoo on his neck, but Karasuda was also an artist, and it was possible that he, too, had once visited France and had the same tattoo done in Marseille.

But he didn't want to disillusion the young woman, so he kept his doubts to himself.

Kimiko was beaming. Her well-shaped lips opened slightly, showing a glimpse of her white teeth. Her coloured cheeks were proof of her excitement.

'Mr. Onitsura, as you now see, the culprit is Mr. Karasuda. You weren't able to catch the murderer, because the investigation mistakenly assumed it was Mr. Okabe. The real person you're after is Mr. Karasuda.'

Kimiko seemed almost possessed as she repeated her accusation and recited all her efforts to get at the truth: what she learnt at Deidosha, what the concierges of the Kōryō Building had told her, what happened when she visited the artists who received the mysterious parcels, and of course how she had sneaked into Karasuda's home.

As she was speaking, the chief inspector's gaze started to wander. He pretended to be listening, but he was actually thinking about another matter. When Kimiko noticed, she suddenly stood up with her handbag in her arms. It was only then that Onitsura realised how rude he had been and tried to stop her. Kimiko was outraged. She felt like accusing him of thinking about dinner instead of listening to her.

'I've taken up too much of your time. Please make sure you catch Mr. Karasuda.'

'Of course,' replied the policeman confidently. And that while he's only shown how incompetent he is, thought Kimiko.

'I expect results.'

'You can count on us. We will inform you the moment we've found him. It will all be due to your information.'

Onitsura knew she was furious at him, but he didn't mind.

10

Five days passed seemingly without any developments. Kimiko made sure not to miss the newspapers and the news on the radio, but there was nothing to indicate anything had happened. She assumed the police were still on the wrong trail, which frustrated her. But on the sixth day Onitsura called her to say that they had found Karasuda and that the case was now solved. He invited her to come over.

Kimiko was an aspiring actress, and had been watching a rehearsal of *The Cherry Orchard* performed by the senior actors in her group, but she quickly left the rehearsal hall and headed for the Metropolitan Police Department. She had a very low opinion of Onitsura, so she was surprised the chief inspector had actually succeeded in capturing Karasuda. She was not particularly pleased, however, and actually felt outdone by him.

It was her fourth visit to the chief inspector's office. There was a discoloured sheet of paper taped to the door which said *Decapitated Body - Investigation HQ*. Kimiko couldn't help feeling all kinds of emotions as she read those words. Although she was fiercely competitive, she was also a very emotional person.

Onitsura greeted her with a friendly smile and offered her a seat.

'Where is Karasuda?'

'Here. The case is solved, so you don't need to worry anymore,' said the chief inspector in his usual calm manner. Karasuda was probably being detained in one of the underground cells of this building, thought Kimiko, secretly laughing. How ironic: the case had started in an underground room and was now ending in one.

'Last time, it was you who was telling me about the fingerprints on the can, so now it's my turn.'

'I'm listening.'

Kimiko was still a bit angry, which showed in the way she spoke.

'You see, we only arrived at the true conclusion of this case because the key to solving the mystery had been hidden in something you told me.'

'Oh, and what was that?'

'Just a small matter. You told me that you'd visited the concierges' room in the Kōryō Building to talk with the men there. Your conversation with them held a vital hint. It was a truly trivial matter, so it was no wonder you overlooked it.'

Kimiko looked at the chief inspector in bewilderment. The case should have been solved the moment they found Karasuda and arrested him. Did that mean that it was her talk with the concierges of the Kōryō Building that had led to the arrest of Karasuda? She tried to replay the conversation in her mind, but she couldn't recall anything significant.

'You don't remember?' asked Onitsura. Although she didn't like admitting it, Kimiko shook her head.

'No, please explain.'

'You told me that the two of them had carried something into one of the storage rooms, not knowing that there was a dead body in the room next door. They hadn't gone there since, because they felt it was too creepy to go down alone. As I listened to you, I wondered what they could have carried down. Because they said they hadn't been down there since, it meant that nothing had been added or removed from the storage rooms and so the item they had carried down was still there. But we only found a chair and a wooden screen in the other storage room, which meant that one of those two items had been carried in by them. Obviously, it wouldn't have taken the strength of two adult men to carry that light chair down, so it must have been the screen, which would have been much too heavy for one person.'

Kimiko could follow Onitsura's reasoning, but had no idea what it meant. She had previously thought very little of the man, but now he seemed to be going through a whole chain of deduction. Surprised by this side of him, she couldn't help staring.

'The crime had occurred in the farthest storage room down the corridor, as reported in the newspapers. The culprit shot the revolver twice there. One bullet penetrated the victim's body, passed through the window in the dividing wall to enter the room next door, and made a hole in the screen. But consider this: if the body was already lying in the room next door when those men carried the screen downstairs, then why was there a bullet hole in the screen? You have to agree that it's awfully curious that a screen which wasn't there at the time of the murder, still managed to be damaged by the bullet.'

'Couldn't he have returned a few days later to the crime scene for some reason, and shot the screen on purpose?'

'For what reason?'

'Hm...'

It annoyed Kimiko that she wasn't able to come up with an answer. It was embarrassing.

'I decided to pursue that line of thought, so after you left my office the other day, I made a phone call to the Kōryō Building to see if my deductions could be confirmed.'

'And were they?'

'I learned that it had indeed been the screen that they had carried there. I asked them what day that was, and the reply was around noon of the third of March. It was a Sunday, and Doll's Day, so they were sure about that date. But now you have to listen carefully. The murder must have occurred after they carried the screen into the storage room. The bullet hole in the screen could only have been made if the crime happened after it had been carried there. That meant the victim was shot after noon on the third of March, which turned the whole case upside down.'

Kimiko fully understood Onitsura's explanation, but she wasn't able to fully grasp how the case was turned upside down by it. But the attractive, obstinate woman didn't want Onitsura to know, so she pretended to have understood everything.

'It was truly unfortunate for the killer to have shot the screen, and truly fortunate that we realised that trivial fact. Once we did, counting backwards then provided the answers we sought. Simple arithmetic even a first grader in elementary school can do. One minus one equals zero. Only the person who received the revolver in a parcel on the third of March, and presented it to the police the following day, could have committed the murder.'

'... But that means Ms. Ui is the culprit.'

'Exactly. Utako Ui is the murderer of Otsugorō Okabe.'

Having once been convinced that Karasuda was the murderer, Kimiko could only gasp in surprise when she learned the truth. But once the initial shock had worn off, she could feel her hate towards the murderer well up inside.

'Why... why did she kill him?'

'Her motive was jealousy, because he had dumped her for another woman. Let me repeat: the perpetrator of that horrendous crime was a woman, and her motive was revenge born out of jealousy. Soon after the crime was discovered, I myself had visited Ms. Ui. She told me she had been the one to have had enough of Mr. Okabe and that she had thrown him out of her house. In fact, the opposite was true, and he had dumped her because he had fallen in love with you.'

Kimiko's face turned pale and her whole body trembled. When she had believed the culprit to be a man, she hadn't thought much of it, but she had to shudder at the thought of how that woman had committed the murder in that dark underground room.

'She's like a witch from the Middle Ages, killing the man she once lived with and cutting his head off. But what was the meaning of that business with the parcels, then?'

'It's quite simple once you know the trick. Let me explain it to you in order. Once she had decided to commit murder, it became necessary to take measures to avoid suspicion. Any clever murderer would do that, but the exceptionally intelligent Ms. Ui devised a particularly ingenious plan. She would make it appear as if the victim himself was the culprit. The idea was that the police would go around desperately looking for a dead person, which would make it impossible for them to catch the killer.'

Kimiko nodded silently, and Onitsura continued.

'In her confession, Ms. Ui stated she had come across that underground room by accident. She had lowered the victim's guard by getting him drunk, and then led him to the storage room, where she shot him once. But he got up again, so she quickly fired a second shot. The she dragged him to the sofa, still alive, and strangled him. Afterwards she decapitated him and burned his fingerprints off.'

Utako Ui had stated she had lured Okabe to the crime scene by saying Kimiko was waiting for him. He had been heavily intoxicated, but upon hearing the name of the woman he loved, he went down into the cellar unsuspectingly. The name Kimiko had been as effective on him as Ali Baba's magical phrase, a fact which only served to strengthen Utako's fury.

Onitsura's account of the murder had intentionally been brief to minimise the pain on Kimiko, which was also why he avoided naming Okabe and merely referred to him as the victim. But when he began to describe the actual murder, it seemed his considerations had been in vain. Kimiko's mouth was contorted as she listened in pain. But being the strong-willed woman she was, she never told him to stop. She was prepared to listen to how her lover had been beheaded.

'The purpose of the decapitation was, of course, to make it impossible to identify the victim. It was necessary to cut the head off starting at the base of the neck, due to the tattoo. It was quite difficult, she said.'

'How horrid, strangling a living person to death. Why didn't she just kill him with the revolver?'

'I'll explain that in a minute, but first let me determine when the crime actually occurred. She presented the revolver at her local police box on the fourth of March. Given that the screen had been moved downstairs around noon of the third, it became obvious the murder had been committed sometime between the evening of the third and the early hours of the fourth. We, however, had erroneously assumed the crime had already been committed by the time the revolver was delivered in a parcel to Ms. Ui. In fact, that strange parcel was actually a prop, to make us believe the murder had already occurred, to imply that Ms. Ui herself was not the murderer, and to suggest that Mr. Okabe was the culprit. We were completely fooled and became convinced that Mr. Okabe was indeed the murderer. I'm terribly sorry,' said Onitsura, from the depths of his heart.

'How did the parcel suggest he was the killer?'

'Let me go through it from the beginning. On the first of March, Mr. Okabe was invited by Ms. Ui to her atelier in Hayashichō. They were about to go their separate ways, but since they had lived together for so long, she hoped they could at least spend their last days together in a nice way. He was touched by this gentle side of her, and he also felt pity for her, so he agreed. On the second of March he went to Deidosha to buy some frames because she had asked him to. I don't know whether Ms. Ui is skilled at controlling men in general, or whether she had learned how to get on his good side by living together for two or three years, but he did what she asked of him. And that was handy in making him appear as the murderer. She had made the face of the victim unrecognizable, but she had left his clothes and other possessions untouched. This contradiction was her first misdirection, and it led us to jump to the conclusion that Mr. Okabe might not have been the victim, but was instead the murderer. The second misdirection was when she viewed the body of the victim at the Medical Examiner's Office and lied about it not being that of Mr. Okabe. The third was when she had Mr. Okabe visit Deidosha on the second of March. And, finally, because the parcel with the gun had been posted on the second of March, it was assumed that the crime had been committed in the early hours of that day. That was the fourth misdirection. They were all pitfalls that Ms. Ui had dug for us, and we fell into every one of them. We truly believed that Mr. Okabe was the murderer, exactly as she had planned.'

'So it was also Mr. Okabe who took the parcels to the post office?'

That sounded too good to be true. Kimiko couldn't help feel angry at Okabe for staying at Ui's atelier in Hayashichō, even though he was already engaged. Onitsura knew very well what was on Kimiko's mind.

'No, that was Ms. Ui herself. She couldn't risk anyone else opening those parcels for any reason. Mr. Okabe was quite a controversial figure, but from what I've heard he was always a gentleman when it came to women. He only argued with men, and when it came to female artists, he always tried to find something to praise no matter how bad the work was. I don't believe you should think too harshly of him for so easily agreeing to spend some time with Ms. Ui after breaking up with her. He was that kind of person.'

Realising Onitsura had read her mind, Kimiko quickly changed the subject.

'So why did she send those parcels using Mr. Akutagawa's name, and why did she also send them to Mr. Ikeda and Mr. Egi?'

'She said she used Mr. Akutagawa's name because his name was at the top of a members list that happened to be lying around. She also knew that if she sent the parcels to Mr. Ikeda and Mr. Egi, they'd probably assume they had come from Mr. Okabe, as he and they were always arguing. She expected, correctly, that they would simply think he was harassing them. But she did tread very carefully when it came to the contents of the parcels. If all she'd done was to send the revolver to herself, and the police discovered that Mr. Okabe had been shot by that same revolver, well, obviously we'd conclude that something odd was going on. But by also sending the empty bottle of sulphuric acid and the rope, and also strangling the body and burning the fingerprints off with acid, she strengthened the impression that the victim had been shot, strangled and then had his fingers burnt by acid. In so doing, she cunningly managed to use the subsequent police investigation to her own advantage.'

'So that rope wasn't used in the actual murder?'

'Correct. I'm repeating myself perhaps, but at the time Mr. Egi received that rope and Mr. Ikeda the empty bottle, Mr. Okabe was still among the living. Ms. Ui used a different piece of rope and bottle of acid during the actual crime. She had no particular reason for picking a vinyl rope, it was simply easily obtainable. Of the three parcels sent, only the revolver sent to her was actually used in the murder.'

The chief inspector paused briefly, then continued his explanation.

11

'I forgot to tell you that Ms. Ui had sent the parcel with the revolver on the second of March, knowing it would arrive on the third. She had invited her disciples to her home to celebrate Doll's Day. One of them was a young man familiar with firearms, and she persuaded him to declare in front of them that the revolver she'd received had been fired recently. Of course, she had simply fired it secretly somewhere before placing it the parcel, so it was only natural there was a smell of gunpowder. And when she spoke to the detective, he didn't doubt that the residue had been from the shots fired at the victim. Of course, when she presented the weapon the following day, on the fourth at the police box, the gunshot residue *had* been from the shots fired at the victim.'

Kimiko gasped out loud. What a frighteningly calculating woman! A true witch. It was no wonder that even a man like Okabe had been caught in her spell.

'She had an important reason for choosing that underground cellar room, where people hardly went any more. Her plans would fall apart if the body had been discovered early, as a medical examination would expose the trickery she had pulled off with the date of Mr. Okabe's death. That's why she picked that spot. But after ten days, not even an autopsy would be able to determine an exact time of death. That is why she could call the police herself then without any worries.'

'What a wicked person.'

'Yes, she's quite unique. Speaking of unique, I've never heard of another case where the murder weapon had been in the possession of the police from the very start. And it wasn't even the result of diligent police work. The murderer herself had brought it to us. We didn't have to do a thing. It was a truly remarkable situation.'

'Did you arrest her?'

'Yes, about three hours ago. She knew we had the evidence, so she gave up and confessed to everything,' said Onitsura, but he didn't seem happy the case was now over. It had left a nasty aftertaste. As Kimiko looked at him, she suddenly recalled an important question she needed to ask.

'You said that Mr. Karasuda was here, too. Was he connected to the case as well?'

'Yes.'

'Was he her accomplice?'

'No. Would you like to meet him?'

A suggestive grin appeared on Onitsura's face. Later, whenever Kimiko would look back on the case of the headless body, she would remember that the scene which had left the greatest impression on her was when he had smiled at her at that moment. Compared to his colleagues, Onitsura could be considered polite, but he was still far from being a true gentleman. A true gentleman would never have smiled in such a vulgar way. And she was sure a gentleman would never have done what Onitsura did next.

But to be fair, Kimiko had misunderstood the meaning behind his grin and had also conveniently forgotten that she herself had agreed to meet Karasuda.

'Do you want to see him?' Onitsura repeated his question. Kimiko didn't notice the expression on his face that said she probably shouldn't, but even if she had, she would have ignored it.

'Of course!' she said eagerly. She had made a tremendous error in her deductions because of Karasuda's disappearance. Why hadn't he come forward, telling everyone that the skull found in Iwakura wasn't his, and that he was still alive? She couldn't let the matter rest until she'd prised the answer to those questions out of the chief inspector. And she'd probably feel better once she had given him a piece of her mind.

Onitsura walked over to the wall and pulled back the black sheet covering the desk. Beneath the sheet were five abstract plaster sculptures.

'Mr. Karasuda was murdered too. His limbs and head were cut off, and hidden inside these plaster sculptures. We broke one of them open already, and out came Mr. Karasuda's head, sealed inside a plastic bag.'

'Oh, it's too horrible, cover it again. Please, quickly, I don't want to see it!'

Kimiko cried hysterically, her face red. Once Onitsura had covered the desk again, she almost collapsed back in her chair.

'I am sorry for surprising you. Perhaps you'd like some tea?'

Kimiko drank the tea down in one gulp, which seemed to calm her.

'It was of course Ms. Ui who killed Mr. Karasuda. These sculptures are exactly the same as the sculptures she had submitted to an exhibition about a year ago, when she won an award. I'd seen them in an art magazine before, but I never suspected anything would be hidden inside. But they're only plaster sculptures, so it's only logical that she's able to make duplicates of them.'

Kimiko's curiosity was once again aroused as she listened to the chief inspector.

'It was already a shock to learn how she killed Mr. Okabe in such a horrible manner, but to think what she also did to Mr. Karasuda... She's a monster, that woman. But why did she kill him as well?'

'It was due to an unfortunate turn of events. Ms. Ui had initially only planned to murder Mr. Okabe. All of her efforts were solely focused on his death. She had gone to Iwakura to bury the head there. She had not picked the location for any particular reason, she had simply visited the place a few times in the past for sketches. Then an unforeseen act of nature caused the skull to be discovered. She told me that it was only at that moment she recalled something, and it caused her to turn pale on the spot. What did you think it was?'

'I have no clue.'

'It was the answer to the question why Mr. Okabe used Mr. Karasuda's name when he went to the dentist. About a year ago, Mr. Okabe had had a toothache—a molar—and needed to see a dentist. Mr. Karasuda had been visiting at the time, and he told Mr. Okabe he should use his health insurance card and that nobody would ever find out. It would cut the treatment costs in half. Mr. Karasuda had never become ill since getting his health insurance, and because he didn't like the idea of paying every month for nothing, he reckoned he might as well help Mr. Okabe out. So Mr. Karasuda offered him his insurance card.

'There was a Literature and Art Health Insurance Association formed by literary authors and artists. Mr. Karasuda had become a member, but Mr. Okabe had not. Mr. Okabe borrowed his friend's card, and pretended to be Mr. Karasuda during the treatment for a crown. This trivial act of misconduct was what led to Mr. Karasuda's murder. Ms. Ui could feel the ground slipping from beneath her feet when she heard that the head had been found in Iwakura and that the police were looking for cooperation from dentists. I guess I don't have to explain her fears. If the dentist Minai were to testify that the skull belonged to Mr. Karasuda, Mr. Karasuda himself would, of course, have to come forward and explain everything to the police once it was in the news. Then it would come out that the victim was actually Mr. Okabe, and we'd realise that Ms. Ui had committed the murder. So, after some desperate thinking, she headed to Chigasaki, lured Mr. Karasuda to her own atelier, and killed him there. She then returned to Chigasaki to get rid of his diary and letters. If she could make Mr. Karasuda disappear, the corpse in the cellar would be assumed to belong to Kanichi Karasuda, and we'd start looking more intensively for Mr. Okabe as the killer. Basically, it was almost over for her when the head was found in Iwakura, but she managed to turn the discovery to her advantage by eliminating Mr. Karasuda. Up until then, there was the unsolved mystery of who the victim had really been. In such cases, someone eventually appears to identify the corpse as their father or husband. It was highly unusual that nobody had appeared to identify the body. But Mr. Karasuda was the perfect "victim" for her plan: he was an eccentric artist who lived in solitude. He had no other family, so nobody would become worried about him, even if he disappeared.'

'She turned the situation completely around.'

'Precisely. Mr. Karasuda was exactly the person she needed. She set fire to his diary and letters, because she was afraid there might be something in them about him lending his insurance card to Mr. Okabe for a treatment. But that was not the only reason. Those documents also had to be burned because Mr. Karasuda was supposed to have died on the second of March, so she had to get rid of the diary, which would prove he was still alive after that day. If Mr. Karasuda had written someone a letter on the third of March or later, or had gone out on a stroll and been seen by one of the locals, Ms. Ui's plans would all have been in vain. But fortunately for her, the eccentric man hardly left his home. His bought his groceries at night so he wouldn't run into fishermen, and he wrote letters as seldom as he received them. That's why her plan was successful. If he had sent even one letter, Ms. Ui's crime would have been revealed, but she had luck on her side. She was lucky on other occasions too. There's a strong west wind in Chigasaki in the spring. So after he was murdered, the wind blew sand inside his house, and it would only have taken one or two nights before any signs he had been alive after the second of March would be covered by sand. So when I went to the place, it appeared as if he hadn't been in his home for three months. If there had been any other houses in the vicinity, we might have learned that he had been alive until recently. Even Chigasaki's weather was on Ms. Ui's side. How lucky can one be?'

The chief inspector sighed out loud. He had finished now, and was staring at the cold teacup in his hands, which he placed on his desk. His pursed lips turned into a smile, as if he were laughing at himself. He was thinking back to the visit he had paid to Ms. Ui at the start of the whole case. It was pathetic. He'd had no idea she was the murderer, and she had played him like a fiddle.

'I have to apologise to you,' said Kimiko.

'For what?'

Onitsura smiled at her. His high forehead and gentle eyes gave off a sense of warmth, a spark that wasn't there while he was still working on the case.

'I had completely underestimated your deductive skills. But now I think you're wonderful. I just wanted to tell you that before I left.'

'Thank you.'

Onitsura's answer was short but sincere.

The Blue Locked Room

1

'Let me go, Aida, let me go now!'

'You have to calm down first, Mr. Shinano. Just calm down and get a grip on yourself.'

The concierge Aida was holding Fuyuto Shinano in a full nelson while he attempted to pacify the young man. But it was no easy task for a man of sixty-or-so years, and he was being swung around by Shinano.

The stage director Katsuhiko Kashimura had been watching television in the canteen of the Villa Notus, when a drunken Fuyuto Shinano had returned from outside and started yelling about killing him.

A glass ash tray was lying on the floor, and cigarette stubs and ash had spilled out.

'Mr. Aida, you can let him go. I'll have to teach him how to behave with my fists.'

The situation didn't seem to impress Kashimura much as he sneered at Shinano. The stage director-cum-actor was standing in a relaxed manner, with both hands in the pockets of his dark brown gown. He was tall and muscular and looked more like a flyweight-class champion than a director of theatre plays.

Fuyuto Shinano, on the other hand, was a slender and frail individual. He usually took off his thick glasses when on stage, but he looked even punier now with them on. His red cheeks were pulsating with anger.

'How—how dare you seduce my dear Chisato…'

'Come on, Shinano, don't come crying to me about it. I simply have this effect on women, which is why Hara was okay with it. I can't begin to understand how a good-for-nothing like you could attract any woman.'

'Damn, let me go, Aida!'

Fuyuto Shinano started to struggle more aggressively. His voice had gone slightly hoarse. The blood on his chin came from a cut he'd received when he'd tried to attack Kashimura and flipped the table over.

'Mr. Kashimura, would you please go up to your room? Your presence only excites Mr. Shinano further.'

'A good punch in the face will sober him up.'

'Please, don't say things like that. We're all members of the Notus Troupe, comrades living under one roof. Mr. Shinano, you're drunk, please stop,' the elderly concierge pleaded, before being thrown onto the couch and landing on his backside. Relieved of the weight, Fuyuto Shinano raised his fist and jumped at Kashimura, but he stood no chance against his muscular opponent. A dull noise rang through the room, and the next moment Fuyuto was sprawled pathetically on the floor.

'There's more for you where that came from. Get up!'

Kashimura stood with his legs spread, looking down at the actor at his feet as he rubbed his fist.

'Here I come!'

Shinano got up unsteadily. He looked pale, but his eyes were still burning red. Instead of attacking Kashimura, he slid backwards across the floor until his back was against the entrance to the canteen.

'Don't tell me you're running away?' mocked Kashimura, but his expression suddenly changed.

'Wait, put that knife down.'

'I'll kill you,' said Shinano in an eerily calm voice, his right hand clenching a large switchblade. The knife looked very sharp and new, and he'd probably picked it up at a hardware store on his way there.

'Get rid of that knife! Coward!'

'Seducing women is cowardly!'

For every step Katsuhiko Kashimura took back, Fuyuto Shinano took two forward. There were no other exits to the room. All the windows were locked.

Aida was still sitting on the couch, wary of getting up. He was afraid that if he said something wrong, Shinano would get angry at him and stab him. Both he and Kashimura had their mouths open, breathing heavily, with shoulders heaving.

Kashimura took a few more steps back and stepped behind the overturned table. He watched Shinano carefully as he swiftly grabbed a nearby chair and held it up.

'Now we can fight. I'll beat you up with this,' he said, challenging Shinano with renewed vigour. The profile of Kashimura with his long sideburns made him resemble a villain in a play.

'Come on then, you chicken,' Kashimura taunted again. Shinano didn't say a word. Instead of replying, he took another step forward. Aida could feel himself shaking as he watched the scene, something that had never happened to him before in a long life. Raising his hands, he tried to say something, but no words came out of his mouth. He couldn't even swallow his saliva. Perspiration ran down his back.

But then he heard footsteps approaching. At first, he thought he was imagining things, but fortunately, he was not.

The door was flung open and a powerful-looking police officer in his mid-thirties barged in. He was holding a pistol in one hand, ready to fire a warning shot. Behind him Aida could make out the frightened look on Fujie Takeda's face.

Thank heavens she had called the police, he thought, as he cast a grateful look at her. The young actress, who specialised in playing elderly women, always seemed to shrink from everything, and hardly seemed alive.

The officer had probably been trained for such a situation, because he stepped purposefully towards Shinano and relieved him of the knife in mere seconds.

Fuyuto Shinano looked in surprise at the officer and started wailing some incomprehensible words, but then ran out of the canteen, pushing Fujie out of the way.

'What happened here?' the police officer asked as he looked calmly at the three people remaining.

'No—nothing. We just had a—a small argument,' said Kashimura quickly, as he saw Aida was about to speak. 'As you saw, he was drunk.'

'What were you arguing about?'

'Nothing. About the casting of the roles.'

Kashimura put his hand in his pocket to look for his business card, but then remembered he was wearing a gown. He straightened up and introduced himself to the police officer.

'I am Katsuhiko Kashimura. I direct the plays of the Notus Troupe. The man who ran out of the room just now is Fuyuto Shinano, one of our actors. Actors being dissatisfied with the part they've been given happens all the time. Nothing special.'

Kashimura brushed his long hair back. The police officer didn't seem satisfied with the explanation, however.

'But he was brandishing a knife. If something like that occurs every time someone's not happy with their part, sooner or later somebody will get badly hurt.'

'Well, that's true,' muttered Kashimura, fiddling with his hair again.

At that moment, the door opened again and Chisato Hara stepped into the canteen. She was a small, tanned woman with a sharp look in her eye. She was wearing a green mid-length coat. Her looks and her fashion made a dramatic impression.

'Oh,' she said as she looked around the room in surprise. 'What happened?'

'Nothing much,' replied Kashimura. Fujie Takeda was still looking pale, while she played with her cameo brooch.

'Anyway, I'll accompany you upstairs. I think it would be wise to remain in your room this evening,' said the police officer as he tried to move Kashimura to a safer place.

'What happened?' Chisato Hara asked again, as the officer was leaving the canteen. There was note of hysteria in her voice.

2

'Thank you for last night,' said the concierge Aida, bowing as he entered the police station. He was wearing the same khaki cargo pants he had been wearing the night before, and the end of a towel hanging from his trousers peeked out from beneath his coat. His hair was cut short, which suited him.

'It's all in a day's work,' replied the police officer. 'I was just doing my rounds, and as I was passing in front of the building that actress came running out onto the street.'

'Aha,' replied the concierge absently. It appeared he was trying to raise another topic.

'And how's Mr. Shinano doing?'

'He's calmed down. He had a bottle of milk at breakfast, but then he went back to his room.'

'And Mr. Kashimura?'

Aida frowned.

'Mail addressed to him arrived this morning, so I tried to call him down.' He explained that there were call buttons in his office for all the rooms in the building.

'I tried ringing him several times, but there was no answer. So I went up to his rooms on the first floor and tried calling out to him, but he still didn't answer. That does worry me, considering what happened last night.'

'Perhaps he took a sleeping draught?' suggested the officer.

'Even so, it's strange that he wouldn't wake up after all that ringing. And there was light shining through the gap under his door, which was strange because Mr. Kashimura is in the habit of turning off the lights when he goes to bed.'

The officer didn't say anything.

'His bedroom is right next to his living room, and I noticed from the street that the window was open. He always said that the cold night air was poison to an actor's throat, so why would he sleep with the window open?'

'That is strange,' conceded the police officer. 'Let me take a look.' He gave a sign to his colleague and left. The sky was clear and they could hear black kites cawing above him.

'I can't help worrying. He's not very well-liked,' explained the concierge as he led the way. He walked with a stoop. It appeared he was uncomfortable talking about Kashimura behind his back, even though he himself had brought the subject up.

'It's not nice talking about people this way, but I heard he had treated his ex-wife quite horribly. It was he who had been head-over-heels in love with her and badgered her to marry him, but when he tired of her, he would often hit her and kick her and do other terrible things to her.'

'Doesn't sound like a sane person.'

'No. But if he continues to act like that, I'm afraid that one day karma will strike back.'

The Villa Notus was less than three hundred metres away from the police station. The paved road was completely empty, as the morning rush was already over.

'You have some strange people living in your building. I don't believe you have office workers or other people with regular hours living there, am I right?'

The officer had only been assigned to the area recently, so he knew hardly anything about the Villa Notus.

'Not a single one. It was built especially to house those people in the theatre group Notus Troupe who are still single,' replied Aida.

The two-storied Notus Villa came into view. As the residential area was close to downtown, the grounds of the villa were not particularly large. The Spanish-style building made a colourful impression, due to its celadon bricks and blue earthenware roof tiles. The wall encircling the grounds was made of rough concrete blocks, however, and looked out of place.

One of the windows on the upper floor facing the street was open.

'That's the window of Mr. Kashimura's bedroom,' said the concierge, pointing up at it. Cream-coloured curtains danced in the spring wind.

'I'll try from the inside first,' replied the policeman.

The concierge's office was located to the right of the front entrance. A hallway extended to the left and right, while opposite the entrance was a staircase with handrails going up to the first floor. About halfway along the upstairs hallway were Kashimura's rooms.

As they approached, the door opposite Kashimura's opened to reveal a tall woman, who had probably noticed the noise of the footsteps. She had a short haircut and was dressed like a Western female beggar.

'Oh.'

She seemed about to say more, but then decided just to follow the concierge. Her large face, free of make-up, wore a clearly interested look.

When the police officer saw for himself there was indeed light shining through the gap around the door and the keyhole, his suspicions seemed to grow. He knocked loudly on the door a few times and called out to Kashimura, but there was no answer.

'This is not normal.'

He turned the door-knob several times and tried pushing and pulling the door, but it wouldn't budge.

'See what I mean?'

'Please bring the master key. We need to open the door quickly.'

'There is no master key,' replied the concierge ruefully.

'Huh? Isn't that key hanging in your office a master key?'

After taking Kashimura up to his rooms the previous night, he'd had a cup of tea in the concierge's office and noticed the key then.

'Oh, that key,' replied the concierge, rubbing his grey hair. 'I dropped it on the tracks when I was crossing the street. The tram ran over it before I could pick it up.'

'Oh.'

A puzzled look appeared on the policeman's broad face.

'We'll have to open the door without a key then,' he muttered as he eyed the door hinges, noting that they were covered, so it wouldn't be possible to pull the pins out. The only way to enter the room through the door would be to break it down.

'Let's try through the window. Do you have a ladder somewhere?' he asked. Unconsciously, the two had started speaking more loudly, which led to several actors sticking their heads out into the hallway to see what was going on. As expected from people with such a colourful occupation, some of the residents were wearing colourful red or pink negligees. Fuyuto Shinano already had his trousers on, and a cardigan, and was holding a rolled-up magazine in one hand.

'The lumber dealer nearby should have a ladder. I'll borrow it,' said Aida.

'I'll come with you. I also want to ask everyone here not to touch this door. Mr. Shinano, I'm going to ask you keep an eye on it, so you'll be responsible,' said the police officer forcefully. Shinano nodded reflexively and shot a nervous glance at the door.

One of the employees helped them carry it, but they still had trouble avoiding getting it tangled up in the overhead electricity lines as they made their way back to the Villa Notus. Going through the entrance gate, the police officer walked inside along the concrete wall until he was under the open window, then suddenly stopped dead in his tracks. On the previous night, he had not noticed the presence of a neat flower bed there. Light green buds were shooting up through the dark soil.

Little wooden stake labels like grave markers accompanied each plant, with its name carefully inscribed: China aster, Indian cress and Cydonia. If anyone had climbed in or out of the bedroom window, they would have to have left traces in the flower bed. Yet there were not even signs of a dog having walked there.

The policeman gave the concierge a quizzical look.

'We'll just have to try not to step in the centre of the bed.'

'What a shame, it looks as if they had just grown buds.'

After a short struggle, the three men managed to get beneath the window and place the base of the ladder against the wall. The young lumber dealer held the ladder firm, while the police officer and Aida climbed towards the window. Each time they took a step up, the bamboo ladder would bounce like rubber.

Eventually the two reached the window, grabbed the frame and climbed inside surprisingly easily. They could see nothing out of the ordinary as they looked across the bedroom. There was a gown on the bed, next to which was a table with a half-read book placed face-down on it, together with an empty water jug. The door to the living room was closed, and no sound came from the other side. The total silence made the men uneasy.

The policeman used his handkerchief, so as not to disturb any fingerprints as he gently turned the knob of the door to the living room. Once it was open, the concierge gasped as he saw what he had already anticipated.

'Please stay here, I'll take a closer look,' said the officer, sounding agitated.

3

The hallway door to Kashimura's rooms was eventually opened by officers from police headquarters. Just as Aida and the other policeman before them, the reinforcements had climbed the ladder to get into the bedroom, which they proceeded to search. Two keys were discovered, one in the pocket of the victim's gown, and the other in the drawer of the table. They were the only two keys in existence that could open the door to Kashimura's rooms.

The Villa Notus had been built by three persons of means who were members of the troupe's fan club. They had given serious consideration to the actors' wishes, which is why each apartment had two rooms. Each hallway door led to the living room, which in Kashimura's case was also the scene of the crime.

The bedroom was reached through a door in the living room, and housed a double bed. Some might think it was odd to have a double-bed in an apartment for single persons, but the patrons knew very well how nice it was to have a double-bed all to oneself.

One of the two windows in the bedroom was open. It was through that window the police had come in, and it was also assumed the murderer had made his escape the same way.

If he had brought a rope, climbing down would have been quite an easy task. Furthermore, the room below was the kitchen, which was usually empty at night (even an elephant hanging from a rope wouldn't have been noticed.) However, that possibility was ruled out by the absence of footprints in the flower bed.

There were also no signs of the bed having been used that night, nor had any of the lights in the bedroom been switched on.

'And this door was closed, is that correct?' asked Chief Inspector Tadokoro, an extremely ugly man with mean eyes and horse teeth, who had come from headquarters.

'Yes sir.'

'Was there anything out of the ordinary? Was there a smell of tobacco, even though the victim might not have smoked, or the scent of perfume, or anything like that?'

'No, nothing.'

'Hmm,' said the chief inspector, and he turned around to the pretentious-looking man behind him.

'Is there anything you would like to ask?'

'Nothing at all,' replied the other in an arrogant tone, not even bothering to turn around as he polished a snake wood walking stick. He was neatly dressed and had a pencil moustache like the deceased film star Ronald Colman.

Despite the man's pretentious airs, Tadokoro seemed to think very highly of him, and the two of them went into the living room, where the forensic investigators were still busy taking photographs. They could handle the corpse without giving it a second thought, like dry goods salesmen handling dried cod.

Katsuhiko Kashimura's body had turned cold and was lying bent so far backwards in a swivel-chair that his long hair almost touched the floor. His beloved Italian necktie had been wrapped around his neck twice and tied tightly behind his head.

He had been due to appear on television at the end of the week and appeared to have been studying his lines. On the desk lay a copy of a script for *He Who Whips*.

The room was illuminated by a blue fluorescent light in the ceiling, and there was also a standard reading lamp with a blue shade on the desk. Next to the lamp, which was still on, sat a saucer in which a short candle had been placed, of which only about three centimetres was left. The wax drops at the foot of the candle had hardened and reflected the light above dimly. The candle had still been lit when the police officer and the concierge had entered the room, but they had extinguished it before calling police headquarters. There had been a blackout in the whole neighbourhood the previous night.

While the candle obviously had burned in a different colour, the murdered Katsuhiko Kashimura had been a fan of blue light. That was the reason for the blue shade on his reading light and the blue fluorescent light in the ceiling. The blue aura gave the crime scene a surreal atmosphere.

The other actors had all been rounded up in a corner of the hallway and were looking anxiously at the ugly chief inspector. Fujie Takeda, a timid woman, shuddered at the very thought of being questioned by such a scary individual. The actors all felt afraid to stay alone in their rooms and felt safer congregated together.

The usual examinations were finally completed approximately two hours after the door was opened, and the remains of the stage play director were carried out.

A white cloth covered the body as it was being carried past the actors. The silhouette of the nose stood out like a pyramid. Many an actor had looked at that characteristic nose with hate whenever they'd had a row with the director. Even now, as they watched the body being carried away, there were cold looks in the eyes of many of them.

Immediately afterwards, they were ordered to convene in the canteen. As they had feared, the ugly chief inspector was going to interview them, like a high-ranking manager doing job interviews with applicants.

There were six men and women currently living in the Villa Notus, not counting Katsuhiko Kashimura, but including the concierge Aida. Tadokoro waited until they were all seated before reading out the names he had written in his notebook, in order to check which face belonged to which name.

His meticulous style made the actors even more nervous.

'Fuyuto Shinano. You are Fuyuto Shinano, am I correct?'

'Yes.'

'Fuyuto Shinano is a stage name, I assume. What is your real name?'

'Tarō Ōsaka.'

'And where were you born? In the Shinshū region, or in Kansai?'

The former Shinshū province was also known as Shinano, while Ōsaka is a major city in the Kansai region.

'Here in Tōkyō.'

Fuyuto had often boasted about having snatched a police officer's baton during a demonstration and hitting him on the helmet with it, but he showed none of that bravery now.

'What was the real name of Katsuhiko Kashimura?'

'Yoshihiko Kawamura.'

The chief inspector nodded as he wrote it down in his notebook, then looked up at Shinano.

'I believe you had a fight with the victim last night. Quite a show, I heard.'

Shinano gasped, and a moment passed before he replied.

'Yes, we had a fight. I'd had a bit too much to drink.'

'I like a drink myself, but I've never wielded a knife and said I wanted to kill someone. There must have been a reason. What was it?'

'Ye—yes, there was something. I'm engaged to Ms. Chisato Hara. That fellow Kashimura tricked her into drinking too much, and then took her to a hotel room. That's why we fought.'

Tadokoro continued writing in his notebook, then looked sharply at Chisato Hara.

'Was it consensual?'

'Consensual?'

'Did you have relations with that man of your own free will, even though you're engaged?'

'How dare you!'

Chisato Hara's eyes flashed angrily. She was a small woman, with a gypsy-like, wild beauty.

'Then you had a reason to kill Kashimura too.'

'Of course! Once wouldn't have been enough, I'd do it a second and third time.'

'Chisato, don't say that. He'll think you're the murderer,' the tall woman with the sizeable chest advised her. She sounded as if she didn't like the police.

'And you must be Terumi Isogawa.'

'Yes.'

'It was you who found the patrol officer, I believe.'

'No, it wasn't.'

Her eyebrows rose, as if to sneer at the policeman's defective memory. She had pronounced eyebrows, almost like a man's.

89

'That was Fujie Takeda here. Chisato and I only came in after their fight had ended. I didn't even know there had been a fight, and had simply gone to my room.'

'And did you have a reason to dislike Kashimura?'

'Of course not, don't be silly,' replied Terumi Isogawa, taking a deep breath, as if she were about to laugh. But the person who actually laughed was Yoneko Kaneko, who had just come into the canteen.

Yoneko had almond-shaped eyes, like a fox. Her long, sharp-angled face and her hair dyed red further strengthened her likeness to the animal. She crossed the canteen slowly and sat down in an empty chair. Her silent steps, too, were reminiscent of a fox.

'And why are you laughing?'

Terumi turned around to confront Yoneko. Her chair made a squeaking sound.

'Don't you think it's hilarious? You hated Kashimura enough to want him dead, too.'

'That's nonsense.'

'Really? I believe that television producer dumped you because of Kashimura's slanderous talk.'

'Lies! Who told you that!?'

Yoneko looked at Terumi and sneered. She took no notice of her adversary's protests, and took her cigarette case out from the pocket of her suit. It had a gaudy, red-and-white checkered motif.

'Does it really matter who told me?' she replied, lighting a cigarette and watching the exhaled smoke drift towards the ceiling.

'But for Kashimura, you'd be that producer's wife by now. You might not be able to dine with him every night, but a producer is a fantastic job, working with the cream of the cream.'

'If what you're saying is true, Ms. Isogawa has a motive for murder as well. But tell me, Ms. Kaneko, why would Kashimura spread slander about her?'

Tadokoro's unpleasant look was now fixed on Yoneko.

'I don't know, probably because she didn't do as he wanted. He always needed to make any woman he fancied his own. He tried his tricks with me too when we were in Atami.'

'Oh.'

'But it's his ex-wife who's really the victim here. You couldn't call it a marriage. Sometimes he'd be away from home for one or two months and other times, he'd bring home a different woman every

90

day. And when he was in a foul mood, he'd hit her, even with guests present. She became a nervous wreck, and I hear she's now in a mental institution.'

'Aha, so he was married once before. I thought it was strange that a man in his forties was still not married.'

The chief inspector turned to his pretentious companion and talked to him in a coaxing manner. But the man did not react and kept on polishing his virgin briar pipe.

Tadokoro gave up and turned back to Yoneko.

'So you weren't fond of Kashimura either, I presume?'

'Absolutely not. There were plenty of times when I wanted to kill that monster.'

A sinister grin appeared on her face as she looked around at the detectives and the head investigator of the local police station sitting at the tables.

'But I didn't kill him. I was recording a video from yesterday evening until this morning.'

'So you were at the television studio all night?' asked the chief inspector, pausing in his note-taking.

'Yes. There was an actor there who kept flubbing his lines, so we were all stuck there until this morning. That's why I'm exhausted.' She realised she should have been emphasising something else, so she quickly added: 'That's why I couldn't have committed the murder.'

'And where would the studio be?'

She supplied the address and Tadokoro made a sign to a police detective, who went out to use the telephone in the concierge's office.

4

'What did you learn?'

'Ms. Kaneko is telling the truth. Both the producer and his assistant confirmed her alibi.'

'Very well,' said the chief inspector, and he turned his attention to the concierge.

'Mr. Aida, is the front entrance left unlocked throughout the night?'

'Yes, actors often have to work late into the night, so I don't lock the front door. But I do lock the back door, the canteen and the kitchen before I go to bed.'

'By the way, I believe there was a blackout last night.'

'Yes, there was.'

Aida bowed his grey head. There was no need for him to apologise, but to Fuyuto Shinano, who was standing next to him, it appeared the old man really seemed sorry.

'When was this?'

'Oh, I think the lights went out at about twenty to twelve. It was after that police officer left here at half past eleven. I had just closed the main gas tap and when I returned to my room to have a cigarette, the lights went out.'

'Yes, the blackout occurred immediately after I returned to the station, sir.'

'Was there an incident of some kind?'

'No, they'd made an announcement in advance that they'd be repairing the electricity lines and there would be a blackout between half past eleven and one o'clock.'

'When were the repairs done?'

'At exactly half past midnight, sir. I checked my watch, and my colleague was there too, standing guard.'

'All right, but just in case, someone make a call to the power company and ask for the exact times. Because this is quite important.'

A detective from headquarters nodded this time and went out.

Tadokoro turned back to the actors, ready to continue his questioning.

'We now know that Mr. Shinano, Ms. Chisato Hara, Ms. Isogawa and Ms. Kaneko all had motives for wanting to kill Kashimura, so that leaves you, Ms. Takeda. Were you harassed by Kashimura too?'

Fujie Takeda stared at the floor. She specialised in playing elderly women, and while she was not ugly, she didn't really look young either. She lacked the bright, energetic attractiveness young women usually had.

'Don't be afraid,' Yoneko said to her. At first it sounded as though she was trying to encourage her to speak to the chief inspector, but she wasn't.

'I know a good doctor, I'll introduce you to him. Even if it already has little limbs like a frog, he'll get it out. You'll be given anaesthetics, so you won't feel a thing.'

'But....'

'It's all right. It's less complicated than an appendectomy.'

The discussion was going off the rails.

'Excuse me.'

'Oh,' the red-haired girl said suddenly, as if she had forgotten about the chief inspector's presence. 'This girl, she's pregnant. She's in her eighth month.'

'Oh.'

'It's Kashimura's child, but he wouldn't admit it. No matter how much poor Fujie cried, he pretended he'd had nothing to do with the baby. Pig-headed all the way, until he got murdered.'

'Yes, a baby with a brute like that, you're better off without it,' said Terumi Isogawa, agreeing with Yoneko.

Tadokoro couldn't believe his ears. What had once been a major crime before the war, was now being done by everyone. And they didn't even feel ashamed, daring to talk about it in front of others.

'So, Ms. Takeda, I take it you also detested Kashimura?'

'Yes.'

She was still looking at the floor as she spoke. Just then, the police detective who had been sent away returned.

'Sir, the blackout lasted between twenty to twelve and half-past, exactly fifty minutes.'

'Well then, I need to know everyone's movements between those times. Kashimura was murdered while he was studying his lines.'

The women looked away as the chief inspector spoke. Even the most innocent would be afraid under his frightening gaze.

'Mr. Shinano, what were you doing last night?'

'I was asleep. I was still worked up, so I took six sleeping pills instead of the usual three. Even so, I didn't fall asleep immediately.'

'What about the rest of you?'

The actresses' replies were similar and none of them could offer a solid alibi. They had all gone to bed when the blackout started, but nobody could confirm their story. Fujie Takeda hadn't been able to fall asleep either, and she too had taken sleeping pills.

'I took them around midnight, and fell asleep about thirty minutes later.'

'You had water in your room?'

'No, I found my way to the drinking fountain in the dark. There's a water tap right near the stairs.'

'Aha,' muttered Tadokoro as he leant his large body forward.

'The murder must have happened around that time. Did you perhaps hear the sound of footsteps walking down the hallway, or a cry, or the noise of a struggle?'

Fujie shook her head slowly.

'No, I noticed candle-light through the gaps around Kashimura's door, but I just assumed he was studying his lines.'

The chief inspector seemed dissatisfied with the answer, and consulted his notebook.

Nothing of value had been taken, so he could omit the possibility of a robbery gone wrong. That meant the problem could be condensed into the following three questions:

Who killed Kashimura?

How did the killer escape from a locked room?

If he escaped through the window, why were there no footprints in the flower bed below?

No matter how hard he racked his brains, Tadokoro was stumped. There was no way to get out of Kashimura's room other than through the door or the window.

His only option was to turn the case over to his pretentious companion, the celebrated private detective Ryūzō Hoshikage. It was for that reason he had sent a car to pick the maestro up from his office and bring him over.

The chief inspector coughed once and announced that the questioning was over for the time being, and the actors and the concierge could leave.

'You will be free to go anywhere you want in another thirty minutes, but until then, please don't leave the building. My men will be watching,' he continued in a stern voice.

Hoshikage had the unfortunate habit of demeaning the chief to his face, and the latter had to live with that to get the job done, but he certainly didn't want to be belittled in front of the actors. The thirty-minute pause was in order for Hoshikage to do whatever he needed. To be honest, Tadokoro didn't really like the fellow, but he was well aware of his gifts.

After everyone had left, the chief inspector turned to Hoshikage.

'Well, that's what we have. If you've formed an opinion about the case...'

Ryūzō Hoshikage stared down at his well-manicured nails. There was no reply for a while, but then he suddenly spoke in a supercilious voice, without looking at the policeman.

'It's obvious that the murderer left through the door and escaped down the hallway. If he had gone through the window, there would have been footprints in the flower bed.'

'But the door was....'

'...Locked, so it was impossible to escape through the door? But the culprit did in fact escape from the room. The door was open, so he could get out.'

'But then who locked the door?'

'The culprit, of course.'

'Why would he do that? Wouldn't he want to get out of the building without being spotted, rather than lose time locking the door?'

Whenever Tadokoro spoke to Hoshikage, he was always careful to end with a question. Declaring anything as a fact was sure to annoy the amateur detective.

'The culprit had his reasons. One was to delay the discovery of the murder. And the other was... no, I'll come back to that later.'

'Very well.'

'Now, regarding the key. The murderer took it with him, but by the time we arrived at the scene, it had already been returned to either the gown pocket of the victim, or the drawer of the desk. Who put it back?'

'Who?'

'You don't know? It seems you're becoming more feebleminded by the day.'

The chief inspector swallowed his pride as he asked the question.

'So who did return the key, then?'

'That fellow over there.'

Hoshikage's delicate finger pointed to the police officer from the local police station, who was standing by the wall.

'The concierge climbed up the ladder into the bedroom together with the officer, but he got no farther than the bedroom. The only person who went into the living room was that officer.'

Tadokoro didn't know what to say.

'It was simple for him to distract the concierge and slip the key back, either in the desk drawer or the gown pocket.'

'But Mr. Hoshikage, I admit he'd have had an opportunity to return the key, but he couldn't have gone out to kill Kashimura. After he'd completed his rounds, he continued his shift at the police station in the presence of a colleague and never left.'

'Oh, you're such a dim-wit. Didn't he say he'd gone up with Kashimura after the fight in the canteen? That's when Kashimura was killed.'

'But wasn't Kashimura still alive up until the blackout? He was killed while he was studying his lines by candlelight. Even supposing it was the murderer who lit the candle, the officer had already returned to the police box by then. He couldn't have lit the candle.'

Tadokoro felt he couldn't stand by while a fellow police officer was being accused of murder. He gingerly tried to refute Hoshikage's accusation.

The detective cast a pitying look at him.

'The blackout had been announced in advance. The police officer knew it was going to happen, so after killing Kashimura he lit a candle while the lights were still working. Then he left.'

The chief inspector was silent.

'The only person who gained an alibi from that trickery was your officer. It wouldn't have helped any of the residents here.'

'I see.'

'That's why he couldn't risk anyone noticing he'd lit the candle before the lights had gone out. The case would be over if we learnt that fact. The reason the door had been locked was not just to delay the discovery of the corpse in order to make it difficult to determine the exact time of Kashimura's death, but also to hide the lit candle.'

'And the bedroom window had been left open to make it seem as though the murderer had escaped through there,' added Tadokoro carefully.

'Exactly. The murder had been committed on impulse, so he did not know about the flower bed. If the ground there had been hard, I might have deduced who the murderer was, but been unable to prove it. It was the absence of footprints in the flower bed which identified the murderer, in fact.'

At that point Hoshikage suddenly stopped talking and started to polish his pipe again.

The police officer, who had not said a word or moved a muscle, suddenly started to talk.

'My younger sister went crazy in a mental institution, and died there. It was her husband, Kashimura, who killed her. I loved my sister. I wanted to meet him myself just once, to have him apologise for all he had done. Last night, I happened to run into him, and when he introduced himself as Kashimura, I could feel my blood boil. I couldn't control myself anymore, and no damned apology would be enough.'

'And he didn't know you?' asked Tadokoro gently.

'My sister had decided to marry him all by herself and so my family had broken off all relations with her. That's why Kashimura didn't recognise me. He didn't suspect anything as he led me up to his living room, which is when I attacked him. I was in a frenzy as I grabbed for his neck...'

His voice trembled with emotion, but then he turned silent. The other officers all looked at the man who had now confessed everything.

Only Ryūzō Hoshikage seemed to take no notice of him, as he continued polishing his pipe.

Death in Early Spring

The case turned out to be one Chief Inspector Onitsura would never forget. Not because the details were exceedingly morbid, nor because the culprit turned out to be the least expected person, but because Onitsura found himself helpless when confronted with the culprit's perfect alibi. He had been close to his own personal Dunkirk, but by desperately hanging on, he managed to avoid being thrown into the English Channel. Even today, thinking back to the case caused him to shudder.

To understand the full detail of what happened, it is unfortunately necessary to examine a dry series of railway timetables. Only by doing so will it become clear how the culprit managed to mystify the chief inspector without utilising any special trickery of their own.

1

The body was discovered on the bone-chilling early morning of the ninth of January. It was found at the construction site of the Nippon Building, on the outskirts of Gofukubashi 3-Chōme, a one-or-two-minute walk from the Yaesu Exit of Tōkyō Station. The discovery had been made by the site foreman of Nagatani Group, the contractor. Despite the proximity of the Yaesu Exit Police Box (1) and the bustle of the nearby Tōkyō Station, the area was apparently a blind spot: two months earlier, another victim had been murdered there and she, too, had not been discovered until the following morning.

The victim this time, a young man of less than thirty, seemed to have struggled with his assailant and put up quite a lot of resistance. One of his red shoes had been kicked all the way to the centre of the construction site, while his broken horn-rimmed glasses were found three metres away, beneath the concrete mixer. The top two buttons of his overcoat had also been ripped off. It seemed clear that, during the violent struggle, the victim had fallen and hit his head on a log, leading to a concussion. He had then been choked to death with a muffler while still unconscious.

(1) A small police station with only two or three policemen

99

Frost coloured his overcoat white, and the reflection of the morning sun made it gleam.

According to the business card retrieved from the inner pocket of his coat, the victim's name was Kazuomi Kokuryō. He worked at the Far East Paper Mill in Chigasaki and had been staying at a boarding house in Nagano.

The assailant had left almost nothing behind. Even the muffler used as the murder weapon appeared to have belonged to the victim. The only clue found was a lighter, lying in a corner where planks had been piled up. It was a New Gold Dunhill lighter, but it was unclear whether it belonged to the assailant or a passer-by. It was clear, however, that the lighter did not belong to the victim. No cigarettes were found, either in his overcoat or in the rest of his clothes, and his fingers did not bear the typical yellowish stains of a smoker.

As the investigators went about their work, the workers at the site gathered to watch them, warming themselves at a brazier before eventually going about their tasks. The morning mist dispersed as the mixers started to growl and rivets started to be hammered, in an incessant machine-gun-like ruckus. The stream of office workers pouring out of the Yaesu Exit grew larger by the minute. The early-morning silence of the metropolis became a cacophony. Only the area around the victim seemed like an oasis, a slice carved out of a large cake.

2

In order to determine the time of the crime, it was not enough to simply wait for the autopsy results. It was also necessary to verify the movements of the victim on the fateful night. On the orders of Chief Inspector Onitsura, Detective Tanna headed immediately to Tōkyō Station, to take the Shōnan line to Chigasaki and visit the Far East Paper Mill there.

For Tanna, who had been working non-stop in the dust of the city, the short trip was more than welcome. He could at least forget about the case while riding the train. Once it had passed Yokohama and was starting to approach Tozuka, Tanna looked out of the window at the hilly, undulating terrain and imagined how nice it would be to have a property there and tend flowers on his days off. He started dreaming about how his own house would look.

100

Seventy minutes after it had left Tōkyō, the train arrived at Chigasaki. As he looked at the long, open platform, Tanna realised how wrong he had been to expect a bustling train station. The realisation continued as he stepped out into the station yard. It was peaceful enough, but it appeared to him that the town lacked verve and he began to miss the never-ending ruckus of Tōkyō. Nevertheless, he did enjoy the bracing air, which was due to the town's proximity to the sea.

He asked at the local police box for directions to the mill, then followed the Tōkaidō road in the direction of Tsujidō. The mill was only 800 metres away, so walking would be faster than waiting for the bus. He followed the concrete wall on the left side of the walkway, and when it ended he had arrived at the entrance of the Far East Paper Mill. An elderly guard sitting inside the janitor's room was looking his way.

'Mr. Kokuryō was murdered? I can't believe it.'

His face turned pale and he stood up from his chair, his hands pressing down on the desk.

'You really can't tell what destiny has in store for you. Why, he looked so cheerful when he left here yesterday,' sighed the man sadly. Tanna offered him a cigarette and had one himself, as he expertly steered the conversation in order to quickly learn all he needed to build a picture of the late Kazuomi Kokuryō.

'He came here three years ago. About the same time I started working here. He was a happy person, and very athletic. He participated in the National Sports Festival last year,' he explained. 'He didn't smoke, but he did like his drink. I sometimes had a beer with him. It's hard to imagine him having done anything that would make anyone want to kill him. But...'

He paused and stared at the pine grove just beyond the walls of the mill. They could hear the loud clucking of partridges there and the singing of the birds in the trees.

'Yes?' urged Tanna.

The guard, his thick glasses pushed up on his forehead, looked grim and seemed reluctant to talk. He looked uneasy as he stared at the withered chrysanthemums in the flower bed outside the window.

'It may just be my imagination,' he began slowly. 'You see, Mr. Kokuryō worked overtime yesterday, and he had a little chat with me on his way out. He was going to meet a female friend at eight o'clock at Tōkyō Station, and they were going to go dancing. He seemed to be really looking forward to it. He took a look at the clock over there and said he mustn't miss his train, so he said goodbye and left.'

He pointed to an octagonal wall clock on the wall behind him.

'What train did he take?' asked Tanna. The information would help him determine the earliest time Kokuryō could have been murdered.

'He said he was going to take the 18:38 train. He used to board in Nakano and commute here every day. Whenever he left work on time, he'd take the 17:37 train home.'

The only public transport serving the small town was the Shōnan train line, and the guard had memorised the times of the trains.

Chigasaki (Departure)	Tōkyō Station (Arrival)
17:37	18:40
18:08	19:11
18:38	19:50
18:47	19:56
19:25	20:38
19:39	20:53

'After he left, I became absorbed in a novel and didn't really pay more attention. It was only when the nine o'clock siren sounded that I looked at the clock, and realised that it had stopped running at twenty-past six.'

So what if the clock had stopped running? What Tanna wanted to know was the name of the female friend Kokuryō had been planning to see.

'Sorry, I can't help you there. But he left here not knowing the clock had stopped, so maybe he didn't even make it in time for the 18:38 train. I fear he may not even have made it to the train after that, the 18:47, in which case his return to Tōkyō would have been quite late. I have a feeling the two of them may have had a fight because of that, which ended in the most terrible manner.'

So that was the reason he had hesitated to speak. If Kokuryō's death had been related to the office clock which had stopped running, the guard must have felt some responsibility himself.

'That doesn't really seem likely. You said Mr. Kokuryō was athletic, so I can't imagine, even on the spur of the moment, how a woman could have killed him.' Tanna tried to soothe the man, but in his own mind he thought the guard might actually be right. Perhaps the wound on the back of the victim's head hadn't been caused by him falling on a log. What if the victim hadn't been on his guard, had turned his back on her and been hit from behind by some kind of bar the woman had been concealing? The two might have struggled, and in his dazed state the woman could have managed to strangle him. And if he had been drunk, the task would have been even easier.

With this in mind, Tanna became even more curious about Kokuryō's time of arrival in the city, so he took the railway timetable out of his pocket. Fifteen minutes was ample time to walk from there to the station, even slowly. Hence, even if Kokuryō had left the mill at exactly twenty past six, he could still have easily made the 18:38 train. And if he had missed it, he would only have needed to wait nine minutes for the next one, the 18:47. The two trains arrived at Tōkyō Station at 19:50 and 19:56, respectively, which would get him there in time for his eight o'clock appointment with his female friend, giving her no reason to get upset.

But if he had missed both trains, he would have arrived in Tōkyō at 20:38, and he would have been almost forty minutes late for his appointment. Unless the woman was extremely patient and didn't care about him being on time, it was clear she would have been far from happy.

But because the office clock had stopped, it was impossible to determine the exact time Kokuryō had left the mill. Tanna could imagine all kinds of scenarios, but none of them would establish exactly what time Kokuryō arrived in Tōkyō.

After thanking the guard, Tanna proceeded to interview Kokuryō's superiors and colleagues about the victim, but he learned nothing more of importance.

'He was doing all the work that had been delayed by influenza on his own, so it's impossible to say how late he worked. The name of his girlfriend? Oh, he did mention something about her, but I don't remember him telling me her name.'

So the long trip Tanna had made to Chigasaki had left him no further forward, and he returned to Tōkyō.

3

Tanna had not succeeded in finding out in Chigasaki what train Kokuryō had taken, nor the identity of the woman he had been going to meet, but those facts were uncovered several hours later due to a completely different lead. Determining the time at which Kokuryō had arrived in Tōkyō was an especially crucial element for investigating a new suspect's alibi.

A different investigative team had gone to the victim's boarding house in Nakano Uchikoshichō, where they had found his address book with the names of four women in it. All four women were paid a visit. The first of them, named Hanako, turned out to be an elderly lady nearly seventy years old. The results were equally poor for the second and third names, but when Detective Teshigawara went to see Shizuko Shibazaki in Shibuya Hachiyamachō, he felt invigorated, knowing he had found his target.

As he stood in front of her residence, by the side of the busway to Meguro, the sun had already begun to set. The porch light hanging above the front door shone dimly on a garland beneath, a souvenir of the New Year celebrations.

As she led him into a traditional Japanese room and offered him a seat at the *hibachi* brazier, Shizuko Shibazaki told the detective that she had just returned from her office job in Kyōbashi. The name Teshigawara might sound like that of an experienced master in Japanese flower arrangement, but it was actually the first time the young detective had been invited into the private dwelling of an adult female. He looked at the vibrantly decorated room as if he were Hindbad being invited into Sinbad's home. He warmed his hands awkwardly at the brazier, but when his fingers accidentally touched those of his host, almost as delicate as glass, he quickly pulled away.

Her beauty was more than enough to make him feel nervous. A pretty, pink two-piece dress did nothing to conceal her well-proportioned figure, and her wide eyes and oval face gave an intelligent, even innocent, impression. The powerful scent of perfume that wafted towards the detective almost made him cough.

'I learnt what had happened to Mr. Kokuryō from the newspaper I bought on my way home. He had invited me to go out dancing last night. We were to meet at eight o'clock on platform 12 at Tōkyō Station.'

In his mind, the young detective was thinking how lucky the victim had been, to have been able to hold hands with such an attractive woman and dance with her.

'But for some reason, he didn't arrive on the ten to eight train, nor the one after that, at four minutes to eight. I got angry with him for letting a lady like me wait, so I went home. If only I had just waited for the next train.'

An expression of regret appeared on her lovely face. The next train would have been the local train starting from Ōsaka, departing from Chigasaki at 19:25 and arriving at Tōkyō Station at 20:38. Teshigawara knew he needed to determine at what time the victim had arrived in the city.

'How do you know that Mr. Kokuryō arrived on that train?'

Shizuko stood up and left the room, returning shortly with an open envelope in her hands.

'This is a letter from Mr. Kokuryō which came this morning. I only read it just now, after I got back from work.'

Teshigawara took the envelope and checked the postmark. It was postmarked Tōkyō Central Office, and had been collected between six and twelve p.m. With a six-hour range, the collection period wouldn't tell them much, even if Kokuryō had posted the letter himself at Tōkyō Station.

Shizuko, guessing what was on Teshigawara's mind, told him he could read the contents of the letter.

It was immediately obvious it had been written on a train. The shaky writing immediately spoke of love, in such passionate terms that even Teshigawara, someone of the younger generation, could feel his face turn red. Shizuko Shibazaki, however, sat still with her hands on her lap without a sign of embarrassment, merely gazing expressionlessly at the detective's forehead.

It appeared that Kokuryō's plan had been to flatter Shizuko in the first half of his letter and to explain why he had been late for their date in the second half, hoping to appease her anger. The first half conjured up an image of him kneeling in front of Shizuko, asking for her forgiveness. His shaky writing wasn't just due to the vibration of the moving train, but also to his passionate feelings.

In the second half of the letter, where he explained his tardiness, he seemed calmer, but as this part, too, had been written on the train, there were a still a few spots where the writing was hard to make out. Even so, the second half was far easier to read compared to the first. The gist was that Kokuryō had missed his planned train and was now riding in the 19:25 train from Chigasaki; that he guessed that by the time he arrived in the city that Shizuko would already have left angrily; that it wasn't his fault he'd missed his train, because a clock had stopped running; that he was writing the letter in the train and would post it if Shizuko wasn't there by the time he arrived, etc., etc.

Thanks to the letter, Teshigawara discovered that the victim had indeed taken the 19:25 train. Just thinking that this man, so desperate to soothe his girl friend, had turned into a corpse a few hours later made young Teshigawara realise just how fragile and fleeting life could be.

'Are you sure the handwriting in this letter is that of Mr. Kokuryō?'

'Yes. But I want to make one thing clear first.'

'Yes.'

'The feelings of love Mr. Kokuryō had towards me were one-sided.'

'Ah.'

'Mr. Kokuryō had proposed to me once already, and I had declined. I only saw him as a friend. I had no special feelings of love or admiration towards him.'

She expressed herself quite clearly, to make sure Teshigawara would not misunderstand their relationship. He nodded vigorously to show he understood what she meant.

'By the way, would you happen to know anyone who might harbour a grudge against Mr. Kokuryō? His wallet was still inside his overcoat, so it is unlikely he was killed during a robbery.'

Teshigawara's sharp eyes didn't miss the fact that, for a brief moment, the expression on the girl's face changed, as if she had thought of someone. She remained silent for a while, but then shook her head.

'No, sorry.'

The detective was disappointed by her reply, but decided to not press the matter further and try a different angle.

'One more question, please. A shiny gold-coloured New Gold lighter was found at the scene of the crime. It looks to have been used extensively, judging by the scuff marks. It's what's usually called a Dunhill-type lighter, manufactured in Japan. Would you happen to know anybody who uses such a lighter?'

As she listened to Teshigawara's description of the lighter, her expression changed visibly. It was obvious it did ring a bell. Her curved red lips pouted.

'Yes, I do.'

'And who would that person be?' Teshigawara raised his voice as he leaned towards her. Shizuko, however, did not reply immediately, but only looked coolly back at the detective.

106

'Suppose I'm wrong? It could be quite awkward in that case, so will you promise not to mention my name? Otherwise I won't tell you,' she said clearly. From the curve of her eyebrows, Teshigawara was sure that, unless he promised, she would never speak, not even if she were hung upside down.

'I promise that I will not mention your name nor cause you any trouble.'

'Then I will tell you. I have a Mr. Fukujirō Fuda among my friends. He owns a New Gold Dunhill-type lighter.'

'Fuda?'

'Yes. He is a securities broker, working for a firm in Kayabachō. And, just like Mr. Kokuryō, he asked me to marry him.'

'So the two men were rivals?'

'Yes.'

'Was Mr. Fuda aware that Mr. Kokuryō had asked you marry him as well?'

'Yes. That's why those two hated each other. As I just told you, I only saw Mr. Kokuryō as a friend, and I felt the same way about Mr. Fuda. Mr. Fuda asked me to marry him about three weeks after Mr. Kokuryō did, but I declined both their proposals, saying politely I would like to stay friends forever. But Mr. Fuda seems to think I turned him down because of Mr. Kokuryō, and he's been telling me awful things, untrue things of course, about Mr. Kokuryō since.'

'How petty-minded.'

A wry smile appeared on Shizuko's face.

'But Mr. Kokuryō was the same. Each man was pointing out the other's bad points in an attempt to woo me over. With men acting like that, I really don't feel like ever marrying anyone.'

'That would be a shame.' Teshigawara accidentally let slip his honest opinion. He felt awkward, but she didn't seem to notice.

'Each man seemed to hate the other, so I was afraid something like this would eventually happen.'

Although she had a childish, innocent-looking face, Shizuko's outlook on the situation was quite mature. Pleased with his unexpected catch, Teshigawara asked for Fukujirō Fuda's address and about what kind of person he was. With Kokuryō's letter and his own notebook tucked safely in his pocket, he took his leave from the beautiful woman.

4

After Teshigawara's phone report to the investigation headquarters, Tanna was sent immediately to Taisei Securities in Nihonbashi Kayabachō 4-Chōme. Cases where a romantic rival is murdered in order to win over the girl are far from rare. With a suspect now identified, everyone at headquarters seemed to feel somewhat relieved.

Tanna went to the rear of the Taisei Securities building and found the service entrance already open. He had called in advance, and an elderly section chief with thinning hair was waiting for him in the janitor's office. Tanna was led to a waiting room near the front of the building. All the employees had already gone home, and the offices with their vaulted ceilings gave off a cold feeling.

A small blackboard had been scribbled full of long numbers, probably the day's rates. Every minor change in the global economy or politics was reflected precisely, but that didn't interest a man like Tanna, who understood nothing about the subject.

'Fuda is still young, but he's quite daring when it comes to cutting a deal, and is not be outdone by veterans who have been in the job for ten to fifteen years. He's easily moving three or four million yen a day. What about him?'

Tanna briefly explained the case without going into details, but to his surprise, the section chief seemed to be relieved at hearing why Tanna had come.

'Oh, I see, you're from Investigative Division I. I feared you might be from Division II, and that Fuda may have violated the trust of one of our clients.'

'Has that happened before?'

'No, no, and we'd be right out of business if it had. Our line of work is based solely on trust.'

The section chief became solemn.

'Fuda wasn't himself yesterday, and this morning he didn't show up for work. I was worried, so I called his boarding house and was told he hadn't come home last night, which made me nervous.'

'What kind of person is Mr. Fuda?'

'Well, he's perfectly normal, until he starts drinking.'

'And then what?'

'Some people become cheerful and generous, but Fuda becomes pale and gets a nasty look in his eye and becomes really unpleasant.

At the year-end party last year, he started a fight with a young colleague and fell down the stairs.'

That was the only fault his superior could find with Fuda, whose performance he otherwise praised.

But where had Fukujirō Fuda gone? Detectives had been sent to his rooms in Ōmori, to friends he might have stayed with, and even to his parents' home in Shizuoka City, but after three days there was still no sign of him. The only lead they got was when the female proprietor of Bar Tyltyl appeared at the police station. She testified that Fuda had visited her bar opposite Ueno Station on the night of January 8 at half past seven. He had borrowed fifty thousand yen from her, with his Vacheron Constantin watch, which he valued more than his own life, as collateral. He then had three highballs and left her bar.

Fuda had visited the bar five minutes after Kokuryō had stepped on to the train in Chigasaki at twenty-five-past seven. It was clear that, before killing Kokuryō, Fuda had prepared sufficient funds to escape. He had thought of everything, as might be expected of an experienced securities broker.

'He'd often come to my bar, and I never could have imagined he might kill someone, so I thought it wouldn't hurt to help him out with a hundred thousand yen. But I only had fifty thousand in cash around, and the banks were already closed, so I hoped it would be enough.'

Thus spoke the slightly plump but attractive woman, as she handed over the expensive Vacheron Constantin watch.

On the fifth day after the murder, the police received a tip that Fukujirō Fuda was hiding in Tanogun, Onishimachi, in the prefecture of Gunma. The female proprietor of Fukube, a traditional inn, had recognized Fuda's picture from the newspapers, but it took another full day for the tip to make its way from the prefecture to the Metropolitan Police Department, and for Tanna to head north with an arrest warrant in his pocket.

He took the Hachikō Line from Hachiōji and got off at Gunma-Fujioka. He visited the police station there and was assigned an officer as a guide. The short Tōkyō detective and the large Gunma detective took a bus, which swayed as they chatted casually about the local produce and famous local food. Fields of leafless mulberry trees could be seen for miles on end on both sides of the national highway. A northern wind made the dried leaves on the grey road dance up into the sky.

Eventually the inns of the Yashio Spring in the foothills came into view. Tanna thought about his target possibly hiding there, while his colleague was still blathering on about how cherry trees were still blooming in this cold, how thrilling families were where the wife was in charge, and how to grow konjac.

The chatter went on until their bus arrived at the outskirts of Onishimachi. It was a dull, dreary town, whose residents all appeared to be asleep in their beds. The houses all looked new because a huge fire had burned down large parts of the town.

A large illustration of a gourd decorated the white walls of the Fukube Inn from the first floor up, so the detectives could already spot their destination from the far end of the street. The Fujioka detective knew the proprietor already, and she led them up to the first floor, where there were two rooms on either side of the corridor, all with their *shōji* sliding doors shut.

The woman indicated which room they wanted, and left the detectives, whereupon they pulled the sliding door open. Fuda was inside, warming his hands over the *hibachi* brazier, munching on some peanuts and reading a book. When the detectives appeared, he jumped up, his eyes darting across the room to look for some way of escape.

When he realised there was no way out, he seemed to calm down again. There was even a defiant smile on his face.

'Who are you? You can't just barge into someone's room!' he protested as he glared at the two men. When Tanna presented the arrest warrant, Fuda tried to tear it up, but the large Fujioka detective stepped in and put handcuffs on their man.

'I didn't do it! Let go of me! Get these off! Damn you!'

He resisted violently, and even after the two detectives each grabbed him by one arm he kept shrieking, eventually kicking through the paper door.

5

After they brought Fukujirō Fuda back from the lonely corner of the country to the bustling Tōkyō metropolis, he immediately became his normal self. At his questioning the following day, he denied he had tried to flee.

'I never did anything wrong, so why would I run away? I've always wanted to stay in a small rural town, to relax for a week or so. You won't know what I'm talking about unless you have to make every meal yourself every day. I'd made a mistake at work and was completely down, so I decided take time off and travel a bit, for a change of mood. You detectives didn't need to come, I was already thinking about returning to the city because my funds were running low.'

Once he got started, Fuda kept on chatting, but his dry hair and pale, tired face betrayed the psychological impact of his life on the run. It was not unusual for a criminal to show relief when finally caught and become chatty as a sort of reflex.

'What time did you leave work that day?' asked Onitsura. It was first necessary to learn the suspect's movements on the night of the crime.

'I left as per schedule, at five.'

'Where did you go next?'

'As I told you, I felt blue, so I didn't feel like going home right away. I strolled over to Kyōbashi, where I visited a mah-jong parlour I frequent.'

'What time did you arrive there?'

'Well, I wasn't checking my watch all the time, so I can't tell you exactly. I'd guess around half-past five. I did one full game, ate something there and left. The time? I can't be more precise, but I'd say half past six.'

'And then?'

'After that, I strolled along the Ginza. At a bookshop I noticed a book on travelling, which gave me the urge to go somewhere. On the spur of the moment I decided to go to the Kamimoku hot springs. I checked the timetables and took the eight o'clock train to Niigata.'

Onitsura had never visited the hot springs himself, but had heard they were located in a beautiful place, in a valley upstream from the Tone River, with many ties to famous female criminals. It was home to the family of O-Koma Shirakoya, also known as O-Kuma, the heroine of the Kabuki drama *Kamiyui Shinza*, and also to the family of the famous vixen Oden Takahashi.

'And then?'

'I took a cab to Bar Tyltyl in Ueno. The owner is quite wealthy and generous too, so I wanted to borrow some money with my watch as the collateral.'

'When did you arrive at the bar?'

'I think around half-past seven. But she only had fifty thousand. I could hardly leave immediately after borrowing her money, so I had two, or maybe three, drinks first. But I had to catch the 20:00 train, so I couldn't hang around too long. I left Tyltyl at ten minutes to eight. I checked the clock, so I know that for sure. I took the underpass and passed the ticket gate five minutes before departure. I made it just in time.'

The chief inspector was listening very attentively. He needed to pay careful attention. He couldn't allow himself to be fooled by this man. Around the time Fuda's train left Ueno, the train with Kazuomi Kokuryō on it was still somewhere around Yokohama. If Fuda had killed Kokuryō, that would mean he had not actually taken the train to Niigata and that he had remained in Tōkyō. He frowned as he checked his notes on the movements of both Fuda and Kokuryō in his notebook.

Time	Fuda	Time	Kokuryō
17:00	Leaves work.		
17:30	Visits Kyōbashi mah-jong		
18:30	Leaves, walks to Ginza		
19:20	Takes cab to Ueno		
		19:25	Takes train from Chigasaki
19:30	Borrows money at Tyltyl		
19:50	Leaves Tyltyl	20:00	Passes by Yokohama
20:00	Takes train from Ueno Station to Niigata	20:38	Arrives at Tōkyō Station

'I arrived at twenty-past midnight at Kamimoku and, after a ten-minute walk from the station, I found an inn called Hanaya near the river. I woke the people there up and got a room. If you don't believe me, you can check with them. But I was trying to escape from being Fukujirō Fuda, the securities broker, so I used a fake name. I stayed there for three days, but then I decided I wanted a more rural place, so I moved on to Onishimachi.'

Fuda appeared self-confident, irritatingly so. If Fuda had really taken that eight o'clock train from Ueno, he could not have killed Kokuryō.

'Can you prove you took that train?'

'I'm sure you'd love to hear that I can't, but I can,' replied Fuda sarcastically.

'It appears there's a shortage of eligible men these days. I was sitting opposite a lady and her eligible daughter in the train all the way from Ueno. She told me her husband was a member of the prefectural assembly and that her parents run a large apple orchard in Nagano Prefecture. It was obvious she was trying to hook her daughter up with me. She kept talking to me, and when she learned I was single, she gave me her business card. A fortune teller once told me I was a ladies' man, and I guess he was right, ha ha!'

'Do you still have that business card?'

'I tore it up and threw it away when I arrived in Kamimoku. I have a woman in Tōkyō and we love each other very much, so I have no interest in some daughter of a member of a prefectural assembly. But I remember her name was Namegawa of Ryōtsu, Sado. I hope you can find her and have her confirm my story. I need to be able to walk free again. One night in a small cell is more than enough.'

He was so confident, Onitsura was inclined to believe him. He produced the lighter, which Fuda took and clicked on.

'This is mine. Where did you find it?'

'Lying next to the victim. Can you explain that?'

'Actually, I lost it at the beginning of the month. Perhaps the killer stole it from me and left it at the scene of the crime to implicate me?'

Fuda had an answer for everything. Onitsura suspected that he had read the details in the newspapers while he was on the run, which would have given him time to think of an excuse. He was going to have to send someone to Sado to locate that wife of an assembly member.

6

The investigation had come to a halt. Tanna had crossed the turbulent Sea of Japan to Sado, and had returned with confirmation of Fuda's story. That meant that Fuda's movements after he arrived at Tyltyl had now been determined, without any holes in his story. Yet it had to be false somewhere. There had to be some trickery. Onitsura went over Fuda's alibi countless times and also visited the owner of Tyltyl again. But all his efforts only led him back to the same place.

Meanwhile Tanna had become fixated on his earlier idea that Shizuko Shibazaki had got into a fight with Kokuryō when he arrived late for their date and accidentally killed him. He, too, tried to break her alibi, but he learnt that she had indeed become angry with Kokuryō and returned to her home in Shibuya from Tōkyō Station immediately, with no room for any doubt.

Onitsura had placed a potted primrose on his desk the day the case started, but with his mind preoccupied, he had forgotten to water it and it had eventually died. The fate of the dried-up flower seemed to be a harbinger of the Kokuryō investigation.

At the next investigation conference, several voices suggested letting Fuda go before the end of the detention period. The number of supporters grew quickly, like victims in a plague outbreak. Even Tanna became a supporter, which left the chief inspector isolated and in a miserable state.

Of course, nobody thought Fuda was innocent, and nobody believed that he went on a trip to get a load off his mind. But there was nothing they could do as long as his alibi held up. They could not ignore the testimony of the mother and daughter Namegawa, or the people at the Hanaya Inn. The fact that so many were in favour of letting Fuda go meant they were beginning to doubt Onitsura's talent for breaking down alibis.

On the same day that Fuda was released from custody, over his objections, the chief inspector decided to take a few days off in a countryside inn in Okuizu. He was tired.

Given the time of the day, it was not unusual for the second-class compartment coach to be completely empty, and it was almost as if Onitsura had rented the whole coach for himself. The bright sun shining in through the train windows managed to cheer him up, for the first time in a long while. That alone made the trip away from Tōkyō worthwhile.

It was when the train had passed Yokohama, Ōfuna and Fujisawa, and was about to enter Tsujidō, that Onitsura noticed that the shaking of the train diminished sharply, almost as if it were gliding along. The jarring chugga noise had now almost completely gone. How odd, he thought, but he quickly realised the cause. The train was now running on long-welded rails.

Normal rails are twenty-five metres long, but by utilising long-welded rails, some longer than two-hundred metres, not only is the noise and shaking of the train reduced, the train wheels also sustain less wear and thus require less maintenance. Once it became clear that no special steel was needed to cope with the expansion and contraction of the rails during the summer and winter season, provided that macadam was used instead of gravel and concrete sleepers were used to secure the rails, long-welded rails had been installed across the country by National Railways. Onitsura recalled having read in the newspapers the previous summer that the rails between Fujisawa and Hiratsuka had all been replaced by long-welded rails in a single night. There had also been advertisements in all the stations.

Onitsura was just thinking how comfortable the long-welded rails made the ride, when Kokuryō's letter came to mind. It had been obvious that the distorted, unclear writing was due to it having been written in a moving train, but he hadn't agreed with Teshigawara's assertion that the writing in the first half of the letter had been especially awful, not only because of the shaking of the train, but also because of Kokuryō's excitement. Onitsura had thought there must be another reason, but had been unable to put his finger on it.

But now he had personally experienced long-welded rails, he realised that the difference in the shaky writing in the first and second half of the letter was not due to some romantic, psychological reason, but by the physical difference between normal and long-welded rails. On the former, the train would shake and chugga chugga every twenty-five metres, so the words written during that part were naturally worse than the part written while the train was on the long-welded rails.

At the risk of belabouring the point, the reader needs to know that regular, twenty-five-metre-long rails link Tōkyō, Yokohama, Ōfuna and Fujisawa, but after Fujisawa, long-welded rails link Tsujidō, Chigasaki and Hiratsuka. With this in mind, it would appear that the change from the first half of Kokuryō's letter to the latter half occurred just as his train was passing through Fujisawa.

It was at this point that the chief inspector noticed, to his great surprise, that an odd contradiction lay within Kokuryō's letter. Kokuryō himself had declared that he was writing the letter in the train to Tōkyō, which would naturally mean that the train he was on must first have run on the long-welded rails and then switched over to regular rails at Fujisawa Station. Following that logic, his writing should have been shaking less in the first half, when he was riding on the long-welded rails, and become worse as the train started running on regular rails. But, in reality, the opposite was true, with the first half of the letter featuring the worst writing. There was only one logical conclusion to draw. Even though Kokuryō had claimed he was writing the letter on the train to Tōkyō, it had actually been written on the train leaving Tōkyō.

It had probably been written the morning of his death or the morning before, while he was commuting to work. But the very fact that he wrote it in advance meant that missing the 18:38 and 18:48 trains, and standing up Shizuko Shibazaki at Tōkyō Station had been his plan all along. But why?

Onitsura couldn't sit still anymore and started pacing up and down the aisle, focusing his mind solely on solving this mystery. The mountains closed in on the train as it approached Kōzu, and the red mandarin oranges peeking out here and there from between dark green leaves were beautiful.

7

Several days later, Onitsura's efforts came to fruition and Fukujirō Fuda was arrested. He had been chatting and joking with his colleagues in a conference room at Taisei Securities, but the moment he saw Teshigawara arrive he turned pale. He realised instantly that the authorities must be very confident to be arresting him a second time, and at his interrogation he spilled the beans.

Tanna had been assigned to another case after Fuda was released and only learned about the second arrest from a newspaper while he was in Kōbe.

It was a few days later, after both Onitsura and Tanna had wrapped up their cases, that the two of them sat down in a nearby park to feed the swans. It was a while before the subject of Fuda's case came up. Tanna had no idea how Onitsura had managed to break down Fuda's iron-clad alibi.

'How could he have been the murderer if his alibi was sound?'

'Of course he was the murderer. Mr. Itō, the prosecutor, had him indicted immediately.'

Tanna frowned, unable to follow.

'What do you mean, he was the murderer even though he had an alibi?'

'Haven't you ever heard the details? Let me explain it all then,' said Onitsura, taking some bread-crumbs out of his pocket and throwing them to the swans.

'Fuda's alibi seemed too good to be true. There was not a single moment unaccounted for, from the moment he turned up at Bar Tyltyl until he checked into the inn at Kamimoku. So did that mean he committed the murder before he showed up at Tyltyl? That seemed to be the only possible conclusion.'

'But that can't be. Kokuryō was still in Chigasaki at that time.'

'Just wait and listen. Fuda claimed that, during the period after he left the mah-jong parlour and before he arrived at Tyltyl—the hour between half-past six and half-past seven—he had spent his time wandering around the Ginza. But he never had an alibi for that period, which meant that was the only time he could have committed the murder.'

'In theory, yes, but you can hardly commit a murder if your victim isn't around, and Kokuryō was still in Chigasaki.'

'That's why I assumed that Kokuryō must already have been in Tōkyō by that time.'

The little detective muttered something as he stared at his boss. The latter's reply had been so blunt that Tanna couldn't believe his ears.

'Well, you can assume all you want, but there's actual proof that Kokuryō was still in Chigasaki at that time.'

'You still don't see it?' said Onitsura, as his eyes followed the departing swans. He turned to look directly at Tanna. 'And what was that proof based on?'

Tanna took out his notebook and checked his notes on Kokuryō's movements and the railway timetable before answering.

'Didn't he himself write that he left Chigasaki on the 19:25 train? Are you saying that a man who took the twenty-five-past seven train was strangled between half-past-six and half-past seven? That's a little hard to swallow.'

'It's not just a little hard to swallow, it's downright impossible. But since you mention the letter, I made an unbelievable discovery about it,' said Onitsura, and he went on to explain what had dawned on him a few days before. Tanna's expression became grimmer and grimmer as Onitsura's explanation continued, and he looked quite troubled by the end of the story.

'What a horribly calculating man, willing to use even the woman he loved. But what could his purpose have been?'

'That's exactly what I mulled over in the train. Kokuryō prepared a fake letter in advance, which meant he had something planned. That was my first step towards the solution.'

The chief inspector looked at Tanna again as he continued.

'We were fixated too much on only one side of the coin. Fukujirō Fuda had a motive to kill his rival, in order to win over the woman he loved, but the same holds for Kokuryō. It was our oversight not to have thought of that.'

'Oh.'

'So what if Kokuryō was the one who had evil plans in mind? Then standing his girlfriend up and writing that fake letter can be assumed to be all part of his fabricating an alibi for himself. I started thinking about what could have happened next. And finally it dawned on me that *Kokuryō had prepared a fake alibi for himself in order to kill Fuda, but that, unfortunately for him, his target had fought back and it was Kokuryō himself who was killed.*'

Onitsura sounded quite weary, talking about such foolish people.

'In other words, the time that Kokuryō was murdered was actually the time at which Kokuryō had planned to kill Fuda.'

'Yes, I think I understand most of it now, but there are still parts I don't get. So Kokuryō lied when he said in his letter he'd taken the 19:25 train from Chigasaki?'

'All lies. Listen, Kokuryō had planned to commit a murder. One mistake, and he himself would've ended up on the gallows. That's why he prepared his alibi so carefully. You must have realised by now that it had been Kokuryō himself who had stopped the clock in the janitor's office at twenty past six.'

The hexagonal clock appeared once again in Tanna's mind. He could almost hear the clucking of partridges and the sound of the wind blowing through the pine trees again.

'I gave up on my hot spring trip and took the train back to Chigasaki. I visited the Far East Paper Mill and had a talk with the old guard there. He told me that on that evening, someone had thrown a piece of stone at the gate light and that he had gone out to find the culprit. It was of course Kokuryō who had thrown the stone to lure the guard away and had sneaked into the office to stop the clock's pendulum. It's quiet at night at the mill and nobody ever complains about the guard just reading books in his office. So the guard didn't notice immediately that the clock had stopped running. Of course, it was a bit careless of him not to have noticed until nine.'

'No, I can definitely imagine it happening to that fellow,' laughed Tanna.

Having visited the mill himself earlier, Tanna could envision everything as if he were watching a play. Kokuryō hiding in the darkness and throwing a pebble at the gate light, the old guard running outside. Kokuryō swiftly slipping inside and stopping the pendulum, like a mouse sneaking around.

Then the grumbling guard returning without even glancing at the clock, returning to his adventures of the legendary warrior Jūtaro Iwami, or whatever he was reading.

Kokuryō waiting in the darkness for a few minutes before he showed himself at the office as if he had just finished work. The guard noticing his footsteps.

'Overtime, Mr. Kokuryō?'

'Yes, I was running behind. Oh, my shoulders!'

It was then that Tanna suddenly recalled something and quickly read through his notes again. He tapped Onitsura, who was watching the swans again, on the arm.

'I still don't get it. Even if he didn't take the 19:25 train, but an earlier one, he still wouldn't have made it back to the city in time for the murder. Even if we assume he stopped the clock exactly at twenty past six, the earliest train he could have taken would have been the 18:38 from Chigasaki. That train arrives in Tōkyō at ten minutes to eight. But that was the time Fuda was drinking highballs at Tyltyl.'

'Being so fixated on your memos is what's tripping you up,' retorted Onitsura, waving away the protest.

'Listen carefully. Kokuryō stopped the clock to create an excuse for missing the 18:38 and 18:47 trains. Do you agree?'

'Yes. He wanted to create the impression he'd been forced to take the next train, the 19:25. He wanted to create an alibi that he had left Chigasaki late, that he could not have been at the scene of the crime at the time of the murder.'

'Exactly. It's a rather commonplace trick, and anyone noticing it is likely to leave it at that. They don't realise what lies beneath.'

'Lies beneath? What do you mean?' asked Tanna expectantly.

'He made you think he stopped the pendulum of the clock at twenty past six.'

Tanna was confused. Onitsura continued.

'Contrary to what you think, Kokuryō did not throw the pebble at the gate light and lure the guard away at twenty-past six. It all occurred at a far earlier time. He didn't just stop the clock, he also moved the hands forward to indicate twenty-past six.'

The penny still didn't drop.

'Both you and the guard were taken in by the illusion of the clock and were convinced Kokuryō had left the mill just after twenty past six, but in fact, he left before twenty past six.'

And the penny still didn't drop.

'At what time did he leave the mill, then?'

'Around ten minutes to six.'

'Where did that time come from?'

Tanna's question was quite natural.

'You can simply count back. That's my own personal way to approach problems. When you can't solve a problem, approach it from the other way round.'

'The other way?'

'Yes. Assume what must be, based on what is. Take Fuda's alibi, for example. His alibi is perfect and he is the murderer, therefore I imagined the murder must have occurred earlier. I calculated the time Kokuryō must have left the mill, by counting back from the end.'

Tanna still didn't seem to grasp it.

'To put it simply, if Kokuryō left the mill at ten to six, he'd be in time for the 18:08 train. You can check it on the railway timetable. That train arrives in Tōkyō at eleven minutes past seven. He would therefore arrive smack in the middle of the blank period in Fuda's own alibi, between half-past six and half-past seven.'

'Ah, now I get it,' said Tanna weakly. He had not even considered the earlier trains until now.

'Fuda confessed everything, which cleared up a lot of questions we had,' continued Onitsura. 'Kokuryō told him he'd given up on Shizuko and asked Fuda to wait for him at the Tōkyō Station because there were things they needed to talk over first, and that he'd arrive on the 19:11 train. After he left work, Fuda spent some time at the mah-jong parlour and then walked to the station, where he waited for Kokuryō's train to arrive, which it duly did. The letter was posted by Kokuryō himself at the Yaesu Exit postbox. Fuda had actually watched him post the letter, never imagining that it would have a significant role to play regarding the alibi Kokuryō had prepared in order to kill Fuda.'

'What must he have felt when he learned about that later?' wondered Tanna out loud. 'But why did Fuda follow Kokuryō so obediently all the way to that construction site?'

'Kokuryō said he wanted to talk over a drink and told Fuda that there was a short cut through the construction site. Fuda went first and Kokuryō suddenly attacked him. He got three or four blows in, but then the tables were turned and Kokuryō ended up the victim. That's why Fuda claims it was self-defence.'

'The time?'

'Around twenty past seven. Fuda's first reflex was to flee, so he took a cab and went to the bar in Ueno, where he borrowed money.'

'And did he plan to use that wife of an assembly member as a witness for his alibi?'

'No. He was trying to stay low actually, as he would be a wanted man. He was really nonplussed when that mother and daughter suddenly spoke to him in the train. But to his great surprise, we were not interested in the actual time of the murder, but in a completely different time. Relieved by that, he dared to speak about his real alibi, but for a different time. He said he was really taken aback by us focusing on the wrong time.'

The chief inspector's explanation had been methodical, but Tanna still hadn't managed to take it all in. He needed time to absorb everything. But he still nodded as if he now understood everything. He didn't want anyone thinking he was slow, even the always easy-going Onitsura.

A cold gust of wind swept the white paper debris from the street into the water. The swans approached it, mistaking it for food.

'I can't laugh at those swans. We were even more short-sighted than they are,' laughed Onitsura, for the first time in a long while. 'By the way, I was thinking of buying a new potted primrose. Come with me, there's a place with delicious Russian cakes right next to the florist.'

Onitsura stood up and patted the sleeves of his overcoat as he looked at Tanna, whose solemn face showed he was still thinking hard about the matter.

The Clown in the Tunnel

1

After crossing the Hijiribashi Bridge, the car continued to follow the dirty Ochanomizu stream for approximately one minute, with the Yushima Seidō Temple to the right. Although the neighbourhood was not far from downtown Tōkyō, it was calm and peaceful, perhaps due to the high density of schools and hospitals.

'You can stop there. I believe that's the building.'

The car turned right from the main street with its tram line and followed the curve of the half-moon shaped flower bed to stop beneath the car porch. Entertainment reporter Azusa and his photographer Tori'i looked up at the building. A floodlight had been attached to a telephone pole on the corner, so it was as bright as daylight and the blinds had been lowered on all the windows. The leaves of the hibiscuses on the walls swayed in the night spring breeze. It was only a two-storey building, but because of the tall ceilings it looked higher. Two years earlier, a jazz pianist had fallen from an upper floor window to instant death. Seeing the building for themselves, it became quite clear how it could have happened.

Azusa got out of the car and looked at the large sign to the right of the entrance door. Engraved on it were the words: Fujimi House – Swing Wagon Lodge.

'This is the place. Come along.'

He beckoned to the photographer and rang the bell, which was immediately answered by Toshihiko Ajiro, clarinettist and bandmaster of the Swing Wagon Band. He was wearing blue denim trousers and a striped blue and yellow sweater reminiscent of wasps, the band's outfit.

'I've been expecting you. Thank you for coming.'

The man, who had exceptionally large hands, bowed as low as he could, thrilled that the entertainment section of a major newspaper was going to write about the band. His frank, open demeanour made a good impression on the journalist.

Azusa already knew that Fujimi House was owned by the patron of the band, one Junzō Miki. Before the war, it had been a well-known luxury building, but—as often occurred after the war—it had been requisitioned as lodgings for American army officers and most of the ground floor had been converted into one large hall.

When the building was eventually returned to Miki, it was no longer suitable as an apartment building and would have taken significant resources to restore, so he offered it to the Swing Band for their use. Not only was the hall spacious enough for twenty couples to dance, there was enough accommodation for all the band members. Now its walls were a warm, cream colour and were festooned with photographs of jazz bands from across the ocean and multicolour posters of the Swing Band promoting their night club performances. There was a red carpet on the floor, probably left by the Americans.

On the wall opposite the front entrance were three windows and what appeared to be the back door. Four doors painted in light green were lined up on the right-hand side of the hall, in the near corner of which was a staircase leading to the upper floor. Ajiro led the way across the hall to a door immediately adjacent to the staircase, leading to the drawing room, a very comfortable, spacious room of about 26 square metres, with indirect lighting and pink wallpaper which gave the room a soft feeling.

After the two men were seated, Ajiro offered them cocktails, but they were teetotallers and declined. Nevertheless he poured vermouth and bitters into three glasses and proceeded to drink. Azusa and Tori'i sipped politely, like the bride at the sake ritual at a traditional Japanese wedding.

'Who wrote your article on the Hot Peppers?' asked Ajiro, interested in the rival band. He seemed to be enjoying his drink, judging by the way his cheeks were turning red.

'I am afraid the true identity of our writer Paprika Kid will have to remain a secret,' said Azusa, smiling politely.

The entertainment section of his newspaper was working on a ten-part series introducing up-and-coming jazz bands. The reviews were mild, in order to encourage the young musicians, and the series was a great success.

'That Paprika Kid is pretty good with his criticism, although I thought there were a few times when he was rather harsh.'

'Well, it's like needing some wasabi with your sashimi. Or adding bitters to a cocktail.'

Ajiro laughed and finished his cocktail. He did not appear to be a strong drinker. Azusa noticed that his fingers were very long and thought that was why he was so good on the clarinet. Although Azusa would not be the one to write the article, it was his job to collect information, so he tried to move the discussion towards other topics.

Ajiro's eyes looked red as he reminisced about forming a band in college and deciding to become professional over the objections of his mother, who wanted him to be an accountant. He was well-educated and a good speaker. He was laughing joyfully and loudly when a loud knock on the door interrupted him.

'There's something I have to ask you,' shrieked a woman as he opened the door. Azusa and Tori'i looked at each other in surprise.

'It's not a good time.'

'Just come out here, there's something I need to tell you.'

The woman was adamant, so Ajiro gave up and stepped out of the room. He said a few things to try to calm the woman down, but that seemed only to make her angrier. The more excited she became, the more roughly she spoke.

'Don't yell,' said Ajiro. 'There are people from the newspaper in the room.'

But this warning only made the woman more agitated. Azusa and Tori'i tried to distract themselves with idle chit-chat until the conversation between Ajiro and the woman was finally over. She seemed to have calmed down after she had spoken her mind, and the men could hear her footsteps as she left. Ajiro came back into the room, even redder in the face.

'I'm terribly sorry.'

Azusa and Tori'i pretended to have heard nothing, which was the normal etiquette in such situations.

'Please don't think badly of her. She's our vocalist, Mayumi Urihara, and she's a nice person at heart.'

Azusa had seen Mayumi on television before. An American magazine had once made fun of Japanese jazz singers trying to sing in English, even though they couldn't differentiate between Ls and Rs. Also Mayumi had a rolled R, as with some German accents, which made her very hard to listen to, and had trouble staying in tune. But she was attractive and appealed to the drunken nightclub crowd. In Azusa's opinion, Mayumi's membership only detracted from Swing Wagon, adding nothing positive to the band at all.

Ajiro was aware of this too, even though he praised Mayumi's skills.

'Anyway, I'd be grateful if you wouldn't be too harsh on her. She knows people are very critical of her, and it frustrates her a lot,' begged Ajiro. 'I'll pass on your wishes,' said Azusa, who could easily imagine the hysterical fit she would throw if her antics were to be revealed in the newspapers.

They continued talking for several more minutes when there was another knock on the door. The reporters learned later that everything in the building, including the doors and windows, had all been soundproofed. So when someone knocked on the door, simply answering from inside was useless because the person outside wouldn't be able to hear anything. Hence it was necessary to answer the door personally.

Ajiro opened the door to find a man and a woman standing there.

'You're late. I've been holding the fort here all by myself.'

'I cut myself shaving,' said the man, who had a small forehead and narrow eyes. Ajiro looked relieved as he turned around to introduce the newcomers.

'This is our bassist, Jūrō Esashi, and Atsuko Ogose, who plays the piano.'

'Nice to meet you.'

Esashi had a hoarse voice, like Louis Armstrong, and looked like a banana salesman at a night market. He offered two business cards to the journalists, who didn't care for his subservient attitude. Atsuko Ogose's eyes were set far apart and she had a round chin. She bowed her head silently, but didn't offer a card. She was wearing a distinctive sweater the colour of a Jorō spider above a green-red checkered skirt.

'I asked Mayumi Urihara to come as well, but she seemed very angry. What happened?'

Ajiro ignored the question and asked them what they wanted to drink. Esashi asked for apple knocker, which was served to all present. Atsuko Ogose remained completely silent, but Ajiro and Esashi spoke more than enough.

As Esashi spoke it transpired that he had an interest in 8 mm films and seemed more eager to talk about cameras than jazz, which earned him several reprovals by Ajiro.

About ten minutes later, the photographer Tori'i said he wanted to take a picture of the whole group, including Mayumi Urihara. Although he had already taken five or six photos, he still didn't have one with the whole band.

'Atsuko, could you get her?'

The jazz pianist turned out to be very light on her feet, and her movements were as swift as a deer. She left the room and was back in less than a minute. When she poked her head around the door, her expression had changed completely. Her eyes had lost their sparkle, and were now nothing but glass beads.

'What's the matter?' Ajiro asked as he got up hurriedly and went outside to talk to her.

After some whispering on the other side of the door, Ajiro's head popped round the door again.

'Esashi, please come with me. Mayumi's dead!'

2

It was clear from the expression on Ajiro's face that Mayumi's death was out of the ordinary. The two reporters followed Esashi out of the room and up the staircase to the floor above, where a corridor ran parallel to the street outside and ended with a white door to a storage room. In the afternoon, it was possible to see Mount Fuji from the windows to the left.

Another corridor extended to the right from the middle of the first, like a T-junction. There were eight closed doors in this second corridor, four on each side. The six nearest rooms were reserved for band members, while the last room on the left was a toilet, and the last room on the right was a bathroom. Ajiro led the way and opened the door to the bathroom. There was a long sink along the left wall with six faucets.

Ajiro took one step inside and stopped immediately. He looked anxiously around. There was another, half-open, door in the back of the room. Red sandals were strewn haphazardly in front of it.

'We'd better go and see what's inside,' said Ajiro to Esashi, who tried to say something, but just nodded. Although it was an emergency, they were hesitant to walk into a bathroom where a young woman was supposed to be bathing. He finally pushed open the door and the two of them went in. There was a bathtub in front of them, in which a woman was submerged. She was almost completely below water level, with her face raised and her legs bent. The water was crimson. Green tiles, a white bathtub and red water: it was a vivid, colourful composition. Tori'i gasped: what a brilliant picture it would be if he could take a colour photograph. But the people at the editors'

127

desk didn't like pictures of corpses, and neither did the peaceful readers of the newspaper. But this was different: this was art, and Tori'i was already considering various compositions in his mind.

Azusa was currently an entertainment reporter, but he had once earned his pay at the city news desk. Like a shepherd dog suddenly recalling its wolf instincts, he immediately knew what to do. He rolled up his sleeves and plunged his hands into the red water. He raised the woman up to make sure she wasn't still alive, and to get a good look at the wound in her chest. It was a light pink colour, and like a crater in the skin. The heart had already stopped beating, as if it were an extinct volcano.

Based on the wound, Azusa surmised the murder weapon was a small knife. He asked Tori'i to hold the body, whilst he searched the bottom of the bathtub with his hands. He looked like a suspect undergoing a *kugatachi* trial (1). Light red water droplets dripped from his arms whilst he searched the entire bathroom, but he failed to discover any weapon.

'I can't tell whether it's murder or suicide,' he said, wiping his arms. 'But calling a doctor won't do her any good. It's better to call the police.'

Azusa threw his handkerchief in the corner of the bathroom and looked at everyone.

'I used to be assigned to the Metropolitan Police Department, and I've been present at many murder scenes. I can tell you that the police don't like anyone messing with the crime scene, so it's best if we all wait in one of the rooms downstairs. Make sure you don't touch anything.'

'I'll make the call,' said Ajiro.

The party were already in the corridor when Azusa called out to Ajiro.

'Is it possible that she committed suicide?'

Ajiro turned around to face Azusa. For a moment, a strange look appeared on his face, but it was gone in a second. It was as if he hoped it was suicide, that it would have been for the best.

But he replied that she wasn't the type to have taken her own life.

'But she did act quite agitated earlier,' insisted Azusa.

---

(1) An ancient trial form in Japan, where the suspects had to place their hands in boiling water. It was believed that only the wicked would get scalded and that the righteous would go unscathed

128

'To be perfectly honest, I wish it had been suicide. It would be a great scandal for a while, certainly, but with time, people would forget. But she wasn't someone who'd kill herself. She was a strong-minded woman, burning with passion and pushing aside everything and everyone in her way. What's more, we were scheduled to record an LP soon, and Mayumi was really excited for the future. She would never have committed suicide.'

Esashi had been listening to Azusa and Ajiro.

'I also think suicide is out of the question. But if it's murder, the assailant might still be in the building.'

'We'll have to leave that to the police. We might get hurt if we try to do something on our own.'

As he said that, Azusa seemed to recall something, and he hastened down the stairs and out onto the porch. His chauffeur was standing outside the car, smoking a cigarette. When he noticed Azusa, he turned around.

'Already done?'

'No, not yet. Did anyone leave the building after we arrived here?'

'Through this door?'

'Yes.'

'No, nobody.'

'And did anyone go inside?'

'No, nobody went inside. What's the matter?'

'Somebody just died. I think she was killed.'

The chauffeur stubbed the cigarette out with his shoe.

'Who was it?'

'A jazz singer. We already called the police, so they should be arriving soon. If you see someone leave the building, sound the horn.'

As Azusa was speaking, he thought he could hear the faint sound of sirens. He paused but could hear nothing but the rumble from a tram on the other side of the river.

He went back into the building, crossed the hall, and headed for the back entrance. Before the police arrived, he wanted to have a look at the escape route the murderer might have taken. It was unlikely he was still hiding inside. There had been ample opportunity for him to escape, as everyone had been together in the downstairs drawing room at first, and also later when they were gathered in the bathroom examining the corpse.

129

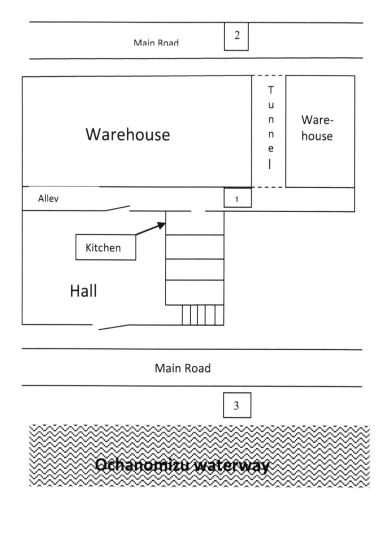

Main Road

2

Warehouse

Tunnel

Ware-house

Alley

1

Kitchen

Hall

Main Road

3

Ochanomizu waterway

1 = Overhead Light
2 = Accident
3= Sweet Potato Stand

130

The back entrance was slightly to the right of the middle of the wall, and thus closer to the ground floor rooms. The door was not locked, and opened easily with one turn of the knob. Immediately behind the door stood a grey wall, which Azusa later learnt was part of a warehouse belonging to a pharmaceutical company owned by the same Miki who owned Fujimi House. Thus Fujimi House faced the main road with the tram line, while the warehouse faced the street at the back. Only two metres separated the rear walls of the two buildings.

Azusa turned right and walked down the narrow alley. The floor was concrete and the alley reminded him of the bottom of a ravine, which was fortunately illuminated by a lamp hanging to his left at the far corner of the warehouse wall.

When he arrived directly beneath the lamp, Azusa noticed something he had not expected. He found himself in front of a tunnel quite unlike anything he had ever seen in any ordinary building. The ceiling was curved, reminiscent of a train tunnel, and it crossed right through the warehouse and into the back street, effectively splitting the ground floor of the warehouse into two parts.

The walls of neighbouring buildings blocked the left and right end of the alley, so the tunnel itself was probably a necessary emergency exit under the Fire Prevention Act. Azusa imagined the murderer must have made his escape through the tunnel and, satisfied with this knowledge, he decided to return to Fujimi House. As he put his hand on the door-knob, he could hear the noise of sirens approaching, becoming louder by the second.

3

It was nearly ten o'clock by the time Chief Inspector Tadokoro had finished overseeing the examination of the corpse and had made his way to the drawing room to conduct an examination of the circumstances surrounding the death.

'Is everyone present?'

'Well, everyone in the band is here. But we also have a maid,' said Ajiro.

'And where is she?'

'In the maid's room.'

'Or she might be in the kitchen,' Ogose added, as if she had suddenly remembered something.

'The kitchen?'

'Yes, I had begun to bake an apple pie, and she was helping me with it.'

'Why a pie all of a sudden?'

She explained how she had started to prepare the pie for the journalists' visit, and had asked Chizu, the maid, to take over when she went to see the men. But she was unreliable and easily distracted, often reading magazines instead of working.

'You go.' The chief inspector raised his finger and Detective Mizuhara immediately left the room. He tried the maid's room first, but when he saw she wasn't there, he tried the kitchen. The light was off and there was a smell of burnt clothing. Mizuhara could hear a woman sobbing. But why would Chizu be crying in a dark room if she was supposed to be reading magazines? He found the light switch and turned it on.

The whole kitchen was illuminated, revealing a gas stove, a large oven, and a refrigerator. There was also a woman tied to a chair near the window. She had been gagged and her teary eyes were begging Mizuhara to untie her.

He picked up a kitchen knife and quickly cut the rope. Not even the kid at the greengrocer's chopping up bunches of daikon radishes could have done it faster. Chizu staggered up from the chair, removed the gag herself, and started to howl. Mizuhara didn't know what to do, so he did nothing. His experience with his own wife had taught him that she wouldn't stop until a certain amount of tears had flowed, so meanwhile he stared with interest at the red stains on Chizu's nice one-piece dress and on the rope lying on the floor.

When she seemed ready, Mizuhara led the slightly plump Chizu back into the drawing room. Even after she was seated, she continued to howl, sniffing between the cries. When she finally noticed Ajiro and the others in the room, she seemed to calm down and she eventually stopped.

'Tell us about who attacked you. Please be as detailed as possible.'

Tadokoro's tone was gentle, so with some encouragement from Atsuko Ogose, Chizu finally managed to tell her story in a coherent manner.

'After I had finished washing the dishes after dinner, we started to make an apple pie, but it took us some time to bake the apples and make the dough, so we still weren't finished by the time the guests arrived.'

While she had no accent, Chizu did speak with a nasal twang, which told the chief inspector that she probably originated from Fukushima or somewhere in that region.

'But we soon finished the pie and put it in the oven, and Ms. Ogose said she'd go to welcome the guests.'

Chizu described how she was wiping the dishes dry when a figure suddenly entered the kitchen.

'Who was it?'

'I don't know. He was wearing a mask and a baggy outfit.'

'A baggy outfit? What kind?'

'A clown's outfit. White clothes with red spots, and a triangular hat.'

She had been scared and had let the metal bowl she was holding fall on the tiled floor as she screamed. But the soundproof doors prevented anyone outside from hearing.

'While I was being tied up, I noticed he was wearing cotton gloves, drenched in red. I was so afraid he was going to kill me. After tying me up, the clown washed his hands in the sink, switched on the gas stove and burnt his gloves.'

After that, the clown stood in front of the mirror to check his clothes carefully for blood stains. But blood stains were not likely to stand out against a red polka dot motif. Eventually, he noticed a spot on the right side of his chest and used a cloth to wipe it, but after a while he gave up and threw the cloth away. Then he peered out of the window into the back alley, and after making sure there was nobody there, he switched the lights off and disappeared into the hall.

She twisted her tied-up body around to peek through the curtains at the passage outside. The back door suddenly opened without a sound, like a scene in a silent film. Out came the figure in the baggy clown's outfit. Chizu held her breath. She could feel her body trembling again. But the clown walked down the alley with his large shoes and disappeared into the tunnel.

'Where does that tunnel lead?'

The question was addressed to Ajiro. Tadokoro hadn't examined the back alley himself yet, so he dispatched Mizuhara to take a look and turned once again to Chizu.

'I'm glad you weren't harmed. Could you tell me the exact time this happened to you?'

'I was so afraid, I didn't keep track. For all I know, it could have been a minute or an hour,' replied Chizu. The chief inspector thought that was quite natural. A woman fearing for her life wasn't likely to remain cool-headed.

'How long did it take for the clown to appear after I left?' asked Atsuko.

'I think about ten or twenty minutes,' replied Chizu, as she straightened the creases in her dress.

'When did you leave the kitchen?' Tadokoro asked Atsuko Ogose after licking the tip of his pencil.

'Well, that's a difficult question, because there's no clock in the kitchen. But it was right after Mayumi and Toshihiko's spat.'

'Atsuko!'

Ajiro looked angrily at Atsuko and leant towards her. The look in his eye was unexpected from the usually friendly bandmaster. Tadokoro continued with his questions.

'So she had a row with Mr. Ajiro. When was that?'

'Don't misunderstand, it wasn't a real fight. We had a difference of opinion, and discussed it rather loudly. That's all.'

'Please don't interrupt. We'll decide what occurred,' said the chief inspector, bluntly reproaching Ajiro. He wasn't about to ignore the fact that the murdered woman had been in an argument right before she died.

'What kind of conversation did Ms. Urihara and Mr. Ajiro have? You can tell us the truth. Please be as accurate as possible.'

Atsuko Ogose seemed to be torn about what to do, as she looked from Ajiro to Tadokoro. The bandmaster had turned his face away, but he was obviously unhappy that she was about to talk. Nevertheless, Atsuko felt obliged to respond to the chief inspector, and she replied in a soft voice.

'I didn't hear everything, only a part. Chizu and I were preparing the pie in the kitchen. Mayumi and Toshihiko were standing in the corridor, just outside the door to the drawing room, but the kitchen door was open, so we could hear them speaking. I peeked out and saw the two facing each other and talking loudly. I thought it wasn't polite to listen to other people's rows, so I went back inside and closed the door.'

'And what were they talking about?'

'Well, I think it was "You don't understand anything about my style of singing," or something like that.'

'I'll say what it was about. You can shut up now.'

Ajiro directed the angry words at Atsuko and lit a cigarette.

'We're recording three songs to be part of an LP to be sold in the UK, featuring Japanese jazz musicians. Her singing style wasn't a good match for what we were planning. And I was the one who told her she had to change her singing style. She became angry about that and had come to vent her frustration.'

Tadokoro shot a glance at Atsuko for confirmation and she nodded silently in agreement.

'And when did this happen?'

'About five minutes after the reporters arrived, so I'd say at about five minutes to nine,' said Ajiro nonchalantly, as if he didn't care anymore.

'Five to nine...' Tadokoro noted the time in his notebook and continued his questioning.

'Did anyone see Ms. Urihara after that?'

'We—I mean Ms. Ogose and I—saw her. I wanted to shave first before I went downstairs, but I cut myself,' said Esashi, pointing to his chin.

'It wouldn't stop bleeding, so I had to put some healing cream on it. That's why I was late.'

'After I left the kitchen, I went upstairs to my own room to redo my lipstick,' added Atsuko. 'Then I called Mr. Esashi and when we were about to go downstairs together, Mayumi was still in her room.'

'We asked her to go downstairs with us to the drawing room, but she declined. She was really angry and said she was about to take a bath. I had heard from Ms. Ogose that they had quarrelled, but I didn't realise how upset she was with Ajiro. I was really surprised, so I quickly went downstairs.'

'At what time?'

'Just after nine?'

He wasn't quite certain, so he answered with a question.

'Did you see a person dressed as a clown?'

'Of course not, I wouldn't have stayed silent if I had.'

The door opened and a detective entered to whisper something in the chief inspector's ear. The latter announced to everyone that a witness had been found who had seen the clown entering the building.

'How did they get inside, Chief Inspector?'

'Through the front entrance. You are familiar with the roasted sweet potato stall across from your building, on the other side of the main street near the water? The man there saw the clown. No wonder he noticed him, in that get-up. This was at eight forty-five. He is absolutely sure.'

Needless to say, the musicians were all very interested.

'It was a coincidence that Mayumi ended up all alone on the top floor, making her the perfect target for the murderer. Suppose she had been with us in the drawing room instead? What would have happened to her then?'

'Considering the size of the building, the clown could have hidden anywhere inside, in which case, the crime might simply have been postponed until you'd all gone to bed.'

Suddenly a startled expression appeared on Chizu's face, as if she had been thinking about something else.

'Chief Inspector, the person dressed as the clown, I now have the feeling he looked a lot like Mr. Iikura...'

The atmosphere in the room suddenly turned tense. The three musicians aimed angry looks at the maid.

'Why did you tell him!?' Esashi cried out in his hoarse voice.

4

'Who is this Iikura?' asked Tadokoro.

'A saxophonist. He was one of us.'

'"Was," so he is not a member of your band currently?'

'No, he was forced to quit.'

'Oh, and why was that?' asked the chief inspector. Then he changed his mind and turned back to Chizu.

'Why do you think that the clown was this Iikura?'

'Well...'

'Did he have the same physique? Did his voice sound similar?'

'No, it wasn't the voice. The clown didn't speak at all, so I don't know what his voice would have sounded like. And he was wearing baggy clothes, so I couldn't make out any physical characteristics. He just... felt like Mr. Iikura.'

'But there must have been some reason why he made such an impression on you.'

'He obviously had a grudge against Ms. Urihara.'

'A grudge? What about?'

When it became clear they could no longer hide the truth from the chief inspector, Esashi began to explain.

'Ms. Urihara can be selfish and unreasonable, but she's also very skilled at getting on the good side of people who can be useful to her. She managed to get into Mr. Miki's good books, with the result she got everything she wanted. Iikura was our saxophonist and an irreplaceable member of the band, but when he confronted her about her attitude, she became furious. Shortly afterwards, Mr. Miki asked him to leave the band.'

The bandmaster had remained silent up until then, but now he, too, was willing to talk. He lit a cigarette before he spoke.

'The direct cause of their quarrel was how we were going to spend the three hundred thousand yen of our remaining budget. Iikura said he wanted to purchase a saxophone from the French company Henri Buisson, whose instruments are far superior to those made in Japan. Mayumi, on the other hand, wanted an air conditioner installed. She wouldn't budge and took the matter to Mr. Miki, and that was the end of it.'

It had now become clear that the saxophonist Mamoru Iikura had had a motive to murder Mayumi.

Tadokoro asked how to reach Iikura and jotted down the address in his notebook.

'Is he in another band now?'

'He hasn't told us anything, so I don't think so. He's definitely a great saxophonist though.'

'One final question. With the demise of Urihara, could Iikura return to the Swing Band?'

'It's possible,' replied Esashi hesitantly. 'With Mr. Miki, it's "out of sight, out of mind." I hope so, because Iikura is really a fantastic musician, and we need him in the band.'

The chief inspector went to the door and handed a note to the officer who had come in earlier. The he continued taking notes about everyone's whereabouts.

'Ms. Ogose, at what time did you leave the kitchen?'

'I think it was about five minutes after the row with Toshihiko.'

'That means that Chizu was assaulted by the clown between ten and twenty past nine. I have another question, which I want you to answer frankly. Your band consists of three men and two women. If there were romantic relations between you, one person would be left out. What do you say about that?'

'There were no such problems. We're all together just to make music, and...'

137

There was a knock on the door, and the owner Junzō Miki and the reporter Azusa entered. The bandmaster and bassist seemed delighted to see Miki, a small, slender man of about sixty with gentle eyes and a slightly nasal baritone voice.

'Ms. Ogose, I heard about it from the newspapers. It must have been a terrible shock,' he began. But Atsuko suddenly started to tremble, and with a loud noise she collapsed on the table, and then to the ground, where she lay motionless.

Ajiro immediately knelt down beside her to see what was wrong. He was the only person to remain calm.

'She's unconscious. Perhaps it's the stress finally taking its toll, after the relief of seeing Mr. Miki.'

'Let's carry her to her room upstairs. Chief Inspector, I trust that's all right?'

Ajiro and Esashi carried Atsuko's torso, while Chizu lifted her legs as they went out into the hall. Miki wanted to follow, but Tadokoro stopped him. He still couldn't rid himself of the suspicion that Mayumi Urihara might have committed suicide.

'Impossible. A person with her character would never do such a thing,' retorted Miki as he left the room. The chief inspector closed the door and threw his box of cigarettes at Azusa. The two knew each other from the days when Azusa was still on the city desk.

'I did think about the possibility that Urihara committed suicide and Atsuko Ogose hid the knife, but I abandoned the idea. Everyone swears Urihara was not the type, and I can't think of any reason why Ogose would want to hide the knife.'

'Who called Miki?'

'Someone from my newspaper, I guess. Probably someone who thought it would be better to inform the man that the woman he loved was dead. Shouldn't we have done that?'

'It's all right, it saved us the trouble. By the way, I might as well ask you these questions now.' Tadokoro's tone changed. 'At what time did you arrive here?'

'Why, do you suspect us?'

'Don't be funny. I need to confirm whether they were telling me the truth or not.'

'Don't scare me like that, I was already imagining myself in prison,' replied the reporter, with a mischievous twinkle in his eyes. 'We got a call just after half past eight to say that it was a convenient time for the interview. So our driver raced here, and Tori'i and I arrived at ten to nine.'

'Did you overhear the row between the victim Mayumi Urihara and the bandmaster Ajiro?'

'Yes, they certainly weren't silent.'

'What was it about?'

'The door wasn't fully shut, so we couldn't help but overhear them. Mayumi was hysterical about the bad reviews she had been getting about her singing. Something about nobody understanding anything about her singing style. Ajiro was just trying to calm her down, probably because the two of us were there in the drawing room.'

Azusa's version matched the accounts of the band members completely.

The chief inspector was satisfied that Ajiro and the others had told him the truth.

'What time did they argue?'

'It was right after we were led into this room, so I'd say five to nine. I might be off by one or two minutes.'

'Another question, and a vital one. Did Ajiro leave the room after his row with Mayumi Urihara?'

'No, he was here with us the whole time until the incident occurred.'

'You are absolutely sure?'

'Yes. Tori'i is back at the office already, but I could call him for you.'

Tadokoro seemed disappointed that his guess had been wrong, and he looked down at his notes again. He had written down the movements of everybody in relation to the clown's movements.

Time	Movement	Testimony
08:45	Clown enters through front entrance.	Roasted sweet potato vendor
08:50	Arrival of reporters.	Azusa, Tori'i
08:55	Mayumi, Ajiro argue.	Azusa and Tori'i
09:00	Atsuko leaves kitchen, touches up make-up in room upstairs.	Atsuko
09:05	Atsuko, Esashi see victim.	Atsuko, Esashi

09:10 (approx.)	Murder assumed to occur around this time.	
09:15 (approx.)	Chizu assaulted by clown	Chizu
09:15	Mayumi's body found in bathroom upstairs.	Azusa, Ajiro, Esashi, Atsuko
09:20 (approx.)	Clown escapes through back entrance.	Chizu
10:00	Chizu freed from kitchen.	Mizuhara

'Did that officer just leave to check up on Iikura?'

'Perhaps.'

'You don't have to hide anything from me. Everyone's been after the story as to why he got the sack.'

At that moment, Mizuhara entered the room and whispered something in Tadokoro's ear. The chief inspector turned redder with each word, and eventually barked at his subordinate: 'How can that be!? Someone must be lying!'

'No, we made a thorough investigation. There's no doubt about it.'

'I'll look into it myself. It's impossible, I tell you,' he growled as he stood there, his back to Azusa.

'What's the matter?'

'Just shut up and follow me! You'll see!'

Tadokoro was simply venting his anger. The younger police detective and the reporter looked each other and grinned. The chief inspector stubbed out his cigarette and disappeared into the hall.

Just at that moment, Chizu came down from the floor above.

'How's Ms. Ogose?'

'She's awake again. I was about to make some coffee for her. I can make some for you, too.'

'Thank you,' the chief inspector muttered.

'You said you saw the clown leave through the back door, is that correct?'

'Yes,' replied the maid as she walked towards the kitchen.

'You also said you saw him walk into the tunnel, but you didn't see him return. Is that also correct?'

'He didn't come back.'

'Is it possible that you could have missed him?'

'No, absolutely not. I was afraid what might happen if he returned, so I watched the tunnel fearfully. There's no way I could have missed him.'

Trailing behind the maid and the chief inspector was Azusa, who could not understand why Tadokoro was being so persistent with his questions. He knew that Mizuhara's message had upset the policeman, but he could not imagine what it had said.

The three entered the kitchen. The stench of burnt pie was still strongly present. The chief inspector's steps reverberated loudly as he walked towards the window and sat down on the chair Chizu had been tied to. He tried looking outside into the alley through the gap in the curtains. There was enough light outside. It was only seven or eight metres from the window to the tunnel, so there was no way anyone could have missed the clown if he had made his way back.

'So let me rephrase the question. You say you didn't see the clown return, but did you see some other person, dressed in Western or Japanese clothing, for example?'

'No,' Chizu shook her head adamantly. 'Nobody came out of that tunnel. Not even a cat.'

The chief inspector looked disappointed and quite troubled, now his final hope had been rejected. He didn't say a word as he left the kitchen, exited through the back door, and walked into the tunnel. Azusa followed him. There were lights above both ends of the tunnel, but the illumination did not reach far inside, so it was pitch dark in the middle.

Four men stood talking at the far end of the tunnel. Tadokoro knew from Mizuhara's report that two of the men were automobile drivers who had been involved in a traffic accident, and the two others were police officers investigating the incident.

When the four noticed the chief inspector, they all stopped talking and waited for him to approach them. They knew what he was going to ask them. One of the officers spoke up on behalf of the group.

'The accident occurred at eight forty-five, Chief Inspector. The police box is just one hundred metres down the road, so we heard the crash and came running. I guess we arrived at eight forty-six or seven. And the four of us have been here since then. Nobody came through the tunnel during that period. To be exact, Detective Mizuhara came through the tunnel about seven minutes ago and talked with us. But apart from the detective, nobody came through the tunnel, we're absolutely sure.'

Mizuhara had already questioned the officer thoroughly, which is why he had been able to come up with such a succinct summary, and why he emphasised how sure they were.

'But if what you say is true, that would mean that the perpetrator disappeared whilst he was still inside the tunnel.'

'I can't say whether he disappeared or not. But it's a fact that nobody came out of that tunnel.'

The other officer and the two drivers nodded in agreement, so it appeared that the clown had indeed gone up in smoke, to paraphrase the chief inspector.

'Mizuhara, I suppose there were no secret passages hidden in the walls or ceiling? Or any manholes?'

'No, sir.' The firm reply killed off any remaining hope the chief inspector may have had.

'I made a thorough examination with a torch. No manholes, no gaps in the walls or ceilings big enough for an ant to crawl through.'

Tadokoro cursed and glared at the tunnel, but after a moment, he said in a cheerful voice: 'Anyway, once we've got the culprit, we can make him talk and explain how he did it. No need to keep thinking about stupid problems.'

5

Within the hour, Tadokoro was obliged to admit utter defeat. He had placed his bets on Iikura, but then he learned that he had been in the custody of the Tsukiji Police Station since the early evening. He ought not to have been intoxicated, considering he'd only had a double whiskey at his regular bar in Ginza, but he had molested a beautiful female passer-by, by licking her face. And he had done it right next to the police box on the crossing of Owarichō 4-Chōme.

With no idea of how to proceed from here, Tadokoro started thinking about Ryūzō Hoshikage, a gifted amateur detective, whom he had not seen lately. His pride made him reluctant, but after ten days he gave in and took a bus to Marunouchi. The detective's trading company was located on the highest floor of the Maru Building.

There was a cynical smile on Hoshikage's handsome face as he sat down opposite the chief inspector.

'You're here about the business at Fujimi House. Just listen to what I have to say and I'll solve the case for you.'

Hoshikage seemed to be in a good mood. The constant ticking of the three teleprinters in the office was evidence that his trading business was doing well.

The chief inspector recounted the case in meticulous detail to the best of his knowledge. His account of how the clown had disappeared from the tunnel, recounted in the style of Musei Tokugawa (2), was especially captivating, ending the tale on a climax. The chief inspector's only fault was that he pronounced his 's' sounds as a slurred 'sh,' a characteristic of the dialect of his birth region, Kyūshū.

'Well, that certainly sounds intriguing.'

Hoshikage had been caressing his pencil moustache during the account, and once the chief inspector had finished, he asked to see the latter's notebook.

'I'd particularly like to see the timetable you created.'

Hoshikage looked for a while at the times when the clown had entered and left the building, but then looked up with a surprisingly jovial look on his face.

'I assume the clown's outfit was rented. Have you pursued that line of investigation?'

'There's a theatre costume rental shop in Tawaramachi, Asakusa. Someone who could be the killer visited the place two days before the murder and rented a clown's costume for a fancy dress parade. The shop reported that he never returned the costume. Luckily for them, he left a deposit.'

'Do you have anything more to add?'

'Yes. Although everyone has a different idea about what a clown should look like, the costume rented from that shop matched Chizu's and the sweet potato seller's descriptions exactly, so it's almost certain it was the murderer.'

'That sounds plausible. Have you given any thought as to why he chose to dress like a clown?'

'A baggy clown costume is perfect as a disguise. You can put it on and take it off over your normal clothes.'

'Glasses and a mask would be easier.'

'That would be too easy, and wouldn't feel safe psychologically. I think the murderer is someone whose gait and mannerisms are known to the band—someone who often visits Fujimi House.'

(2) Musei Tokugawa (1894-1971) was a storyteller, known for his narration of silent films and later the stage, radio and television.

'I disagree. I believe the culprit selected such a conspicuous costume precisely because he wanted to attract attention. And he succeeded perfectly, because the sweet potato vendor was a witness to him entering the building.'

'But why would the murderer want to be seen?'

Hoshikage just grinned, without explaining himself, and went on:

'You seem to believe that you have to catch the culprit in order to find out how he vanished from the tunnel, but such conventional thinking will get you nowhere. You first need to work out how he managed to disappear from the tunnel. Only then will you grasp the truth and learn the identity of the murderer.'

Hoshikage grinned again as he made the remarks. Tadokoro didn't say a word. The amateur detective was quite eccentric, and it was unlikely he would give a straight answer even if Tadokoro had asked him point-blank to explain. It was better just to listen to what he had to say.

'Here's what I suggest,' continued Hoshikage briskly. 'We'll meet tonight at exactly eight o'clock in the drawing room at Fujimi House. You'll gather everyone involved in the case and I'll bring along two or three guests of my own.' Tadokoro agreed and was about to leave when he was stopped.

'Here's something to think about. The solution of the mystery lies in Atsuko Ogose's fainting spell.'

'You mean when the patron Miki entered the room?'

'Exactly. To solve the mystery of the disappearing clown, start considering the reason she fainted.'

Hoshikage patted the startled chief inspector on the shoulder and turned to continue his work.

6

Five men and women were gathered in the drawing room: the three remaining band members, Mamoru Iikura and the maid Chizu. They were visibly nervous and anxious, like trapped animals. Ajiro was busy with his shaker making drinks for everyone. Perhaps he wanted to hide his anxiety from the chief inspector, or perhaps he wanted something to take his mind off the situation.

Mamoru Iikura seemed the calmest among those present. He had a ruddy face even before he started on the liquor and seemed secretly pleased that Mayumi Urihara was no more. He was extremely

144

corpulent, like the nice little piggy living in a house of cabbage who got eaten by the wolf.

'So you are coming back to the Swing Band?'

'Yes, thank goodness. I just hope we can order that saxophone from France soon.' He tried to speak while drinking, which caused him to cough heavily.

The two women, Atsuko Ogose and Chizu were, as expected of their sex, silent. Chizu's complexion was fine, but this evening, Atsuko's skin seemed very dry, perhaps due to her make up. There was not a hint of her usual attractiveness.

As usual, the bassist Jūrō Esashi's face betrayed nothing of what was on his mind. He smoked continuously, and a mountain of stubs had started to build up in the ashtray.

The tense atmosphere in the room had affected Tadokoro and Mizuhara, who both started checking their watches as eight o'clock approached. At precisely eight, there was a rap on the door and Junzō Miki entered the room, followed by Ryūzō Hoshikage and the two reporters, Azusa and Tori'i. Apart from Hoshikage, the others seemed nervous. Miki, who seemed inebriated, tripped at the entrance and had to clutch the door frame to save himself from falling.

Tadokoro started to introduce the group to Hoshikage, but was interrupted by an incident. As Miki tried to talk to Atsuko, she keeled over and fell to the floor, as if his breath had been poisonous.

'She's fainted again.'

'Let's carry her upstairs.'

Hoshikage watched the busy jazz musicians closely. As Atsuko's body was being lifted off the floor, he suddenly said in a low voice: 'There's no need to take her upstairs. Let her rest on the sofa here.'

'But...'

'Don't worry, I have a lot of experience handling ladies who have fainted. I have something I want everyone here to listen to. It's about the problem of the clown vanishing from the tunnel.'

'Did he use some kind of special method?' asked the entertainment reporter restlessly. Hoshikage ignored him and turned to Miki.

'There is something I wish to ask you. I believe that this lady also fainted on the night of the murder when she saw you?'

'Yes. It seems that all the pent-up stress suddenly got to her when she saw me. But I wonder what's the trouble tonight? If she's so exhausted, it might be wise for her to take a long rest...' he said worriedly, as he looked down gently at Atsuko.

145

'It almost seems like an allergic reaction. Some people become ill when they breathe the pollen of certain flowers. A lady I know, for example, falls victim to chrysanthemums. It's similar to an asthma attack. At times, she looks as though she's almost dying.'

'So you're suggesting Ms. Ogose also has a kind of allergy?' asked Miki.

'Well, she fainted on the night of the murder, and this evening, so twice in total. Has she had similar experiences before?'

Once again, Miki looked gently at the jazz pianist lying on the sofa before he replied. She was still unconscious, lying motionless with her eyes shut.

'No, never.'

Tadokoro knew that Hoshikage's questions weren't without meaning. The things he'd said in his office that afternoon came back to the chief inspector.

'I have one more question. Have you met with Ms. Ogose lately, aside from this evening and the night of the murder?'

'If you mean alone, then no. But I've seen the whole band twice, at the wake and at the funeral.'

'I assume she did not lose consciousness on either occasion?'

'No. We talked, but nothing out of the ordinary happened.'

After he had heard the answer, Hoshikage seemed to have learnt enough and stopped the conversation. None of those present seemed to know what to make of the amateur detective's questions.

Hoshikage appeared to have read their minds, as he decided to reveal his findings immediately.

'You all seem to be under a misapprehension as to why Ms. Ogose has fainted. That is why you can't see the truth behind this case. She didn't faint because of Mr. Miki. The cause of her fainting spell lies with the other person who came in behind him.'

'Do you mean, me?' asked Azusa testily. 'Why would I make her faint?'

'Saying you made her faint would not be correct. For she only pretended to have fainted.'

Everyone in the room seemed in shock, as if a typhoon had hit the building. Nobody had anticipated what had just been said.

'But why would she need to do that?' the entertainment reporter repeated in a slightly higher pitch.

'The answer becomes clear once you think about it. What does she have to gain by pretending to have fainted?'

Hoshikage looked encouragingly at everyone, but nobody seemed to have an answer.

'It's very simple. You don't have to think hard about it.'

'I know,' said the photographer. 'That way, she doesn't have to speak.'

'Exactly.'

'But why wouldn't she want to speak to me? I could imagine her acting like that if there had been bad blood between us, but we hadn't even met before.'

Azusa looked baffled.

'If you think about it that way, you'll never solve the mystery. Ms. Ogose was not opposed to having a conversation with you. She just didn't want you to hear her voice.'

'Her voice? I still don't see it. Why shouldn't I hear her voice?'

Hoshikage's only reply was a gale of laughter.

7

'Let me tell you what I think. Ms. Urihara was discovered in the bathroom, supposedly shortly after her murder. But even if the crime had been committed a whole hour earlier, it would still be possible to fool the doctors, because the body had been lying in a hot bath and therefore the body temperature would not drop much.'

'Maybe so,' replied Azusa doubtfully, 'but I can assure you that she had been arguing with Mr. Ajiro at eight fifty-five. That is an irrefutable fact. It wasn't just me who heard them, but Tori'i here, the not-really-unconscious lady, Ms. Ogose, and Chizu, the maid. The theory that Ms. Urihara was already dead at that time is contradicted by that fact alone.'

Everyone nodded silently in agreement. But Hoshikage didn't seem deterred at all. He beamed as he took out his briar pipe and stuffed it with his beloved Granger tobacco. Tadokoro and Mizuhara knew that smile was a sign of things to come.

'...Allow me to refute your point.'

He lit his pipe with his Ronson lighter and, after puffing some smoke into the room, he continued.

'First I have a question for the two gentlemen of the press. You were in this very room when you overheard the argument. Did you peek out and see Mr. Ajiro and Ms. Urihara argue?'

'Of course not, that would have been rude,' replied the reporter angrily. Still smiling, Hoshikage persisted.

'But if you didn't even peek, how do you know that the person Mr. Ajiro was having a row with was Ms. Urihara?'

'Because he told us so. And Ms. Ogose and Chizu also saw them arguing. That's more than enough, surely?'

The detective didn't comment, but turned to Chizu.

'Now it's your turn. You say you saw Mr. Ajiro and Ms. Urihara arguing at eight fifty-five, but the kitchen does not have a clock. So how did you know what time it was?'

'Because that's what Mr. Ajiro and the other gentlemen told me,' answered Chizu with a pout. She didn't like Hoshikage's tone.

Hoshikage blew another cloud of smoke out and addressed everyone in the room.

'What I've established with these questions is that all the testimonies are dependent on each other, and that, taken separately, they don't prove anything at all. Which means that the quarrel which Chizu saw and the quarrel the two reporters overheard could actually have occurred at different times. It is only by suggestion that you've been led to believe that the two quarrels were one and the same.'

'I guess that's possible in theory...'

'It's also possible practically. Once you examine the details of the case, you will see that hypothesis fits the facts surprisingly well. For example, the pie Ms. Ogose was preparing was ostensibly for you, her guests. But the real purpose was to make sure the maid would see the quarrel and become a witness.

'And when Mr. Ajiro was arguing with a woman he claimed was Ms. Urihara, why didn't he shut the door tightly behind him? It might have been carelessness, but it's far more likely he did so in order for the argument to be overheard.'

Azusa was speechless.

'That started me thinking. Why was it necessary for Mr. Ajiro to enact this foolish fight twice? There's only one answer: to make it seem as though Ms. Urihara was still alive at eight fifty-five. And why was that? Because she had already been murdered by then.'

Hoshikage had been so preoccupied with his story that he had forgotten to puff on his pipe. The others were also listening intently, trying to understand what he was saying. Atsuko Ogose, too, had "awakened" at some point, and was staring hard at him.

'If Ms. Urihara was already dead, then obviously the voice you two reporters overheard belonged to someone else impersonating her. Needless to say, that someone could only have been Atsuko Ogose.'

'Aha.'

'Aha, indeed! That was why Ms. Ogose had to pretend to faint whenever she saw you.'

'Now I get it,' said Azusa. 'If we had noticed that the fake Mayumi Urihara beyond the door had the same voice as Atsuko Ogose, the game would have been up.'

Tori'i, the photographer, had a question.

'Mr. Hoshikage, I understand that Mr. Ajiro deceived us, but Mr. Esashi also said he'd been upstairs and seen and spoken with the victim. Does that mean he lied as well?'

'Of course. You can't have a chat with someone who's already dead.'

'Then does that mean that Mr. Ajiro, Ms. Ogose and Mr. Esashi were all in it together?'

Junzō Miki's voice trembled. It was obviously a great shock for him to learn that the youngsters he had supported had conspired to kill Mayumi.

'Yes.'

'Why?! Why do such a thing? I loved all of them, and this is what they do to me?'

'I'll talk about motive in a minute. But first I want to explain how the murder was committed. I'm speculating, so correct me if I'm wrong.'

Esashi stared at the floor, but Ajiro nodded to Hoshikage. He looked peaceful, as if he was resigned to his fate.

'Ms. Ogose claims she started on the pie in the kitchen at half past seven and I believe her. It takes at least an hour to boil the filling, prepare the dough and get everything ready to put in the oven. Mr. Ajiro and the victim had their row at some point during the preparation of the pie, and my theory is that it occurred before half past eight.'

'Yes, around twenty past eight.'

'I don't know if you had intended to do so, but you had already put her in a bad mood, so she could have been triggered at any time. I assume you lured her in front of the drawing room and then taunted her somehow.'

'Yes. Mayumi was very stubborn, and it was easy to set her off.'

149

'As I said, Ms. Ogose could hear you fighting from the kitchen, and Chizu could too. Ms. Ogose, what did you do next?'

Atsuko had also given up any further attempts at resistance. She had a distant look in her eyes, which looked even more beautifully clear than ever before.

'I put the pie in the oven and immediately left the kitchen to go upstairs. I told the chief inspector that this was at nine o'clock, but actually, it was still twenty-five past eight.'

'And you did not redo your make-up. What did you do?'

'I committed the murder. I....'

'I think you'd better not say anything until you get a solicitor. Don't forget we have two veteran police detectives from the Metropolitan Police Department here as well.'

She was silent for a moment. Not because of Hoshikage's warning, but in order to prepare for her confession.

'But I want to tell you. Kazuo Kakio, the jazz pianist who fell from the upstairs window to his death, was my older brother.'

'Young Kakio was your brother? I never knew,' said Miki, greatly surprised.

'I deliberately kept that from you. My brother's death was officially an accident, but in fact he was murdered. Mr. Esashi saw how Mayumi pushed him out of the window, but as there was no physical evidence, she managed to avoid justice. I decided that if the law wouldn't punish her, then I would. With the help of the others, I joined the band.'

Even Hoshikage had not expected this astounding confession, so he too listened intently to Atsuko.

'It took me two years to find out why she did it. If my brother had been at fault and got killed for it, I could have lived with that. But he was murdered just because he rejected her romantic advances, so I decided to kill her. Toshihiko and Mr. Iikura were also aware of what Mayumi had done and were very sympathetic to my cause. Mr. Iikura devised a detailed plan and Toshihiko and Mr. Esashi helped me carry it out. It would have been easier if we'd been able to make her death look like a suicide, but unfortunately Mayumi wasn't the type. It would have made her death more suspicious, in fact, so that idea was discarded. Everything would have gone according to plan if only that traffic accident hadn't happened, or if it had happened a bit farther down the road. The murder would have been pinned on the clown who got away.'

But neither Atsuko nor the other young musicians seemed truly regretful about that. All four people actually seemed quite relieved.

'When did you kill her?'

'At half past eight. We had rehearsed it several times. Everything went according to the timetable.'

'I was told by Mr. Azusa that a woman had called his office.'

'That was me. We weren't sure when the reporters would arrive here exactly, but it all went as we had hoped. I was afraid my voice would be trembling, but in fact the call went fine. Toshihiko had offered to make the call for me but he was busy carrying the body into the bathtub and placing Mayumi's sandals correctly.'

As she spoke, Atsuko was radiant, like a maiden hearing sweet whispered words of romance.

'Given that Mr. Iikura has a perfect alibi, I assume it was Mr. Esashi who dressed up as the clown and left after visiting the kitchen.'

'Yes,' replied Esashi cheerfully. 'My part in this was to scare Chizu and tie her up in the chair.'

'I know practically everything you did. Washing the blood off your hands and burning the gloves was all just for show. Your real goal was to tie the maid up by the window, so she could witness how you left the building. You couldn't afford to have anyone suspect the people who live here, so it was necessary to leave the impression that the clown had left and never returned. In a way, you had high expectations of your maid.'

After he saw all the conspirators nodding, Hoshikage addressed Jūrō Esashi again.

'At what time did you attack Chizu?'

'The attack was planned for half past eight, and for me to escape through the back door ten minutes later. Everything went according to schedule.'

Hoshikage straightened up in his chair and continued.

'When I was told about the clown disappearing from inside the tunnel, I immediately foresaw what the truth must have been. The maid had seen the clown enter the tunnel, but had not seen him return. The natural assumption would be that he must have exited at the other end. Since we know there were four witnesses on that end, some of them police officers, it's obvious the clown must have gone through the tunnel before the witnesses arrived. In other words, the clown attacked the maid earlier than had been assumed.'

'I still don't get it,' said Tadokoro bluntly. Azusa and Tori'i felt the same way. Hoshikage coughed and turned to the chief inspector.

'Listen carefully and try to keep up. The fundamental point is to understand that you've been deceived about the times. Mr. Ajiro and Ms. Mayumi had their fight at twenty-past eight. The belief that this quarrel happened at eight fifty-five led to the curious incident of the clown disappearing from the tunnel. Oh, how should I explain this?'

Hoshikage's slender index finger twirled with his pencil moustache.

'All right, let's go over it again, starting with the reason for the clown's existence, which was to create a fake culprit. If you take everything at face value, the clown entered the building at the front, committed the crime and then went into the kitchen, where he washed his hands before tying the maid up. Everyone assumed the clown was the murderer. But, since we know the real culprit was Ms. Ogose, the red on the clown's hands must have been paint. The reason he washed them so thoroughly was to avoid any traces of paint being discovered, which would have given the game away. He arranged for Chizu to witness him going into the tunnel. But because an accident had occurred on the other side of the tunnel, the curious incident of the clown vanishing from the tunnel was born.'

'Yes, I escaped through the tunnel at precisely eight forty. The accident hadn't occurred yet,' explained Esashi to Tadokoro and the reporters.

'This part of town has a lot of students, so there usually aren't many people out on the street at night, but just to be sure, I put on the cloak I had previously hidden in the tunnel and exited at the other end. Then I walked around the warehouse back to the front entrance, where I took off my cloak and threw it in the shrubs. Every night there are food stalls on the waterfront, so I was sure someone would notice me.'

Esashi's explanation was intended for Tadokoro and the reporters. He did not once look at Hoshikage.

'So now you can see that everyone had it backwards,' said the detective. 'The clown did not first enter the premises through the front, and then escape through the back after committing the murder. He first exited at the back through the tunnel, and then went back inside through the front entrance later,' explained Hoshikage.

The puzzled expressions on the grim faces of Tadokoro and Mizuhara showed that they still hadn't got the whole picture, but Hoshikage didn't care.

'And now I have a question for Mr. Esashi here. I know exactly what the clown, that's you, did before you arrived at the front door, but could you tell us what you did after you went inside?'

'Not very much, actually. I reckoned that someone would untie Chizu sooner or later, so I just went upstairs to my own room, changed my clothes and hid the clown's outfit in the closet. Later, we shredded the whole outfit. Everyone helped out, so it didn't take long.'

'What did you do with the shredded pieces?'

'We divided them and threw them away the next day in dustbins at stations. The police were still looking for the clown and didn't pay us much attention, so it was easy to take the pieces out of the building. I got rid of the knife the same way.'

'And now let me explain my part,' said Atsuko.

'Let me warn you once again, be very careful about what you say. Do not make things worse for yourself.'

Atsuko nodded to Hoshikage, but proceeded with her confession anyway.

'I went to Mayumi's room with the knife, but she wasn't there. Her clothes were laid out on the bed, so I guessed she was taking a shower. I could not afford to wait for her to come back, so I went to the shower room.'

'I'd just taken the clown's outfit off,' interjected Esashi. 'We had to be careful the two of them didn't get into a struggle, where Urihara might have taken the knife from Ogose, so I was listening carefully in case my help was needed.'

Atsuko looked gratefully at the sturdy bassist.

'I then returned to my own room, dazed by feelings of great satisfaction and relief now that the main task had been done. But I still had things to do.'

'Yes, you had to go downstairs, lure Mr. Ajiro out of the drawing room and pretend to argue with him!'

'I had just taken a person's life, so I wasn't very calm. But later they told me that my shrieking voice felt really genuine.'

'You were truly authentic, I really thought you were the real Mayumi Urihara,' said Tori'i. Atsuko smiled at him.

'And I believe this is what you need?' Hoshikage asked Tadokoro.

'Yes, I've got most of it. But could you go over once again what everyone did and at what time?'

'Of course.' Atsuko put her finger on her chin and thought for a moment.

'I already told you how Chizu and I overheard the row between Toshihiko and Mayumi from the kitchen. Unknown to Chizu, I was listening intently to what they said, because thirty minutes later I had to repeat that same quarrel with Mr. Ajiro, pretending to be Mayumi.'

'By then, Chizu was tied up in the chair, and I had shut the kitchen door so she couldn't hear the second argument,' interjected Esashi.

'Got it, got it. What happened next?'

'So as far as Chizu knew, the quarrel happened only once. She had seen for herself that Mayumi and Toshihiko were arguing, so why would she harbour any doubts about that? The only error in her story was that she believed the quarrel occurred at eight fifty-five, whereas in fact it happened at eight twenty.'

Atsuko looked at Chizu, who seemed angry at having been deceived and had turned her face away.

'Shortly after the first quarrel, I pretended to Chizu that the reporters had arrived and left the kitchen, supposedly to meet them. In fact, they didn't actually arrive until thirty minutes later.'

Tadokoro had meticulously been taking notes. He compared them with the timetable he had written down earlier.

Time	Movement
08:15	Atsuko, Chizu make pie in kitchen.
08:20	Ajiro, Mayumi argue. Overheard by Atsuko, Chizu.
08:25	Atsuko lies about arrival of reporters, leaves kitchen.
08:30	Atsuko kills Mayumi in bathroom.
08:35	Esashi in clown disguise attacks Chizu.
08:40	Esashi leaves through back door.
08:45	Esashi enters through front door.
08:50	Azusa, Tori'i arrive.
08:55	Atsuko pretends to be Mayumi, acts out row with Ajiro. "Mayumi" believed to go upstairs for a bath.

09:05	Esashi out of disguise reunites with others. Tells reporters Mayumi is in a bad mood to make them believe she is still alive.
09:10	(It is made to appear as if the murder had occurred between 09:05 and 09:15.)
09:20	(Time the clown was assumed to have escaped.)
10:00	Chizu freed.

'The way there seems to be something occurring every five minutes leads me to believe that you had a planned timetable. Did you, and if so, who made it?'

'I did,' said Iikura, who had been standing silently against a wall until then.

'I'm a great fan of detective fiction, and own quite a number. Like any self-respecting aficionado, I thought about entering a writing contest. The trick I devised made it seem as though someone who had actually gone out and then in, appeared to have gone in and then out.

'It was my contribution to Ms. Ogose's cause. Mayumi Urihara was a viper in Mr. Miki's bosom. We all knew that she would have to be dealt with sooner or later, and Ms. Ogose was willing to do the job.' He laughed loudly.

'I don't know how good a saxophonist you are, but that was masterful planning. By skilfully manipulating our sense of time, you made it appear as though the clown who had gone out of Fujimi House and returned inside, had actually come inside, committed a murder and then left.'

Ryūzō Hoshikage felt ashamed that he had likened the man to a pig living in a cabbage house.

'I believe it's almost time for us to be taken away, but would you allow us to perform one final time? A parting concert for ourselves...' Ajiro implored the chief inspector. Tadokoro hesitated.

'Let them do it,' urged Hoshikage. 'One song can't hurt.'

The young musicians all cheered, ran out into the hall and climbed onto the stage on the other side of the room. The next moment, a brilliant swing version of *Glow of a Firefly* began (3).

(3) *Glow of a Firefly* (*Hotaru no Hikari*) is a Japanese song based on the tune of the Scottish folk song *Auld Lang Syne*. It features original lyrics and is often played as a theme song at graduation ceremonies or at the end of the day when schools, stores and restaurants close.

The Five Clocks

1

After Tokiko had expressed her gratitude and left the room, Sarumaru gently closed the door behind her and relaxed in his chair.

'She came here at the advice of my professor when I was in college, so I could hardly refuse her.'

After explaining himself, Sarumaru opened his cigarette case, lit up a Peace cigarette and took a puff. After a moment, he stubbed his cigarette out in the ash tray and his demeanour became more serious.

'It's only natural that she believes her fiancé to be innocent. But I am well aware how busy you are, so I wouldn't be bothering you if trust were all she had besides a fancy introduction letter. I couldn't say this out loud in front of her, but I am actually of the same opinion.'

'So you, too, think Nikaidō is not our man?' Chief Inspector Onitsura looked surprised and upset by the statement. 'There's motive and evidence. And he has no alibi either.'

'That's exactly what I mean. Don't you think it's all a little too pat, served up on a silver platter like that? Doesn't it feel as though someone's been pulling strings?'

'What good comes from suspecting everything like that? It would be different if you had something concrete for me, but you can't expect me to rule out Nikaidō as the murderer just because it seems too neatly wrapped up,' retorted Onitsura. It was too late to go over the case again, the expression on his face said.

The details of the case the two men were discussing were as follows.

Exactly one week earlier, at noon on the first of May, the body of Mansaku Sasamoto was discovered in a room in his fancy apartment in Takagichō in Aoyama. Sasamoto had been found by a visitor, who had turned pale at the sight and almost tripped as he made his way to the concierge's office on the ground floor. The concierge had immediately gone up to the room, and found Sasamoto lying stone

157

cold, strangled by the dirty towel around his neck. His eyes were bulging, and the tongue sticking out of his mouth had turned dark.

The usual examinations were conducted and it was discovered that the victim's savings passbook had been stolen from his closet. That was seen as the first clue tying Ryūkichi Nikaidō to the horrible crime, for he was known to be having trouble financing his upcoming wedding. He, however, claimed that although he had indeed been fretting over money, he had accepted Tokiko's suggestion to hold a simple ceremony, with no reception and only an overnight honeymoon. So the problem had already been solved, according to Nikaidō.

Glasses of whisky soda had been sitting on the table at the crime scene, suggesting that the murderer was not a passing thief, but an acquaintance of Sasamoto. That was the second clue. But Ryūkichi claimed he was not particularly close to Sasamoto, and that they only ever talked about work. He had never visited Sasamoto's apartment. It was suspected that the killer had deliberately not touched his own drink, and had attacked Sasamoto when his guard was down.

The new criminal laws placed emphasis on physical evidence, so the police did everything to trace the owner of the murder weapon— the towel which had been left at the crime scene. When it was discovered that the towel belonged to Ryūkichi, who worked in the same accounting division as Sasamoto, suspicion of the former became insurmountable. That was the third clue. When confronted, Ryūkichi turned pale. While admitting it was the towel he used in his office, he claimed he had misplaced it a few days earlier.

Ryūkichi's office desk was searched, and Sasamoto's passbook was found there, hidden at the bottom of the lowest drawer on the right side of the desk. That was clue number four. Ryūkichi only gave vague answers, saying he had no idea where the passbook had come from, but that made a bad impression on the detectives, who seemed to think he was brazenly challenging them.

Lastly, Ryūkichi had no alibi. That was clue number five. The time of the murder had been determined to be between nine and eleven of the night prior to the discovery of the body. Ryūkichi usually spent his evenings reading in his shabby apartment, but on that particular night he had gone out. And his testimony about it sounded like a pack of lies.

'It was just before nine. A woman called me saying Ms. Hario had asked her to pass on a message. I was told to go to a café called Marronier at once. So I got dressed and went out.'

The young man looked very serious as he anxiously explained his movements that night. But the more serious he became, the more he gave the impression he had carefully prepared his answers beforehand. His whole story sounded fake. The Hario he mentioned was Tokiko's surname.

'What's this Marronier place?'

"I was told it was a café near the crossing in Jinbōchō and that it was easy to find, but I didn't see it anywhere. I went by all the streets around the crossing and even checked the back alleys, but there was no such a place. I searched for an hour and half, but eventually gave up and went home exhausted. The following day, I met with Ms. Hario and asked her about the phone call, but she said she hadn't asked anyone to pass on a message to me. It was only then that I realised I had been tricked.'

'Did you meet anyone you knew while you were out?'

'No, nobody.'

And so it was that Ryūkichi Nikaidō was sent to the prosecutor's office while still protesting his innocence.

'So you claim there's actually someone else behind it all?'

Onitsura's question to Sarumaru was answered by a slow, almost theatrically slow, nod back. There was an intellectual air about him, but he was a hard worker.

'Do you remember how disappointed we were when we learnt Sasamoto had been murdered?'

By "we," Sarumaru meant the detectives of Investigative Division II.

'This is between you and me, but early this year, we learned something interesting from an international merchant I know. A young employee at the accounting division of a certain government office was supposed to be living a rather luxurious life: driving a Cadillac, maintaining two mistresses, investing in trading firms and even buying a villa in Atami. That was suspicious, and when we started to follow the lead, it eventually led to Mansaku Sasamoto, the man who was killed.'

'So that's why he was living in such a fancy apartment in Takagichō.'

159

'That wasn't all. He had two other apartments for his two mistresses. He managed to lure a woman called Tonkoma from Kaguyazaka's geisha district and installed her in Akasaka, and he bought a home in Yoyogi Hatsudai for a dancer who had once been Miss Nippon. We were surprised to find that he lived even more glamorously than the rumours had said. But it was clear the income of a simple accountant in his thirties could never have covered his extravagant life style.'

It was obvious he had been getting his money elsewhere, so we investigated his dossiers. We found out that over the last three years, he had embezzled 56 million yen. We wouldn't have been able to earn that much in two hundred years.'

'But he wasn't the only one who had been helping himself to the till, surely? He had to have a partner in crime.'

'Precisely,' said Sarumaru, nodding in agreement.

'It was the assistant division chief. Sasamoto would cook the books, and the assistant division chief would work his ways on the division chief, making him rubber stamp everything. But with age comes wisdom, and he is much craftier than Sasamoto. He lives in a normal home like other office workers and his daily commute is by train in rush hour. He even dresses very simply. He occasionally splurges on food, but as his wife runs a small handicraft shop in Shinjuku, and when you add in that income, there was nothing suspicious about his expenditures at all. He had been very careful, so we were completely fooled by him.'

Sarumaru leaned forward as he told Onitsura how they had asked Mansaku Sasamoto to appear voluntarily for questioning.

'At first he maintained he knew nothing about anything and at times even tried to threaten us, but we had gathered our evidence in advance, so he couldn't maintain that aggressive attitude for long. At the fifth interrogation, he broke down. He asked for a week in order to write a detailed memo about their crime. We were waiting eagerly to get our hands on it, but he was killed on the fourth day.'

'So the mastermind behind it all was the assistant division chief?'

'Yes, Hirondo Sugita.'

Onitsura had met Sugita when the police went to search Nikaidō's desk. A plump man in his forties, with downward slanting eyes, he had given the stereotypical apology about how sorry he was that his lack of supervision had led to his subordinate becoming a murderer. He hadn't left a particularly bad impression on Onitsura at the time, but now he had heard Sarumaru's side of the story, the chief inspector couldn't help feeling that the man had been laughing at him behind his serious expression.

'The corruption seems to run deep. We might even be talking about political payoffs here. Sugita would be the one in the most danger if Sasamoto had presented his memo. In my view, he had a much stronger motive to commit the crime than Nikaidō.'

'Suppose you are right. Why did he choose Nikaidō as his scapegoat?'

'That, I don't know,' said Sarumaru, shaking his head. 'Perhaps Nikaidō's personal circumstances made him perfect for the role, as everybody knew about them. Or it might be that Sugita had another reason for wanting to kick Nikaidō off the cliff. If Nikaidō is indeed an honest young man with a strong sense of justice, as his fiancée claims, then maybe a man like Sugita simply couldn't stand someone like that around. But digging into that is your speciality. What I'm concerned about is Sugita's alibi. If he was astute enough to frame Nikaidō for Sasamoto's murder, he's bound to have prepared a cleverly constructed alibi for himself. Be careful not to fall for his tricks,' said Sarumaru with a warning look.

2

It wasn't done for a detective to have doubts about his suspect, so Onitsura immediately went to his superior to tell him about Sarumaru's warning.

Next, he paid Sugita a visit. The latter's face was already flushed from too much drinking, but when he realised he was a suspect himself, his ruddy face turned purple with anger. Struggling to control his outrage, he told the chief inspector that on the thirtieth of April he had been out drinking with a junior classmate from his college days, and that the police should ask him about his alibi. There was no hint of the friendly face resembling Ebisu, one of the Seven Gods of Fortune, which he had presented when Onitsura and he first met.

Onitsura ignored Sugita's mood and simply asked him about his movements on the night of the murder. He then paid a visit to Sugita's friend, a man called Jōji Kobayakawa, who worked at an Indian trading firm located in Nihonbashi.

Kobayakawa, whose office was on the fourth floor of a small building, had just returned from the Ministry of International Trade and Industry. The skinny young man was obviously nervous and kept blinking his eyes behind thick glasses. His testimony about the night of the murder corresponded to what Hirondo Sugita had told Onitsura earlier.

Early in April, Kobayakawa had received a call from Sugita, who had lost money on off-course betting. He asked Kobayakawa to lend him 20,000 yen, so he could keep it a secret from his wife. He promised he would pay Kobayakawa back by the end of the month. Sugita had often helped Kobayakawa out in the past, so he didn't hesitate to withdraw the amount from his savings.

The next call came on the twenty-eighth. Sugita said he wanted to return the money he'd borrowed. His wife had found out anyway, but he'd managed to smooth things out, so he hoped that Kobayakawa could come over so Sugita could treat him, and perhaps sleep over. It had been a long time since Kobayakawa had last visited Sugita in his home in Shinjuku, so he was glad to take up the offer.

They had met at Tōkyō Station on the early evening of the thirtieth and taken the train to Shinjuku, where Sugita took Kobayakawa to a beer hall near the station. The place was packed, as it was the night before May Day, but they managed to get a corner table.

'Are you familiar with Shinjuku by night?' asked Sugita.

'I guess it depends. I don't really know the darker side of Shinjuku.'

'Perfect. Tonight, I will be your guide.'

After the beer hall, they visited an oden restaurant, a music café, another bar and a cinema. By the time they finally arrived at Sugita's home, the hands on Kobayakawa's wristwatch showed ten minutes to nine. Sugita's home was located in Banshūchō, only a ten-minute walk away from the entertainment district of Shinjuku. It was not particularly large, but the location was very convenient, and it actually became surprisingly quiet at night. Kobayakawa's daily commute to the city was from Hachiōji, so he would have loved to live there.

'Hey, we're starving. Is there anything to eat?' shouted Sugita as he dropped into an armchair in his study. A splendid bookcase with heavy books flanked the right side of the window, and on top of it stood a marble timepiece. "I'd love to have a gorgeous clock like that too, once I have my own house and family," thought Kobayakawa. Sugita's thirty-five year old wife Yaeko looked younger than her age, perhaps because they had no children, but she also seemed to have more beauty than brains.

'How about cheese?'

'How is cheese going to fill us up! Kobayakawa here is starving as well. Let's order some soba noodles with tempura.'

While his wife was on the phone placing the order, Sugita suddenly got up.

'Let me return your money before the soba arrives. Thank you for helping me out.'

He took out a fountain pen and his stamp and opened the chequebook on his desk. Sugita often used cheques, perhaps because his wife ran a store separately on her own.

After Yaeko had finished her call, she sat next to Kobayakawa.

'My husband lost money on off-course betting and foolishly tried to hide it from me. I'm sorry he caused you so much trouble.'

She shot an angry glance at her husband, who pretended not to notice.

'It was no trouble at all,' said Kobayakawa, suddenly noticing the amount on the cheque. It was two thousand yen more than he had lent Sugita.

'Hey, this isn't right.'

'It's interest.'

'This much? I'm not a loan shark.'

'A senior should never be borrowing from his junior, only the other way around. Please accept that interest, or else I'll feel ashamed for the rest of my life,' Sugita insisted. Yaeko stood firm with her husband as well, so Kobayakawa had no choice but to accept.

Just then the soba noodle delivery man called and Yaeko hurried out, to return quickly with a tray with two bowls. As Kobayakawa picked up his chopsticks, he noticed the name printed on the bowl covers.

'Issa-an? That's an unusual name.'

'There's no better place. I heard the name comes from Issa Kobayashi. You know, from the poem "There's the moon, there are Buddhas, but for me, there's soba." The soba there is really good.'

Sugita had stopped his chopsticks in mid-air to boast about the place, when Yaeko suddenly remembered something.

'Did you repay Mr. Narahara?'

'Oh no! It slipped my mind,' cried her husband as he put down his bowl and chopsticks. His wife looked furious.

'Today's the last day of the month. I reminded you this morning.'

'Sorry.'

'It's no good saying sorry. If you don't pay it back today, nobody will ever trust us anymore. You have to go now.'

'But it's already past nine. Let's give up on tonight.'

Sugita looked sour as he looked up at the clock on the bookcase.

'Nine isn't that late. You can make it back here in thirty minutes.'

'Twenty even, but can't this wait until tomorrow?'

'No, a delay of even one day will still mean their trust in you becomes zero. It's simple to lose trust, but not easy to regain it. Especially from a precise person like Mr. Narahara.'

'Okay, I'll go,' said Sugita. He quickly finished his meal and asked Kobayakawa to wait for him. It was just out on the main street, so it wouldn't take too long and once he was back, they could get started on the whisky. He got up and picked up his chequebook.

'Dear, don't forget your stamp.'

'I know, you don't have to tell me!' he barked at her.

'I always have to keep an eye on him all the time. He's like a big baby. And yet he acts like he's a big man.'

Kobayakawa didn't quite know how to react. Yaeko sighed as she sat down in the armchair her husband had vacated.

'The amount he borrowed from you wasn't enough, so he had to borrow another 50,000 yen from the owner of a clothes store we know,' she explained with a frown. She seemed to realise she was making her guest uncomfortable, so she tried to put on a smile.

'Do you like music? I believe there's a concert at nine.'

Kobayakawa checked the radio schedule in the evening newspaper lying on the desk and indeed, Radio Kantō was airing a Mozart piano concerto.

'Feel free to listen. You can turn on the radio.'

A medium-sized radio was standing next to the clock on the bookcase. Kobayakawa stood up, switched it on and turned the dial until he finally found the concerto in C minor. The first movement had just begun, and the pianist's light touch promised an enjoyable performance.

After thirty minutes sitting all alone with someone else's wife, Kobayakawa was feeling quite nervous. Only Mozart's angelic music saved him from the awkward situation. By the time the front door opened again, the performance had ended and the announcer was reading a commercial message. Yaeko switched the radio off, and they could hear Sugita calling out.

He looked quite pleased and there was no sign of the ill temper in which he had left the house.

'How did it go?'

'He was there. He offered me a seat, but I said I had an important guest waiting at home, as well as some good whisky and my lovely wife, so I was only there for about ten minutes. By the way, Kobayakawa, did I write the date on that cheque of yours?'

'The date? Well...,' Kobayakawa mumbled as he took the cheque out of his pocket. The date column was indeed empty.

'It happened over there too. Mr. Narahara had to draw my attention to it. Must be a bad night.'

'You've drunk too much, dear.'

'Nonsense. If anything, it's because I haven't had enough. Bring the cheese and smoked herring.'

As his wife left the room, Sugita took out his fountain pen, wrote the date on the cheque, then took out a bottle of whisky from the bookcase.

'Look at this. Old Parr.'

'Wo—wow!'

As someone who had grown up in the post-war period, Kobayakawa had never tasted the famous brand, and couldn't help salivating at the sight of the amber liquid.

'So you had a few drinks and stayed the night there. And Mr. Sugita only left you once, when he went out just after nine, is that correct?'

'Exactly. After he returned, we drank together for a long time. His wife was with us as well.'

Kobayakawa was devoted to Sugita, and didn't seem to like how the chief inspector was asking all the questions about what they had done that night. He started to blink more frequently the longer the conversation continued. Onitsura pretended not to notice and pressed on regardless. He learned that Sugita had left to visit the tailor around five past nine.

'When did he return?'

'Just after the Mozart ended, so slightly before half past, I'd say.'

So Sugita had been absent for about twenty-three minutes. If he were indeed the murderer, that period was the only time he could have committed the crime. Twenty-three minutes would have been enough to go to the crime scene in Aoyama and return. The investigation needed therefore to concentrate on that time interval, starting with whether Sugita had indeed visited the tailor. Onitsura also had to think of ways to fabricate an alibi, such as moving the hands on the clock to the wrong time. He also had to determine whether the clock on the bookcase had been indicating the correct time.

'Of course the time was correct. My wristwatch and their clock were both set to the correct time,' said young Kobayakawa vehemently. 'And if you don't believe me, you can check with the soba restaurant. Their delivery came exactly at nine,' he said.

3

Tokiko's mother had been busy when her daughter returned home, so she waited until they sat down for dinner to ask her: 'So, were there any leads in the investigation?'

Tokiko had used her lunch break to visit Onitsura for an update on his investigation. She had gone to work full of hope, but now she looked gloomy and didn't even touch her chopsticks. Her small, innocent face suddenly looked many years older.

Her mother repeated her question.

'Your tea is getting cold. What did the chief inspector say?'

'It's hopeless....'

Tokiko looked very depressed.

'Mr. Sarumaru said he suspected that Hirondo Sugita, the assistant division chief, might be the culprit. But he has a perfect alibi. Mr. Sarumaru said it was a miracle it was so perfect.'

Seeing her mother looking anxious, Tokiko elaborated.

'Mr. Sugita claimed to have been having a drink with a friend in his own home in Shinjuku at the time of the murder. The police suspected the clock in the house may have been tampered with, but on checking the clock at the soba restaurant which made a delivery at the Sugitas, they corresponded.'

'How confusing.'

'Mr. Sugita did leave his home for a while to pay back some borrowed money to a person called Narahara, the owner of a clothes shop. But that was true too. Mr. Narahara confirmed Mr. Sugita's story.'

'Tokiko, what if this Sugita had a brother? He could have asked him to act as a double. The tailor could have been easily fooled.'

Tokiko shook her head.

'The police didn't overlook that possibility, either. But Mr. Sugita wrote a cheque for both his friend and the tailor, so his handwriting was on both cheques. They were checked by the handwriting experts at the Metropolitan Police Department, who determined that it was 95% certain that they were signed by Mr. Sugita himself. So the person drinking with his friend at home, and the person who visited Mr. Narahara was definitely the real Mr. Sugita, which means it would have been impossible for him to make a return trip to Aoyama Takagichō to commit the murder.'

'But don't you think it's suspicious that he went out just then to return the money to the tailor? He may have really visited the man, but he could also have gone over to Aoyama in a taxi while he was out.'

Tokiko's mother was desperately looking for some way to break the deadlock. If it could be proved that Sugita was the murderer, Ryūkichi could safely return to her Tokiko.

'That's impossible as well. The shop is just a six- or seven-minute walk from the Sugita residence. The time it would have taken for a round trip, plus the time the two chatted, adds up exactly. He couldn't have gone to Aoyama.'

Sugita had left his house at five past nine, and arrived seven minutes later at the tailor at twelve minutes past. They had talked for about ten minutes. After Sugita wrote Narahara the cheque, he had been invited to stay a bit longer, but Sugita had explained he had a guest waiting and left. He had returned home at twenty-eight minutes past nine. So there was no time for Sugita to have found a taxi and made a round trip to Aoyama to commit the crime. Tokiko felt that listing all those times would only confuse her mother, however, so she spared her the details.

'And what if that tailor is lying? Is he trustworthy?'

'He's not lying. An office worker who lives in the neighbourhood happened to be in the store to buy some shirts and saw Mr. Sugita. With all those details uncovered by the investigation, even I am inclined to believe his alibi....'

'Then someone else must be the culprit.'

'But Mr. Sarumaru said that Mr. Sugita was without a doubt the murderer. He said that Mr. Onitsura must have fallen for a fake alibi. A perfect alibi....'

Her daughter seemed to be sighing to herself, but her mother knew of no way to comfort poor Tokiko. Those peaceful times when Tokiko was counting down the days to her wedding seemed like ancient history now.

'Don't give up now. Hope will surely shine its light upon us sooner or later. Now pick up your bowl. Today's your favourite, fried shrimp,' she said in a forcefully spirited manner, in the hopes of cheering up her daughter. She could not think of anything better to say at that moment.

At the same time, Onitsura was having dinner at his home in Kokubunji. He lived alone, without even a pet, so his meals were always very simple.

He thought back to that afternoon, and the terribly disappointed expression on Tokiko Hario's face as he explained the results of his investigation to her in a café in Toranomon. He grimaced at the unpleasant message he'd had for her. There were no doubts left about Sugita's alibi, due to the testimonies of both the tailor and the soba chef. And, as long as Sugita had an alibi, Ryūkichi Nikaidō's guilt appeared to be indisputable.

Nevertheless, there was still something bothering him, but he couldn't put a finger on what it was. Only after sitting in his armchair for almost an hour did Onitsura finally realise that it had been Sugita's cheques that had concerned him.

According to Kobayakawa, Sugita had forgotten to write down the date on his cheque and had added the date after he had returned from the tailor. While the chief inspector had not given it any particular attention at first, subconsciously he had found it unnatural that a person accustomed to writing cheques would make such a careless mistake, and he couldn't help thinking that Sugita had done it on purpose. He tried to put himself in Sugita's shoes, imagining what reason he could have had not to write the date on the cheque the first time.

Sugita had obviously anticipated that the authorities would check his alibi, and had probably anticipated that the police would be suspicious whether the man who ate soba in the study and drank with his friend was indeed Sugita himself, or a substitute. Sugita had two brothers, Masando and Takendo, so perhaps he had foreseen that the police, in their desperation, would not think it out of the question that one of them had taken his place and acted a role, together with Yaeko, in order to fool Kobayakawa. It was for that reason that it was necessary to prove that it was indeed he himself who had kept Kobayakawa company, and the way to do that was through his handwriting. Which is why he wrote a cheque to Kobayakawa.

If Sugita had written the amount, his signature and the date all at once, he could prove he had been in his home before he left, but there would be no way to prove that the man who returned from the tailor was also Sugita himself. To avoid even the slightest suspicion, and to fill in all the holes in his alibi, he needed to leave evidence to prove that it was indeed he himself who had returned from the tailor. And he could only do that by leaving his handwriting both before he left and after he returned. It didn't need to be a cheque, of course. He could have just written a short note as well, but as it needed to be presented as evidence later, Sugita had to make sure it was something Kobayakawa wouldn't lose carelessly. A cheque would be handled with care by its bearer and also be filed away by the bank once it had been handed in, so it would be available to the police as evidence at any time.

Onitsura was stunned when he realised that such a small action on Sugita's part could hold such significant meaning. At the same time, the fact Sugita had acted with such attention to detail convinced the policeman that his perfect alibi was nothing more than a meticulously constructed fake.

4

Late the following afternoon, just as she was about to finish work, Tokiko got an unexpected call from Onitsura. He wanted her to meet him, as he had something to tell her.

She got off the metro at Jingū Gaien, but spent some time trying to find the designated spot. Eventually, she found him sitting on a park bench.

'Hello, I'm happy you're here. After what I told you yesterday, you must have been feeling rather desperate.'

Onitsura was like a different person from the day before, radiating energy from every pore. Tokiko looked at him with a mixture of hope and trepidation.

'Did you manage to get any sleep last night? No? That's a shame. I have to apologise for that. But today, I bear good news. We might be overheard in a café, which is why I decided to meet you here.'

The chief inspector paused as a young man passed by, walking his dog.

'Last night, I re-examined Mr. Sugita's alibi and concluded that I needed to correct what I conveyed to you earlier. I've found decisive evidence that proves his alibi was falsified.'

'But what could that be?'

'I'll explain later. It had been in front of my nose, but due to carelessness, I had completely missed it until last night.'

Tokiko gasped. How had Onitsura managed to break an alibi that he had deemed to be impenetrable?

'What Sugita did was very simple, actually. The hands of the clock were moved back one hour, that was all. But the real problem was how he managed to fool his witness. As you know, the murder was committed between nine and eleven, and what was supporting Sugita's alibi in that two-hour interval were the hands of the clock. Actually, there were several clocks involved, either directly or indirectly. Let's count them.'

Tokiko started counting on her slim fingers.

'First there's the clock in the study. And then there's the wristwatch of the witness, Mr. Kobayakawa. And I should also count the clock of the radio station which broadcast the Mozart performance at nine. Then there's the clock at Narahara Tailors and finally, the clock on the wall at the soba restaurant. That makes five clocks in total. By setting the time on all those five clocks back one hour, he created his false alibi. So how did he manage to tinker with all those clocks? It took me all day, but I finally solved the mystery.'

Onitsura's eye fell on the watch around his listener's slender wrist.

'What a lovely watch. Could I have a look at it?'

Tokiko hesitated for a second, as it was hardly a watch worthy of praise, then took it off.

'It's just a cheap watch, made here in Japan.'

'No, it's wonderful. Those illegal imports, the ones they call bed bugs, make the wearer look so cheap,' said Onitsura as he held the watch in his hands and admired it. It didn't sound as though he was merely flattering her.

'Anyway, Mr. Kobayakawa testified that when they entered Sugita's study, the clock there was indicating 8:50 p.m. But, as I told you just now, in reality the time was already 9:50 p.m. Naturally, someone had already set the clock back one hour.'

'Mr. Sugita's wife?'

'Almost certainly. She only needed to turn the hands back before her husband and Mr. Kobayakawa came home, which was a very simple task. By the way, it was probably she who made the fake phone call to young Nikaidō.'

'The next problem we face is how Mr. Kobayakawa's wristwatch was set back one hour. You obviously can't tinker with a watch still on someone's wrist, so you would need to find a way to separate the watch from the person. What would you have done?'

'Errr, visit the public bath?'

'That's right. It might not be original, but there's really no other way. So when I questioned Mr. Kobayakawa he said he had indeed been taken to a Turkish bath that night. After their bath, Sugita had probably dressed quickly and picked up both wristwatches, turning Mr. Kobayakawa's back one hour, which the owner put back on without checking. Oh, I've been so busy talking, I've kept your own watch. Here, better put it back on before you forget.'

Tokiko felt somewhat disappointed by Onitsura's explanation, as he seemed to make everything seem so easy. She wasn't familiar with the inside of a Turkish bath, but she assumed there were clocks on the walls there, too. Wasn't it likely that Kobayakawa would have checked his watch with the clocks in the baths?

She looked up to see the chief inspector grinning at her. He seemed to have guessed her thoughts.

'You might think it odd that Mr. Kobayakawa didn't see through Sugita's simple trick, but if he had done, Sugita would just have put off his murder plans. But, since the murder did occur, it means that Mr. Kobayakawa didn't notice the change.'

Despite Onitsura's assurances, Tokiko couldn't help still doubting that the trick would have really worked. The chief inspector smiled again.

'Let me demonstrate in practice. I moved the hands on your watch slightly before I returned it to you, but you haven't noticed. Isn't that enough proof?'

'Oh!' Tokiko immediately looked at her watch, which was indicating five forty-five.

'Can you tell me by how many minutes I moved the hands?'

'No....'

She looked at the face of her wristwatch again, but she had no idea how many minutes it had been moved.

'Once the hands on a clock have been moved, it's nearly impossible to guess the real time. So it was quite normal for Mr. Kobayakawa to be wearing a watch which was running an hour behind, without noticing it.'

Tokiko had to admit that, now she had been shown the trick in person. She looked absolutely perplexed at how Onitsura had fooled her. He stared at her again for a moment, then laughed out loud.

'Hahaha, I fooled you again. I lied to you when I said I'd moved the hands of your watch. Here, look at my watch,' he said as he showed her his Elgin wristwatch. It showed five forty-five.

'Oh, I really believed you. You looked so serious.'

But then the chief inspector laughed again.

'Haha, you are being deceived again. The correct time now is actually five past six. I had already set my own watch back twenty minutes, then set yours back twenty minutes as well, to match mine. Just because both our watches indicate the same time, doesn't mean they are running correctly.'

'Oh!'

'Now do you understand? If two clocks are both running twenty minutes late, it's unlikely you'd ever notice. If I hadn't said anything, you'd have believed that it was now five forty-five. That's the same trick Sugita used. Mr. Kobayakawa didn't notice the clock in the study was an hour late, because his own wristwatch had been set one hour back as well.'

A wry smile appeared on Tokiko's face as she moved the hand on her watch back to the correct time.

'Please don't do that, it's not good for a watch if you keep moving the hands. I was actually lying when I said both our watches were running twenty minutes behind. I never moved the hands on your watch. The same with my own watch. I only wanted to perform a little experiment with you, to show that it's not difficult to move the hands of someone else's watch, that it's not easy to notice if one's own watch has been tinkered with, and that it's very simple to deceive someone with nothing more than the power of suggestion. I am of the opinion that it was a lot easier for Sugita to deceive Mr. Kobayakawa than you and I were initially inclined to believe.'

Tokiko nodded while hesitating about whether she should or should not move the hand on her watch.

'Hahaha, you've lost all trust in me now. Well, let's forget about that and move on to the next clock. According to that night's newspaper, Radio Kantō had a Mozart program starting at nine. But in reality Mr. Kobayakawa started listening to that performance at ten. Needless to say, it's not possible that the clocks at the radio station were all running behind. So that leads us to the conclusion that he had not in fact been listening to the radio waves from Radio Kantō. It's common knowledge that commercial radio stations copy their programs on tape to be distributed to local stations, which can then fit them into their own programming. So I rang Radio Kantō and I learned that the only stations broadcasting that Mozart concerto at ten o'clock on the evening of the thirtieth of April were Radio Akita and Kinki Broadcasting. I don't know which of these stations Mr. Kobayakawa had been listening to, but with a DX Radio which can receive long distance, you can definitely have a clean reception of either station even from Tōkyō.'

Here Onitsura paused. Tokiko looked around at the shrubbery. It had grown dark by now, and there was nobody else in the park.

5

'And at this point, the problem of the fourth clock, the clock at the tailor's, basically solves itself. Mr. Kobayakawa testified that after their soba meal, Sugita had taken his chequebook and stamp with him to visit Mr. Narahara. But we now know their clocks were running one hour late, so Sugita did not leave his house at five past nine, but five past ten. So Sugita had not visited the clothes shop at that moment, he had actually done so an hour earlier, at the real twelve minutes past nine. Which means that Sugita did not leave his home at the false five past nine to visit Mr. Narahara, he went out to commit the murder in Aoyama. But now a new problem arises: what was Mr. Kobayakawa doing when Sugita was visiting Mr. Narahara at the real twelve minutes past nine? Do you have any ideas?'

'Well, perhaps he had passed out in some bar, after too many drinks.'

'It's a good guess. But having him pass out would actually be bad for Sugita, who needed his witness to be able to recall clearly where they had been between nine and nine-thirty. So he couldn't afford to have him drunk before that. When Mr. Kobayakawa went through all their movements that night, he told me that after the baths Sugita took

173

him to a newsreel cinema. A theatre in the entertainment district is, of course, always packed. Sugita had suggested that, because the theatre was so crowded, they would never find two seats together, so they should just sit down wherever there was an empty seat and, once the newsreel had ended, they could meet up again outside. There was no reason to say no, so Kobayakawa found a seat in the front of the cinema and watched the news from there. The reels were short, so it was over in an hour and he found Sugita already waiting for him outside. Afterwards, they headed for Sugita's home in Banshūchō.'

'So Sugita had slipped out of the theatre to make his round trip to the tailor then?'

'Exactly. And to Mr. Narahara he made it sound as if he had a guest waiting at home. So now do you understand what he did?'

'Yes, your explanation makes it clear, but it's still hard to grasp the whole picture,' she admitted honestly.

'That's only natural. I'll show you my notes later. But first we have to discuss the problem of the fifth clock. How did Sugita manage to affect the clock of the soba restaurant? I questioned the cook at Issa-an, the madam at the counter, and the delivery boy, and they all swore that the soba had been delivered to the Sugitas at nine. Orders by phone are immediately written down in the notebook on the counter and Sugita's order had indeed been recorded there. The clock at the restaurant was also running correctly, down to the minute. As I told you, I had worked on the presumption that the clock in Sugita's study had been running behind and from there I'd managed to break his alibi apart. But unless I could prove the testimonies at Issa-an wrong, I would have had no choice but to accept that the clock in the study and Mr. Kobayakawa's wristwatch were in fact running correctly. It would mean my whole line of reasoning had been faulty. I was in a pinch.'

Tokiko had been entranced by Onitsura's story and couldn't suppress a gasp.

'Unlike the other simple tricks, the mystery of the fifth clock really turned out to be the major obstacle in unravelling the false alibi. I really had to rack my brains to come up with a solution. But it's already time for dinner. What if I treat you to a bowl of soba?'

Tokiko had expected to be taken to a soba restaurant nearby, but they took the bus to Shinjuku instead. They got off at the Isetan Department Store and walked past the newsreel cinema Sugita and Kobayakawa had visited. The programming had already changed, but

174

knowing Sugita had used this place for his alibi, Tokiko couldn't help staring at the building with interest.

'This neighbourhood is called Sankōchō, and it's next door to Banshūchō,' explained the chief inspector.

At the far corner of the next crossing, Tokiko spotted a soba restaurant. The words "O-Soba Restaurant – Sunaba" appeared on a glass sign lit by traditional lamps.

'Lately there have been more and more restaurants using the fancy-sounding O-Soba, by putting the honorific 'O' before the word. But I say that plain "soba" is much more like the old days and sounds much more delicious. It's a shame to see how Tōkyō has changed,' muttered Onitsura as they crossed the street. They entered the restaurant and ordered two bowls. Then the chief inspector asked the waitress an odd question.

'Would you happen to know the home of the Sugitas?'

'Yes, it's in a street three blocks behind us.'

'Do they like soba?'

'Not particularly. But Issa-an is closer to their home, so they probably eat there.'

Onitsura whispered something in her ear, which made the waitress suddenly look serious.

'Nevertheless, did you get any orders from the Sugitas recently?'

'Let me think,' replied the waitress, cocking her head and stealing a glance at Tokiko. She seemed confused, but Tokiko was starting to have a vague idea of what the policeman was trying to find out.

'Yes, there was that one evening a while back,' the girl finally recalled. The restaurant was quite small, so their conversation was also overheard in the kitchen. A young man stuck his head out and added: 'Mister, that was late on the night of the thirtieth. I think it was around ten.'

Onitsura went over to the man and had a brief discussion. Returning to his seat, it was clear from the tone of his voice that he was satisfied with the conversation.

'I already suspected what happened that night. The soba and tempura Mr. Kobayakawa ate actually came from this restaurant.'

'Oh,' cried Tokiko in surprise, even though she hadn't yet fully grasped the significance of the chief inspector's statement. He would only explain after they had finished their meal and left Sunaba.

'As the people at Issa-an testified, they made a delivery at nine. But at that time, Mr. Kobayakawa was actually watching news reels,

175

while Sugita had sneaked out of the cinema. So when Issa-an delivered their soba and tempura to the Sugita residence, only Yaeko Sugita was present.

'Approximately one hour later, Sugita returned home together with Mr. Kobayakawa. And, exactly according to the scenario, Sugita said he wanted something to eat and ordered soba and tempura. His wife pretended to be calling Issa-an, but in fact was calling Sunaba.

'After Sunaba arrived with their delivery, she quickly transferred the soba and tempura into the bowls from Issa-an and brought them to her husband and their guest. The tray and disposable chopsticks were of course also those of Issa-an. It was only natural that Mr. Kobayakawa would believe he was eating soba from Issa-an.'

'Now I finally understand,' said Tokiko in an emotionless tone. She had prayed to the heavens for proof that would save her Ryūkichi, but that had left her emotionally drained. Suddenly presented with the solution, she simply didn't know how to express her utter joy.

After the soba, Onitsura took her to a fruit parlour for dessert. The melody coming out of the audio system had a sweet romantic tune, wholly unsuitable for the serious conversation the two were having.

'To be honest, I had quite some trouble with the mystery of the fifth clock, only solving it just before I called you. Because I'd had no time to test my theory, I decided to do my final inquiries in your presence. If I'd failed to get results from that soba restaurant, I was planning to visit another three or four soba outside Banshūchō. I was already afraid you'd get a stomach-ache from eating all that soba, hahaha!'

He laughed loudly as he held a spoon in his hand. His sense of humour was hardly refined, but seeing the smile on his face made Tokiko realise he was quite a pleasant man, and she could laugh with him.

After they finished their fruit dessert, Onitsura took a notebook from his pocket, opened it at a certain page and showed Tokiko. It looked like a timetable.

Correct Time	False Time	Movements
08:40 p.m.		S & K visit cinema.
08:53		Y orders soba from Issa-an.
09:00		Issa-an delivers soba.
09:05		S exits cinema.
09:12		S visits tailor.

09:22		S leaves tailor.
09:30		S returns to cinema.
09:40		K exits cinema, meets up with S.
09:50	08:50	Arrival at S's house.
09:53	08:53	Y orders soba from Sunaba.
10:00	09:00	Sunaba delivers soba.
10:05	09:05	S says he is going to tailor. Goes out to commit murder.
10:28	09:28	S returns after murder. Says he visited tailor.

Tokiko read each line carefully.

'Of course nothing was quite as precise as what I wrote, but setting it down like this makes it easier to understand.'

'Yes, it's perfectly clear now,' said Tokiko as she looked up at the policeman. 'But there is still one mystery I don't understand.'

6

'Another mystery?'

'You said earlier you had decisive evidence that Sugita's alibi was fake. What was that evidence?'

Onitsura placed his bag on his lap and took out two slips of paper. They were the cheques Hirondo Sugita had written out for Kobayakawa and Narahara. He had borrowed them from the bank to confirm the handwriting.

'Here, have a look at these.'

Tokiko held them in her hands, but they looked to her like perfectly ordinary used cheques. One of them was written out for the amount of 22,000 yen, the other for 52,500 yen. Both were dated April 30, Shōwa Year 32 (1957), and both were signed and stamped by Hirondo Sugita.

She turned them over, and on the back of the one with the smaller amount she noticed some unclear writing in ink. The name, address and stamp of Jōji Kobayakawa were also signed on the back.

Narahara Tailors' address and stamp were also on the back of the other cheque, but that cheque didn't have the vague ink markings.

Tokiko looked at both sides of the two cheques several times, but she couldn't work out what Onitsura had discovered.

'Is there something wrong with them?'

'Yes,' answered the chief inspector with an enigmatic grin. 'But first I have to ask you a question. When you write a letter to your friends, how do you use your stationery?'

'How? I start with the page on top and use them in order.'

Tokiko was surprised by the question and had no idea why he had asked it.

He continued without explanation.

'If you look at the back of Mr. Kobayakawa's cheque, you'll see some blurry ink marks left on the paper, some sort of writing. Look very carefully and see if you can make out what it says.'

'...Hmm, this is a money amount starting with "52" and this is Hirondo Sugita's signature. And I think it says "April 30, Shōwa Year 32" here.'

'Exactly. That's more than enough already. You should already know what it says.'

'Oh, this is the writing on the cheque for Narahara Tailors.'

Onitsura said nothing, but nodded vigorously. He then placed one of the cheques on top of the other.

'Look, the writing and the ink marks correspond exactly. That means that before the ink on this cheque had dried completely, the other cheque was placed on top of it, leaving ink marks on the back. That's not unusual. Sugita's chequebook contained fifty cheques in all. Mr. Kobayakawa's was number 14 and Narahara Tailors' was number 15. Since they followed each other, it's quite normal that the ink of one left marks on the other.'

Tokiko listened carefully. She understood that the writing on the front of the Narahara cheque could have left marks on the back of the Kobayakawa cheque, but what did it mean?

'According to Mr. Kobayakawa's testimony, Sugita wrote and signed the cheque right before his eyes and handed it over, before taking his chequebook and stamp and leaving the house. We now know he didn't go to the tailor, but to Aoyama to commit the murder. But even if we pretend that he did really visit Narahara Tailors, as he testified, it's immediately obvious that the cheque he wrote and signed in front of Mr. Narahara could never have left ink marks on the back of Mr. Kobayakawa's cheque, because that cheque was already safely in his pocket, as he was sitting in a chair in the study, listening to Mozart!'

'Oh, you're right.'

Now it had been pointed out to her, Tokiko finally understood what was wrong and almost felt ashamed for being so slow to follow.

'The only explanation is that, for some reason, Sugita wrote the cheque for Narahara Tailors first, skipping number 14 and going straight to number 15. Then, before the ink had dried, the chequebook must somehow have fallen to the floor and left ink marks on the back of number 14. The obvious question is why did he sign the cheques out of order? That's what first put me on the trail.'

Finally, Tokiko grasped what the chief inspector was saying. With hindsight it all sounded so simple, like the Egg of Columbus.

'When you tear a cheque out of a chequebook, there's a stub left inside, so it's easy to confirm to whom the cheque was written. Sugita's trick revolved around making it appear he had written a cheque out for Narahara Tailors *after* he had written one out for Mr. Kobayakawa, so it was imperative for him to write no. 14 out to Kobayakawa, and no. 15 to Narahara Tailors. It was not a particularly difficult trick, so he must have conducted it without giving it too much thought. If he had not made that one mistake....'

If he had not made that one minuscule mistake, Sugita's plan would have gone perfectly. Even Onitsura had accepted Sugita's false alibi until he finally uncovered the truth. Ryūkichi would have been protesting his innocence all the way to the gallows. Tokiko could feel a chill run down her spine as she imagined what would have happened had Sugita not made that one slip.

'This morning I went to the tailor and surreptitiously asked him about how the ink had been transferred to the other cheque,' continued Onitsura. 'Apparently, a sudden gust of wind through the window made the pages of the chequebook flutter. For Sugita it was a fatal wind, but for Mr. Nikaidō it was the wind of fortune.'

The chief inspector, too, had realised how that brief moment had made the difference between life and death. He solemnly closed his notebook and put it back in his pocket.

The Red Locked Room

1

Work in the dissecting room was almost finished. An elderly vagrant sent there by the ward office was having his cause of death determined as he lay silently on the table, his face covered by a white cloth. But to display any emotion that the poor fellow's long life filled with hardships had come to an end would have been mere sentimentalism, the sign of amateurs. Not that the four people in the room were cold-hearted: they were scientists, of whom calm thinking was expected. They were actually relieved when, after almost three hours, they were freed from the tense work.

Professor Amano washed his hands as he glanced outside at the campus yard through the latticed window. Dusk had already cast its shadow outside. He turned to Fumio Urakami standing next to him.

'What happened to Katsuki?' he asked. Emiko Katsuki was a female student in the Faculty of Forensic and Legal Medicine. She was responsible for taking records during autopsies, and the professor thought highly of her.

'Well...' Urakami cocked his head. 'There was a phone call for her around nine this morning, and she went out and didn't return.'

'Maybe she left early?'

'No, she said she would be right back.'

'Hmm.' A worried expression appeared on the professor's face. 'All kinds of unfortunate incidents lately...'

He cleaned his hands with a towel as he tried to hide his concern behind some small talk. He took off his mask, revealing a thick moustache that made his face look even sterner. Amano was the stereotypical stoical scientist who would often lament the post-war moral breakdown to his students.

'I'll check up on her later.'

'Good idea,' replied the professor with a worried look.

Rui Itō stopped tidying up the medical instruments as she listened to the two men, her eyes burning with intense emotion as she stared at Urakami's profile. She came back to her senses when Shigeru Enoki, like Urakami a dissection assistant, called out to her.

'What did you say?'

'You need to listen. That's the third time I've told you.'

'I'm sorry, my mind was somewhere else.' She tried to smile back at him.

Enoki knew very well what was on the mind of the small girl with beautiful hair: resentment that the gorgeous Emiko Katsuki had taken Urakami from her. The feeling of frustration was heightened because the two worked together every day.

As a postgraduate student, it was only natural that Rui was more knowledgeable and experienced than the younger Emiko, but it had been made clear to her that education alone wasn't enough to keep a man. Rui had a nice figure, and unlike most Japanese women, her chest most definitely did not need a padded bra, but that didn't count for much when compared to Emiko's beauty.

'What did you need me for?'

'I'm sorry, I've forgotten.' Enoki's sneering grin implied the silent comment, 'What does Urakami have that I haven't?'

Both men were prodigies under the tutelage of Professor Amano and therefore rivals, but Urakami had the edge over Enoki and it was he who had been chosen to study in West Germany the following spring. Enoki's opinion of Urakami therefore was not very high. Rui could understand why Enoki felt dejected, but she thought that his attitude at times could be quite unmanly, which only resulted in looks of contempt from her. The four young men and women who formed the Amano study group all despised each other.

After the professor had left for his research office, Rui went up to Urakami and whispered in his ear.

'Shall I wait for you?' she said in a flirtatious manner, but he appeared to be cross, not even turning to look at her as he shook his head.

After Urakami had dumped Rui, the smile he had always shown her disappeared completely and he only acted disdainfully towards her, looking at her coldly from behind his glasses. Urakami was tall but not particularly attractive, with a big nose, so why couldn't Rui stop thinking about him? Was it because he had been her first? Even Rui thought that the heart of a woman was sometimes incomprehensible.

Listlessly, she stepped out of the dissection room into the preparation room. She took off her surgical gown, picked up her bag and was about to leave, when she changed her mind and sat down on a chair near the window. Not to wait for Urakami, but because she suddenly felt fatigued. While she stared outside at the campus garden painted in the colours of the setting sun, she recalled the bittersweet days when the two of them would go home together. Rui remained seated there, playing with the buttons of her overcoat.

The remaining two men still had tasks to perform. It was always Urakami's job to write post-mortem and death certificates and obtain the professor's signature and seal on the documents. Contacting a mortician in advance to arrange for a casket and placing the dissected body inside was Enoki's job.

After cleaning the scalpels and scissors, Urakami went to the preparation room. He ignored Rui and sat down at the desk. Enoki came into the room shortly afterwards and seemed surprised to see Rui still there. He lit a Golden Bat cigarette and went outside with a nonchalant expression on his face.

Urakami was silent, but in a bad mood. Even the noise of his pen seemed to annoy him. Rui looked sadly at his forehead.

After a while, Urakami put his pen down and read through the documents once again. He searched for some blotting paper, but couldn't find any, to his further annoyance. Then he started to blow on the ink to help it dry and tapped the floor impatiently with the heels of his shoes. He seemed restless and impatient and looked at the clock no fewer than three times while awaiting Enoki's return. It was forbidden for the person responsible to leave a corpse unattended. His movements reminded Rui of how he had acted whenever they had a date in some coffee house in Ginza. The emotions welling up inside her were unbearable.

About ten minutes later, the smaller Enoki returned with a casket larger than himself on his back. He staggered as he passed by the two in the preparation room, and mumbled, 'I skipped lunch,' to himself as if to explain his uncertain steps. As he carried the casket into the dissection room, Rui muttered to herself that he was a liar, as she had seen him eat enough toast for two.

Just as Enoki was about to close the doors of the dissection room, Urakami, holding a bundle of papers under his arm, left for the professor's office to get his signature and seal.

Rui was still lost in thought when Enoki came out of the dissection room.

'I'm starved. Omagari is late. Did Urakami forget to alert him?'

It was customary for Urakami to go to the concierge's office and tell Omagari that the dissection had been completed before going to the professor's office. Placing the corpse inside the casket was actually Omagari's job, with Enoki acting as supervisor.

Enoki fished around inside his white gown and produced a flattened bag of Bats. He offered Rui one and had one himself. His small body was parked on the desk and he swung his legs as he enjoyed his smoke.

'I know how you're feeling,' he said suddenly.

'I don't need your sympathy,' said Rui, and she glared at the medical student who was known for detesting women. A man with thin eyebrows and yellowish, dried-out skin. People said of him that he was a calculating person, but strangely enough he seemed to have no interest in the opposite sex. It was even said among the female medical students that they weren't afraid of being alone in a room with Enoki.

Just as Rui finished her cigarette, Omagari arrived.

2

The following day, on the second of December, Urakami and Enoki headed together to the dissection room, as they had to prepare for another dissection which had been scheduled a few days earlier.

The simple red brick building containing the dissection room stood all alone in the north-west corner of the spacious campus, about a ten-minute walk from the university hospital and the research offices. The medical students referred to it as "the island," and when they spoke of "another exiled to the island" they meant another corpse had been sent to the dissection room.

It had been built in the tenth year of Meiji (1877), meaning it was already close to eighty years old, but the sturdy exterior walls could probably go without maintenance for another fifty to a hundred years. The sturdy oak double doors at the entrance, secured by a thick iron bolt, had probably been painted once, but time had peeled all of that away.

The building was laid out in an inverted T-shape, with the preparation room as the crossbar and the long, narrow dissection room leading back from it.

The preparation room, directly accessed from the front entrance, was approximately 6.5 square metres in size and rectangular in shape, with one window on the left wall and one on the right. It contained two desks, four chairs and a small cabinet. Opposite the front entrance was a single door that led to the dissection room.

The dissection room itself was also rectangular and about 30 square metres in size, with the door to the preparation room on one of the short sides. The windows were all latticed, with one at the far end of the room, and two on each of the walls to the left and right, for a total of five. Like the preparation room, the flooring consisted of linoleum tiles on top of concrete, and the ceiling and walls were plastered in white. It was a dreary room, reminiscent of a cold prison cell. A rectangular dissection table stood in the middle of the room, and the only other furniture was a desk for the person taking records, a chair and two small electric heaters.

Urakami dialled the combination for the lock on the front door while Enoki, who had been there many times, stood by. They were puzzled to find that the bolt, which could only be slid open once the lock was removed, moved unusually smoothly. They examined it and discovered that it had been oiled and that some of the oil had dripped on the granite flooring, staining it.

'That's odd,' muttered Urakami, almost inaudibly. But he didn't pay the matter any more attention as he stepped inside the preparation room and flipped on the two wall switches to light up both the preparation and dissection rooms. The windows were shuttered from the outside, so it was dark there even in the daytime.

Enoki placed his briefcase on a desk and put on one of the surgical gowns hanging from the wall. Urakami took a small, thin key out of his pocket and used it to open the door to the dissection room. The two men stepped inside, one behind the other, and immediately froze to the spot.

On the dissection table in front of them lay the bloody head and cut-off limbs of a woman. For a moment, the two thought they were looking at parts of a mannequin doll broken in pieces. They stood for a moment at the door while their minds processed the scene in front of them and they realised the gravity of the situation.

Urakami was the first to come to his senses. He left Enoki, who was still standing there with his eyes wide open, behind and went over to the left side of the dissection table, where he found a number of strange packages on the floor. There were five in all, of different sizes, wrapped in oilpaper and neatly tied with hemp cord. At first glance they resembled postal packages. A pair of scissors lay beside them. Urakami picked up the largest one. It was quite heavy, and when he pressed it he could feel the elasticity of the contents. He knew instantly that inside the wrapping was another cut-up body part.

Enoki finally came to his senses as well and crouched down to examine several folded pieces of paper lying on the floor.

'Oilpaper and newspapers,' he said weakly.

'Don't touch the paper. We have to call the police at once. What's that?'

There was a bicycle lamp leaning against one leg of the recording table. It was battery operated and a handkerchief had been placed over it to weaken the light. It was still on and the sepia light was still shining.

Scouring the floor, they also found a scalpel and a roll of hemp cord beneath the dissection table. By now it was not difficult to imagine what the culprit had done and what he had been planning to do. Fearing the ceiling light of the dissection room would be noticed from the outside, the culprit had done his work by the light of a bicycle lamp, but must have been interrupted. Perhaps he was nearly seen by someone and had fled the scene.

Turning their attention to the dissection table, they observed a crimson-stained surgical saw and five scalpels, as well as the head lying face down, a left leg below the joint cut into three pieces and the left upper arm and forearm all lying criss-cross on it. At first sight, it looked to be the work of a complete amateur, but the clean cuts proved that the culprit had to have had specialised knowledge of anatomy or surgical experience.

Due to the wavy haircut it was clear that the head belonged to a female, but Enoki, who had been scrutinising it carefully, suddenly recoiled.

'He—hey, i—isn't this Katsuki?'

'What?'

Urakami turned even paler. He took a hard look. There was no doubt in his mind: it was the head of Emiko Katsuki, famed for her beauty.

'I'll call the police,' cried Urakami as he hurried out of the room, nodding to Enoki, who was having trouble standing and was leaning on the desk.

It wasn't easy running along the gravel path and Urakami quickly ran out of breath. Enoki finally caught up with him.

'He—hey, don't leave me alone in there.'

At that moment neither of them had the presence of mind to reflect on how pathetic they, two top medical students, must have looked.

3

As soon as Chief Inspector Tadokoro received the report on the murder, he immediately had his team driven to the dissection room. While he waited for the forensic photographers to take the necessary pictures of the crime scene from all angles, his team started to open a number of wrapped packages lying on the floor. They cut the cords in order to preserve the knots and opened the first package. Inside was a pale, well-formed thigh. The other four packages were similar. They contained the right thigh, lower leg and ankle, and the right forearm and hand.

'That's strange, where did her torso go?' the chief inspector muttered to himself. He scanned the dissection table and started counting: the head, the right upper arm, the left leg cut up in three pieces, and the left upper and forearm. Just those seven parts.

'The left hand is also missing,' added detective Mizuhara.

Just then a detective checking the large drawer of the recorder's desk called out excitedly. The moment Tadokoro saw the large oilpaper package, he knew it contained the torso, and that the smaller package contained the left hand. The two packages had also been wrapped up with hemp cord, and placed in the large drawer as one would put a piece of ham in the refrigerator.

'What's this? Tadokoro muttered as he picked up some white cards lying beside the large package.

'Shipping labels, sir,' said Mizuhara. It was a new bundle and twenty of them were still unused.

The chief inspector looked grim as he placed the labels on the desk. The labels and the oilpaper were of the kind sold everywhere, and it would be very difficult to trace where they had come from. Finding out who had bought them would be even more difficult.

'It would have been helpful if one of the labels had been filled out already,' lamented Mizuhara.

'We're going to have to work out for ourselves where the killer was planning to send the packages and why.'

Tadokoro crossed his arms. Shipping a cut-up corpse was a risky act. Finding out why the culprit was willing to take such a risk would be an important step to solving the mystery. He remembered a

187

Sherlock Holmes story in which the ear of a victim was sent to a man against whom the culprit held a grudge.

'It seems our man had to leave in a hurry.'

Mizuhara's loud voice interrupted his superior's thoughts.

'Yes, we need to find out why he interrupted his work. Did he hear footsteps, or did he take too much time cutting up the body and the sun had already started rising?'

'Given that he even forgot to switch off the bicycle lamp, I'd say he got out in a real hurry. Of course, we can't be absolutely sure.'

Tadokoro looked grim as he silently removed the large package from the drawer and started to cut the hemp cord. As expected, he found the torso of a young woman inside, wrapped in oilpaper and bloody newspapers.

Torsos shown at art exhibitions are meant to show the beauty of the human form, but the torso of the young woman who had been robbed of her life only symbolised visceral cruelty, a horrible sight which became more horrid the younger the victim. What really hurt to see was the single stab wound right through the heart.

'How horrible,' muttered the chief inspector through pursed lips.

He proceeded to examine a pile of fourteen newspapers on the floor, all dated the twenty-fourth of November or later. Not only the three major newspapers were there, but also various smaller ones like the Tōkyō Newspaper. The most recent one was the evening edition of the previous day's Nihon Keizai Shinpō, dated the first of December. It had been used to wrap the left hand.

'It says sixth printing. Mizuhara, call the paper immediately and ask them when the sixth printing of the evening edition was done and what time it showed up at the stores.'

As the detective was leaving, Tadokoro called out to him.

'Mizuhara, I also want to borrow the key to this place. The graduate student Urakami has it, he's in the research office. Also find Professor Amano and tell him we're done here and that we'd like him to perform an examination of the body. Take the car.'

He then proceeded to examine the six scalpels, the scissors and the roll of hemp cord with great care. The scalpels and scissors were new, so to learn the identity of the purchaser would entail checking with all the sellers of medical supplies. It was clear the killer had been very careful in his preparation and had probably worn rubber gloves, as forensics said there were no fingerprints on the implements.

Mizuhara returned about ten minutes later, accompanied by Professor Amano and Urakami, who followed him into the preparation room.

'That was quick. What about the newspaper?'

'I was able to talk to the editor-in-chief immediately. The sixth printing is the last. Printing was finished at ten to seven in the evening, as usual, and the nearest newsstands started selling the paper somewhere between six fifty-five and seven.'

'All right, that means we can safely assume the murder happened after seven o'clock last night,' said Tadokoro. 'Professor Amano, I'm sorry to impose upon your time, but I hope you can help us with our investigation.'

The horrible murder of Emiko Katsuki had affected the normally jovial demeanour of the professor, who merely nodded silently. But the stern look of the scientist could be seen on his face as he stepped into the dissection room.

After the door had shut, Tadokoro turned to Mizuhara.

'What about the key?'

Before the detective could reply, the tall Urakami appeared from behind him.

'I was told you wanted to borrow the key, but I must respectfully decline. Responsibility for the key to the dissection room is mine entirely. Unless you have the explicit permission of the university, I cannot hand it over to you.'

The chief inspector didn't say anything, but stared into the eyes of the student. He appeared to Tadokoro to be a cunning, cold individual. His large nose was a physiological sign that he was interested in women.

'I can tell you that no one has experienced more trouble from this business than myself. I will tell you now that I didn't do it. Neither has this key left my side for even a second. Furthermore, only I know the combination of the lock outside.'

'So you claim the murderer did not come inside through those doors?'

'No, I can't make any such claim. Perhaps the murderer did enter through those doors. All I can say is they did not open the combination lock outside, nor did they use the key to open the door to the dissection room.'

'Then how did the murderer get inside?'

'I can only tell you that the murderer did not unlock the doors. Maybe he lifted them off their hinges with the bolt still on. Or he could simply have unscrewed the bolt and strike plate.'

'By the way, I wanted to ask you, who oiled the bolt?'

Urakami had no answer and could only blink in surprise.

'I wondered about that as well, when Enoki and I opened the door. But I don't know who did it.'

'Was it oiled yesterday?'

'Yesterday?' Urakami frowned as he thought back to the day before. 'No, it wasn't oiled then. I remember what a nasty squeaking sound it made as I locked it.'

'What time did you lock up?'

'It was after we finished the dissection, so some time after half past four.'

'Thank you, that's helpful. Would you allow me to do some tests with the lock, under your supervision of course. It wouldn't be efficient if I had to wait until the university's permission.'

'Well, I don't know...' Urakami seemed hesitant.

'Urakami, that's all right. I'll talk to the administration, so please cooperate with the police,' Professor Amano called out from the dissection room.

'Very well, sir.'

Urakami turned to Tadokoro.

'I'll tell you the combination then, although it makes the lock sort of meaningless.' Urakami obviously didn't like telling anyone else the combination.

He went out of the building and waited for the chief inspector and other detectives to join him. He held the lock in his left hand while the fingers of his right played with the dial.

'Listen carefully. First you turn it clockwise to 3, then counter-clockwise to 0, clockwise to 8, counter-clockwise to 6, clockwise 1...'

He turned the dial as he spoke. When he was finished, the lock opened without making any noise. Tadokoro took the combination lock in his hands and looked at it.

'Quite the sturdy, well-made lock. So... right 3, left 0, right 8...'

He said the combination out loud as he tried the lock. He looked pleased as he handed it over to a forensic investigator.

'Suppose someone doesn't know the combination and tries them all one by one. How many possible combinations are there?'

'Those are permutations. Please wait a second,' replied the investigator as he started making calculations on his fingers. 'There's a difference, depending on whether the same number may be used multiple times or not, but let's say somewhere around several hundred thousand combinations. It wouldn't be an easy task trying all of them.'

'Let's say it takes five seconds to try one combination, and there are two hundred thousand.' Tadokoro himself started to calculate. 'Eleven and a half days.'

'Something like that. Of course, the probability of getting it right on the very first try, or on attempt number two hundred thousand is exactly the same, and I doubt the murderer was willing to accept the same odds as winning the lottery.'

'Anyway, make sure there are no other combinations that can open it, and whether it can be opened with some kind of tool,' ordered the chief inspector, as he turned back to Urakami.

'By the way, what about the lock on the door itself?'

Tadokoro pointed to the keyhole beneath one of the brass door knobs on the double doors.

'That lock hasn't worked in ages. It was already broken before I started my studies here.'

A forensic investigator tried poking around with a thick metal wire with a curved tip, but the rusted lock wouldn't budge. Tadokoro nodded with satisfaction and examined the bolt. It slid easily, without any resistance. He borrowed a magnifying glass from the forensic investigator to take a closer look at the hinges, and also the screws which secured the bolt to the door.

'No sign of anything having been removed or tampered with. Next up is the door inside.'

The chief inspector seemed cheerful as he had everyone follow him back into the preparation room.

The large door separating the preparation room from the dissection room was a simple flush door, made of one single large board. It appeared to be relatively new. The sheen of the cream-coloured oil paint and the transparent glass door knob with a brilliant cut gave the door a clean, bright look. But because the door was the only new object amidst its aged surroundings, it didn't quite fit in.

'Was this door here replaced recently?'

'Yes, about three months ago. September, I believe. The old one was damaged.'

'Was it damaged due to age, or was it damaged on purpose?'

Tadokoro seemed to be suspicious of the fact the door was new.

'It was so old it decided to break on its own. It would have had to be replaced sooner or later.'

'I see,' said the chief inspector. 'Who was the person who insisted upon replacing it? Was there somebody who actively proposed to have it changed?'

'Well, I wouldn't say actively, but Itō had the chief of the educational affairs section come over to have a look at it.'

'What kind of lock did the old door have?'

'An ugly-looking, primitive lock, dating from the Meiji period.'

Tadokoro nodded again. He was given a small key by Urakami, which he inserted in the keyhole of the flush door. He tried locking and unlocking it a few times.

'The lock isn't oiled. Then again, it's no trouble to turn it, so there's no need for that yet.'

After the door hinges were examined in detail, Tadokoro turned to Urakami: 'We can say for certain that the culprit didn't tamper with the hinges of this door either. That means that, contrary to what you claim, the culprit must have unlocked the door or used the windows to get in and out.'

Urakami's almond-shaped eyes blinked rapidly from behind his glasses. He tried to say something, but the chief inspector stopped him. Next, the policeman examined the two windows on the left and right walls of the preparation room, which were double casement glass windows, with iron lattices over them. On the outside were shutters which swung outwards.

'It all seems very secure.'

Tadokoro seemed puzzled.

'Yes, from what I hear they used to keep specimens here in the preparation room, but they were burgled a few times, so they put those lattices on.'

'Specimen thieves?'

'After that infamous vixen murderess Oden Takahashi was sentenced to death in the first year of Meiji, her body was dissected right here. They say that some of the bottles in which her organs were preserved in alcohol were stolen, and that the ones they now show off at the campus festival are imitations. It was probably some freak collector who stole them,' Urakami explained with a vacant look, as if he were still thinking of something else.

The chief inspector nodded as he examined the windows, but both the windows and the shutters were a tight fit, so there was no reason to assume anything was wrong with them. The bars on the lattice were 1 centimetre and 3 millimetres thick, with gaps of 5 centimetres between the bars. The lattice wouldn't budge no matter how much Tadokoro pulled and pushed. Eventually, he gave up, took a step back and patted the dust on his clothes away with his handkerchief.

Next he entered the dissection room. The professor was bent over the dissection table, and did not even glance in his direction. The chief inspector examined all five windows carefully, but the result was the same as for the windows in the preparation room. The expression on Urakami's face became gloomier by the minute. When it was determined that nothing was wrong with the last window, he sighed and pointed at the ceiling.

'Chief Inspector, what about that? Someone could have taken a ladder from equipment storage and climbed up to the roof.'

In the plaster ceiling right above the dissection table was a square hole.

'What's that?'

'It's a ventilation opening.'

'It doesn't look as though any person could fit through it. What size is it?'

'I saw the blueprints in the library once, but I don't remember the measurements. Professor, would you happen to know?'

The professor looked up at the ceiling, but didn't seem really interested.

'I don't know. It'd be easier if you ask Professor Arai of Architecture.'

'I'll go,' said Mizuhara and quickly left.

'I still think no person could make their way through that. A monkey, maybe.'

'Hahaha, you're thinking of Edgar Allan Poe? With a female victim and a locked room on our hands, I guess this is the Rue Morgue,' a young forensic investigator joked. The professor, however, was decidedly not pleased hearing someone joke about his beautiful deceased pupil.

'A Japanese macaque might be able to squeeze through, but not someone carrying a body. Their head might fit through, but their shoulders would get stuck.'

Urakami looked down and didn't say a word. The chief inspector glanced at him sideways and seemed pleased once again.

'The only other spots connected to the outside world are the three sewer, water and gas pipes. I assume there's no secret underground passage.'

'This is a building dating from the first year of Meiji, it's not completely out of the question. If you think it's necessary, we could strip away some of the linoleum flooring,' said a forensic investigator seriously, which only seemed to irritate Urakami, who couldn't contain himself inside anymore.

'Nonsense. Why would there be an underground passage? You can check the blueprints in the library if you want to be sure.'

'It's better to examine the real thing rather than rely on documents,' said the investigator with conviction.

At that moment Detective Mizuhara returned. His report was that all four sides of the ventilation opening were twenty centimetres long and that it was four and a half metres above the floor.

'And that means the culprit didn't have much choice in how they entered and left this room. You may think it's nonsense, but it appears we might have to strip the flooring here, Urakami.'

4

Several facts were uncovered between that evening and the following day, the third of December. The main points of Professor Amano's report were as follows:

1. All body parts discovered at the crime scene belonged to Emiko Katsuki.
2. The initial cause of death was a nine-centimetre-deep wound to the heart. Death was almost instantaneous. The murder weapon was a scalpel or similar sharp instrument. There were no signs of other wounds.
3. The estimated time of death was between nine and ten o'clock on the morning of the first of December.
4. The dissection of the body was performed by someone with considerable medical experience.
5. Several hours elapsed between the murder and the dissection. The extremely small amounts of blood left on the table indicated that the murder was committed elsewhere and the

exsanguinated corpse was transported to the dissection room by the murderer to be cut up there.

6. The victim was in the first month of pregnancy.

As the dissection on the vagrant had been performed in the afternoon of the first of December and nothing out of the ordinary had been noticed then, the point that the murder had not been committed in the dissection room was, of course, obvious to all.

Following the report, detectives searched high and low for the actual murder location, and it was found surprisingly quickly. This neighbourhood featured many educational institutions, but it bordered a small town with many inns and hot springs. The murder location was found to be a cellar in the branch office of The Safe Economy Society, located at the very edge of that town, facing the walls of the university campus. Despite heavy advertising during the summer, this financial institution was running on a shoestring, which eventually led to a run on them by their creditors. It was all over the news when The Safe Economy Society was ordered to shut down its business for violating lending regulations, since when the branch office had been closed and left unattended.

Emiko Katsuki had presumably been lured to the cellar there by a phone call from the murderer. The floor and one part of the wall had been gruesomely spattered with blood spraying from her torso. Given that Emiko had gone there of her own free will, it could be safely assumed that she knew the killer well. Many couples in the town try to avoid attention, so neither the murderer's behaviour nor Emiko's looks would have attracted suspicion, and the police had to admit that the murderer had chosen the location wisely.

The forensic investigators had conducted a full-scale investigation of the dissection room, but had only found concrete beneath the linoleum flooring of the dissection room and no secret passages. No clues emerged from examination of the windows, door and ceiling. The floor engineers from the Meiji era had not created any secret passageways, and the entire building was very sturdy. It was clear to everyone that the only way the murderer could have entered and left was by unlocking the doors.

Tests also proved that only one combination would open the lock on the front doors and that it could not be opened with any tool. The objects left by the murderer were all new, but attempts to trace him through his purchases of them had been fruitless. The fact that the murderer could only have got in by unlocking the door was the only clue to identifying him.

Such was the state of the investigation when Chief Inspector Tadokoro went to the campus on the morning of the third of December. He first called the concierge into the preparation room for questioning.

Omagari was a large, swarthy man in his forties. He was about 1.80 metres in height, but appeared shorter because of his considerable girth. His most notable features were his deep-set staring eyes, the thick wrinkles chiselled on his brow and his close-cropped hair.

On seeing him, the chief inspector's mind went back to a recent sensational magazine article which described him as "The man who slept with a corpse." The previous night's investigation, however, had revealed to the chief inspector a secret even the media didn't know about.

Omagari pulled out a towel tucked into his cargo pants and wiped his brow with it, even though the weather was not hot at all.

'Sit down,' ordered Tadokoro. 'I hear you sleep with dead people.'

'Sir, you must have read *Weekly Nichinichi*? It's not as though I'm sleeping with them night and day.'

'Don't they scare you?'

Omagari snorted at the question and a creepy smile appeared on his face.

'I can't explain it all logically like, but I don't think dead bodies are scary. Both you and me, we might get there at different times, but in the end, we'll end up as dead bodies. Why be afraid of what you yourself will be?' Omagari explained his odd way of thinking.

'And I must say it's pretty nice sleeping with a beautiful woman. Not that it happens often.'

The policeman thought him simple-minded, but now it was time to get down to business.

'Speaking of beautiful woman, it was you who killed Emiko Katsuki, wasn't it?'

'O—of course not! That's not funny, sir.'

'Who's joking? She was killed not far from here. You could have easily made it there during a break.'

'No, not at all. Or are you saying I had some reason to want to kill her?'

'Are you saying you hadn't? Didn't Ms. Katsuki see how you slept with a corpse, opened its mouth and pulled out a gold tooth? If she'd

196

reported it to Professor Amano, you would have been fired and lost your job and your housing. Luckily for you, she didn't say anything, but as they say, a woman's heart is as fickle as autumn weather. Who knew whether she wouldn't change her mind and tell the professor? It's only natural for us to suspect you of killing her to silence her. Unless you have an alibi, to prove you didn't go out that night?'

Omagari stared back at him. He was desperately trying to keep his calm, but eventually a bead of sweat formed on the tip of his nose.

'Sir, do you have any proof? You can't just threaten me without any evidence. Please don't think I'm the kind of man to confess to just anything.'

The chief inspector slowly pulled a small notebook with a pink cover from his inner pocket.

'I'm not making it up. It's all in Ms. Katsuki's diary. Don't tell me you forgot about the tenth of April? Shall I read it to you?'

'No, no, please!' Omagari waved his hands spiritedly. 'Damn, who would have expected something like that from such a pretty face!'

The veins on his temples were throbbing.

'It's all a lie. Just something she made up. You can't just believe whatever she wrote.'

'Would she have any reason to accuse you of such a thing?'

'Ho—how would I know? You seem to have decided already that I'm the killer, but that night I attended a wake at the morgue and only left to go to the toilet. Ask anyone you like,' Omagari pleaded as he wiped his sweat away with his dirty towel again.

5

Enoki was a small man who acted the part of the insufferable prodigy to perfection and was in the habit of pursing his lips while speaking. He lit a Bat and crossed his legs.

'If you think back to yesterday when you and Mr. Urakami opened the door, was there anything that struck you as odd?'

'…No, unfortunately.'

'Is it possible that Mr. Urakami could have forgotten to lock up the day before yesterday?'

'No. Rui Itō, Omagari and I were all there when he put the combination lock on.'

'And the lock on the flush door?'

197

'Omagari and I went out of the room first, carrying the casket, so I don't know for sure about that door. But I think Itō would have seen.'

'Wait. Where did you carry that casket to?'

'There's a morgue on the third floor of the university hospital. All four of us went there. We left Omagari behind, he stayed for the wake.'

'Did you go home at once?'

'Urakami left right away. Itō and I burnt some incense and sat there for about five minutes before we left as well.'

'What's your opinion of Rui Itō?'

'She's a nice girl. That's all.'

'From what I hear, you have no interest in women.'

Enoki had answered all questions up until then smoothly, but this time he didn't reply immediately. He took a deep pull on his cigarette and an embarrassed grin appeared on his face.

'That's just a rumour that's gone on living its own life. I'm no legendary monk like Kenkō Yoshida, I'm a man and I feel something whenever I look at a woman. But the rumours of me as a living saint have spread, and now I'm captive to them, despite my wishes. But I have to focus all my attention on my research for the time being, so in a way, it's all for the best.'

'By the way, do you know the combination of the lock?' asked Tadokoro casually, in order to move the questioning forward again.

'Of course not. That's the one thing Urakami is absolutely reliable about. He'd never tell another soul. Well, perhaps I shouldn't say reliable. He's just doing it because he doesn't want to lose the professor's trust,' Enoki corrected himself bitterly. He nodded towards the flush door.

'He doesn't even let us look at the key to the dissection room, let alone tamper with it.'

'I understand. One more question, how did you spend the night of the first?'

Enoki's eyebrows rose as he replied irritably: 'Why, do you suspect I did it?'

'It's a question we ask of everyone involved in the case. There's no special meaning behind it.'

'Really? It doesn't feel nice to be asked the question, even if you're innocent. In any case, I was in my room that night, as always.'

'Can you leave your boarding house without anyone noticing?'

'Now you're really acting as though I did it. How would I know, I've never had to sneak out of my room.'

He frowned as he took another pull of his Bat, which had become so short it was about to burn his lips.

6

Rui Itō let her long hair hang down, which made her look smaller, but to counter that she wore red Oxford shoes with high Cuban heels. Her red turtleneck sweater and box-pleated skirt made her appear gaudier than most other students, perhaps in an attempt to attract Urakami's attention. She was not particularly attractive, but she wasn't unattractive either. She might have romance problems involving one particular man now, but she did not seem an emotional type. She was in fact a strong-minded, intelligent woman.

'What's your opinion of the victim, Ms. Katsuki?'

'She was so beautiful. I wouldn't even regret dying young if I'd had her looks. Murder is a different story though.'

'And what did you think about having young Urakami taken from you?'

'What did I think? That's a difficult question. On the one hand, it wasn't all that strange, considering how pretty she was. Nevertheless, I was upset.'

Her straightforward manner of speech betrayed no emotion.

'I want to change the subject now. Have you ever seen the film *Odd Man Out*?'

She seemed puzzled by the question.

'Oh, wait. It was released here under the title *Jamamono wa Korose* (*Kill Those Who Stand in the Way*), I believe? No, I never saw it,' she started to say, but then she realised what the chief inspector was implying.

'Why do you ask me?'

'No, I was just reminded of the film. Aren't you relieved, now that the person who stood in your way is gone?'

'Whatever do you mean?'

'Exactly what I say. With Ms. Katsuki gone, Mr. Urakami is likely to come back to you. Surely you must have considered that possibility.'

Tadokoro observed the woman carefully, measuring her reaction. To his surprise, her shoulders dropped as she whispered an admission.

'Yes, I have. But I didn't kill her.'

The chief inspector nodded.

'At the moment, young Urakami is in a rather precarious spot. As you know, he was the only person able to open both locks. Things would be different if he had ever told anyone else the combination to the outside lock, or if he had been lax in handling the key, giving someone a chance to make a copy of it. Any thoughts on that?'

She looked down at the floor as she thought, then shook her head.

'He was really fussy about the locks. I can't imagine any of those things ever happening.'

Did Rui realise that her answers only solidified the case against Urakami? Tadokoro immediately followed with another question.

'Can I ask you what you did between seven o'clock in the evening two nights ago until the morning?'

'What did I do? Nothing. I was feeling down, and didn't want to do anything. I went to bed at ten.'

'Another question. When you finished the dissection in the afternoon of the first, do you remember whether Mr. Urakami locked the door between the dissection and preparation rooms?'

'Yes, he did lock it. He even pulled the key out of the keyhole and tried turning the door knob a few times. He always tries the door to see if he's locked it properly, but that day he did it especially thoroughly, so it stuck with me.'

'I believe you were the one who wanted the flush door replaced. Was there any special reason?'

Rui looked back at the chief inspector in surprise, but that lasted only for a second.

'Nothing in particular. The door was badly damaged and barely functional. If I hadn't suggested replacing it, someone else would.'

'Do you recall whether Mr. Urakami locked the door outside with the combination lock when you left here two days ago?'

'Yes, he put the combination lock on, and pulled on it a few times. You can tell he's really distrustful from little actions like that.'

This was the first time Rui had said something negative about Urakami, but the chief inspector let it pass and instead asked his final question. Constantly changing the direction of his questions was

Tadokoro's own special technique. At times the confusion it caused led to suspects confessing to things by accident.

'I believe you live in Shinbōchō? It's only fifteen minutes away by streetcar. Could you have left your boarding house at night without anyone noticing?'

'It wouldn't be easy, but I suppose it would be possible by going out through the garden. But I've never tried it myself.'

She spoke calmly, but the chief inspector noticed that she crumpled the handkerchief in her hands.

Urakami came in after Rui Itō had left. The eyebrows behind his thick glasses twitched constantly, and he was clearly nervous. He had obviously realised that his current position was very unfavourable.

'Did you know that Ms. Katsuki was pregnant?'

Urakami turned pale at the question, but the only reaction the chief inspector got were his eyes opening wide. Tadokoro grinned. There was only one thing to do at such a time: make him angry.

'She wanted you to marry her, but you said no, and wanted an abortion. To you, she was just a bit of fun on the side.'

'Wha—what do you mean, on the side!'

'Now, now, keep calm. Perhaps I chose my words unwisely, but her diary did basically say that. She wrote that the baby in her tummy would tie the two of you together, and that was why she wanted to give birth. Now, this is only speculation on my part, but once her belly became swollen, you wouldn't be able to hide the fact you'd had relations with her from the professor. Considering how strict he is, I can imagine him returning your graduate thesis without grading it, which might threaten your career. To you, it would literally be a matter of life or death. So you decided to use that scalpel in your hand. Never did you imagine that she'd leave a detailed diary.'

'Of all the impertinent rubbish! You don't understand anything. I'll sue you for false accusation!'

He seemed about to lash out.

'But everything I've said is the truth.'

'How much of it is really the truth? There was nothing between me and Katsuki, so there's no way her diary would say that. It's just bluff on your part,' he said vehemently, but he was unable to hide how much the accusation had upset him.

'And what if we examine the foetus and find out it's your child?'

'That's a good one. There's no way you can determine the father of a foetus one or two months old.' Urakami sneered at the attempt to bluff a medical student.

'I see you're quite well informed of its age.'

'It would have been obvious to anyone once she was three months pregnant. I do know the fundamentals of obstetrics.'

'There's no need to get excited. Let me ask you about the afternoon of the first, after you'd finished the dissection. I was told you were acting quite irritably that day. Could you tell me why?'

'Huh?' Urakami glared back. 'I don't know.'

'You don't have to be so afraid of my questions. Let's talk about something else. Yesterday's forensic examination determined that the only ways in and out of the building are through the two doors. It also determined that the door hinges and the bolt had not been tampered with. To put it bluntly, that means that you are either the murderer or an accomplice. On the afternoon of the first, you did indeed lock both doors, that is a proven fact. But you could have only pretended to go home, then actually returned here to unlock the doors. Your accomplice could then have got inside later.'

'No—no. You're just making things up. I don't like being treated like a suspect, but I suppose it's only to be expected, given that I'm the one responsible for both locks. But if you say there's an accomplice, then you'd better find him and let me have a look at him. You can't threaten me with a one-in-a-million possibility as your "proof", just because your investigation isn't going smoothly. It's cowardly.'

Urakami was becoming more and more furious, and was already standing in an aggressive manner.

'You call it a one-in-a-million possibility. Let's look at some other possibilities, then. Where were you between the evening of the first and the following morning?'

'At home, of course.'

'That's a lie,' the chief inspector said curtly. 'Yes, you did return home, but then you changed clothes and went out, not returning until the following morning. Would you care to explain yourself? We're not playing games. We questioned each and every other lodger, and have received five separate testimonies about your movements. Or are you still claiming you didn't go out?'

Urakami was at a loss for words. He buried his head silently in his hands.

It was on the following day, the fourth of December, that the investigation hit a wall.

Omagari's story had been a complete lie. On the evening of the crime, he had only remained at the wake for about an hour. The police discovered he had bought some shōchū from a liquor store, gulped it all down and was lying peacefully in bed by nine o'clock. But nobody could testify about his movements after that time with any certainty.

'Damn liar. He had to know we'd find out. Don't know if he's stupid or bold. In any case, I don't like him,' Mizuhara grumbled.

'But the murderer is someone with considerable experience handling a scalpel. That Sego-don doesn't seem like someone with that kind of skill.'[1]

'Ah, he does look like the bronze statue of Saigō in Ueno! I thought he looked familiar. Haha, Sego-don!'

Mizuhara was in a better mood now, laughing out loud.

The objects left by the murderer in the dissection room were still being traced, but, just as they had feared, nothing of importance could be learned from them. No clear answers had been found as to why the culprit had been forced to flee the scene and as to where he had planned to send the body parts. However, that did not seem to disappoint the police particularly, as they expected Urakami to confess to the crime sooner or later. The newspapers and the radio also seemed to have a positive outlook, speaking of "a major suspect being questioned" or "an imminent arrest."

Urakami had been asked to appear "voluntarily" at the investigation headquarters and had been questioned since the early morning, but he continued to deny any involvement in the murder. A dark cloud hung over the interrogation room.

---

(1) Takamori Saigō (1828-1877) was a highly influential samurai and one of the three nobles who led the Meiji Restoration. He is known as the last true samurai. Sego-don was his nickname in his local dialect. A statue of him stands at the southern entrance of Ueno Park.

But around two o'clock of that same day, a geisha called Kikka and a middle-aged woman, perhaps the owner of a drinking establishment, came to see Chief Inspector Tadokoro. Kikka introduced herself as a geisha of the Azuma house in the entertainment district of Ikebukuro, while her companion introduced herself as the proprietor of Kanagawa, a house of assignation also located in Ikebukuro. They said the police should stop torturing that poor "Uh" and let him go.

'Oh, you're so 'orrible. Uh was with me that night, we stayed in Kanagawa. So 'e couldn't 'ave committed that awful murder. You can ask the ma'am 'ere if you think I'm lying.'

'Yes, she's right. Mr. Urakami always comes on the first of the month, to stay with Ms. Kikka. The waitress, the maid, the bath attendant, they all know him.'

As the women were talking over each other, they were also using their alluring almond-shaped eyes to act flirtatiously, bringing some life to the otherwise bleak police office.

Kikka was a slightly plump but attractive woman with a round face. She had a voluptuous body, and if Rui was an apple, this woman would be a coquettish, juicy and ripe apricot. But she was not too ripe, and seemed exactly Urakami's type.

After Tadokoro had questioned them about the exact time and date, he ordered a man to accompany them back to Kanagawa and question the maid and the head clerk there.

After the women had left, Tadokoro pondered over what he had learnt. Urakami had acted so edgily after the dissection because his night with Kikka had been on his mind, which made him impatient. But if Urakami had an alibi, then who could the murderer be? The day before, the chief inspector had hinted at the possibility of an accomplice, but to be honest, he could hardly imagine an intelligent fellow like Urakami with an accomplice. It would be different if he were a professional criminal or even just one of those hooligan students. But Urakami would have been aware that a crime committed by someone acting alone was more difficult to detect, and it was difficult to find a partner in crime unless one already came from the same milieu.

After some thought, he returned to the interrogation room, where Urakami was still sitting with his head buried in his hands.

'You have an alibi, why didn't you say anything about it?'

Tadokoro's tone was different from before. Urakami realised it and looked up.

'I believe you spent the night at an assignation house? A geisha called Kikka just paid me a visit.'

'Kikka was here?'

'Yes. As was the madam of Kanagawa.'

'Aaagh.'

A terrible cry escaped from Urakami's mouth.

'The fool! Why was she so stupid! I—I wanted to keep it a secret, so why did Kikka tell you? Now I won't be able to go to Germany and I won't be able to graduate. Damn, damn!'

If Professor Amano learned that he was regularly spending nights at an assignation house with a geisha, it was indeed likely that Urakami wouldn't be allowed to study in West Germany. He had probably planned to wait until the police found the real murderer, without having to expose his own misbehaviour. The chief inspector could imagine how much anger and despair the young man must be feeling, so he left him alone and went out into the hallway.

Just then he received a call from the detective who had gone to Kanagawa. The man had questioned the head clerk, the waitress and maid, and they all confirmed Urakami's alibi.

He returned again to the interrogation room and spoke to the desolate student.

'A real man knows when to give up. It's clear now that you are not the murderer. But even if the murderer is somebody else, they still had to learn the combination of the lock, and borrow the key from you. So now can you tell me who you told the combination and gave the key to?'

It was pretty harsh treatment, but it was better to go in hard, now the student was vulnerable.

'But I didn't lend the key to anyone.'

'Don't be foolish. Logic dictates that the culprit couldn't have opened those two doors unless you had told him the combination and lent him your key.'

'I can only tell you I that I didn't give that key to anyone. It never left my person.'

The chief inspector shifted to a milder tone, as if to persuade Urakami.

'Why keep holding on to that story? Just think carefully for a second and consider your position. Now your misconduct is known, the professor's trust in you will be close to zero anyway. It won't help you if you keep taking full responsibility for those locks.'

205

'That's exactly it. Suppose the murderer did get inside by borrowing my key and by learning the combination from me. Is there anyone who's been put through more trouble because of it than me? Don't you think I'd be mad at them? You can't believe I'm still trying to protect the murderer's reputation? Hah, if I'd known who the murderer was, I'd have told you long ago without you getting on my back!'

8

The lights in the police headquarters were shining brightly, and Tadokoro and Mizuhara were seated right beneath one of them, a desk separating the two. Most of the detectives had gone home for the night, but the chief inspector prepared to stay there and hold the fort until the case was cracked.

'So now that Urakami's innocent, I assume that the murderer must be one of the other three. Is that right, sir?'

'None of them has a good alibi either.'

'And Enoki doesn't even have a motive.'

'Whereas Omagari has no experience handling a scalpel. He may have been helping out in the dissection room for a long time, but I don't think it's something you can pick up just by watching.'

'So that means that the Rui girl is our most likely suspect.'

'But I don't see how she could have gone in and out of that locked building. That's the big problem.'

Tadokoro had never whined in the past when faced with a difficult case, but this time he sounded beaten and dispirited. The two had run into a brick wall, but neither of them cared to lament out loud, so they sat there in silence.

After a while the chief inspector felt cold, so he got up to add some coal to the heater. He poured some *bancha* (coarse tea) into two cups and placed them on the table. The springs in the wall clock creaked, disturbing the silent atmosphere of the office in the middle of the night. The clock indicated it was one o'clock.

The next morning, the fifth of December, Tadokoro woke up from a short nap on the couch. He could feel his body was still tired. All his joints hurt, his shirt was full of wrinkles and the collar of his shirt was starting to get dirty. The face looking back at him in the restroom mirror was haggard and the stubble on his face told everyone how his battle was going. It was not even clear whether it would end in a satisfactory conclusion.

He went through the morning papers. The fact that all the newspapers featured pessimistic headlines like "Investigation Stuck" and "End Seems Far" did nothing to improve his mood.

That afternoon, when it became clear to Tadokoro that he was going nowhere, he finally made up his mind to visit Ryūzō Hoshikage. Hoshikage was in the trading business and had an office on the seventh floor of the Maru Building, but he had also been blessed with sharp instincts and superior powers of reasoning. He used his talent for deduction to help with criminal investigations, and had repeatedly solved cases which had thwarted the police.

When he arrived at Hoshikage's office overlooking Tōkyō Station, Tadokoro was shown into a brightly-lit room with decor more that of a living room than a reception room. On the other side of a green table sat Mr. Hoshikage.

'Hello,' he greeted Tadokoro with a smile and offered him a seat. 'I just returned from Ōsaka yesterday.'

'From a case?'

'Yes, a decapitated body on Centipede Road. A very clever murderer, indeed.'

He stroked his pencil moustache with his long fingers as he praised the perpetrator.

'It was quite amusing to face such an adversary. Very satisfying.'

Ryūzō Hoshikage was considered arrogant and insolent by some, but, surprisingly, he was able to get along with Tadokoro. A handsome man almost 45 years old, he paid more attention to his looks than the average person. He wore a cravenette jacket of pure wool, a necktie made of traditional *nishijin* textile, a white silk handkerchief in his breast pocket and a greenhouse-grown sweet pea flower in his lapel.

'I had to hurry back on Japan Airlines, but I now have time to help. Can you brief me about your case?'

Ryūzō Hoshikage stuffed Granger tobacco in his virgin briar pipe, and lit it with his Ronson lighter. He offered a Lucky Strike cigarette to Tadokoro and slowly crossed his legs. Tadokoro coughed once before starting to explain the case in great detail. From experience, he knew that a fact he might have thought insignificant often turned out to be the important hint that allowed Hoshikage to solve the mystery.

When the chief inspector had finally finished his story, he awaited Hoshikage's reaction with a mixture of expectation and fear, as if he were a patient about to be told his diagnosis by the doctor. But there was a wide grin on Hoshikage's face.

'What a fascinating case! I am a lover of magic, so I often read detective novels about locked room murders. I even had an antiquarian in Paris trace down the records of the murder of Rose Delacourt, which served as the inspiration for Poe's *The Murders in the Rue Morgue*. But nine out of ten locked room murders involve some form of mechanical trickery, and that I don't like. Furthermore, in most stories of locked room murder there's not even any need for a locked room. The author just thinks of a trick and then writes a locked room mystery around it. But to come back to your case, I've solved most of the mystery already, just by listening to your explanation. Yes, I already know the secret behind your locked room.'

Tadokoro looked in astonishment at Hoshikage, who had spoken nonchalantly.

'When you say you've solved the mystery, do you mean you know how the murderer got in and out of the building? And do you know the name of the murderer?'

'Yes to both,' came the short reply as Hoshikage fiddled with his pipe.

'And there was no accomplice?'

'No, it could all be done by one person. And once you know how it was done, the name of the murderer becomes apparent as well.'

'How did they get in and out? The doors were locked and the only other places connected to the outside were the ventilation opening in the ceiling, the drain, and the water and gas pipes. Don't tell me it was the drain?'

'No.'

'And I don't suppose it was the gas pipe either?'

'Of course not.'

'So it must have been the ventilation opening.'

The only passage left was the ventilation opening in the ceiling. But it was only twenty centimetres long on each side. The murderer couldn't have got in through the opening, nor could they have carried the body in through it.

But Hoshikage shook his head.

'No, the culprit was neither an exceptionally small person, nor a monkey or a snake. The murderer is a fully grown adult with all their limbs, so of course they could not have gone out of the building through that opening. And it is utterly foolish even to consider something like the drain. The culprit went in and out of the building through a different entrance.'

The chief inspector shook his head to indicate he really didn't understand the hint. The two doors had been locked. The windows were covered by both lattices and shutters. With even the ventilation opening ruled out, didn't that mean there was no issue through which the culprit could have entered? It was no wonder that Tadokoro thought Hoshikage's declaration sounded illogical.

'I am not trying to argue with you,' Tadokoro started to say, but at that moment detective Mizuhara was ushered into the room, wiping his brow with a dirty handkerchief.

As they knew each other, Mizuhara nodded to Hoshikage and sat down next to the chief inspector.

'I hurried here when I heard you were visiting Mr. Hoshikage. There's something you need to know.'

'What?'

'It's that Omagari,' said Mizuhara, trying to catch his breath.

'What did he do?'

'I discovered he was in the Philippines during the war, so I visited his old platoon sergeant and first-class privates and learnt a lot about him.'

'Such as?'

'Omagari was an army cook in the field. It was his job to slaughter pigs and cows. By the end of the war, he had grown so experienced, he was basically an expert on skinning and cutting meat and bone.'

'That buffoon?' the chief inspector cried out in surprise. 'Who could have imagined that a concierge could be master of such skills? So was it Omagari who cut up Emiko Katsuki?'

The chief inspector rubbed his nose in his excitement.

'But he still wouldn't have been able to get inside the building without unlocking those doors. How do you explain that, sir?'

'Mr. Hoshikage was about to explain that to me. Let's listen carefully to what he has to say.'

Hoshikage adjusted his seat. Four eyes were focused on him, but he didn't appear to be in a hurry. He seemed to be enjoying the lustrous form of his virgin briar pipe. Finally, he started to speak in a clear voice.

'It appears the both of you got caught in the culprit's trap right from the start. You've been wandering about in the completely wrong direction.'

'Oh.'

'For example, if that man Urakami really were the murderer, he'd have no reason to transport the corpse to the dissection room and cut it up there. He's the only person who can unlock the doors, so he must know he would attract your attention, which makes it obvious he's not the murderer.'

It sounded so logical now he had pointed it out to them.

'If you want to learn the truth about the murder you need to reconsider everything from the very beginning. You still don't see it?'

Hoshikage grinned mischievously as he looked at the two men.

9

'Tadokoro, did you ever wonder why the murderer didn't put all the packages in the desk drawers?'

'No...'

'You should also consider the opposite.'

'The opposite?'

'Why were only the torso and the left hand put there?'

'I thought it was because the murderer was suddenly disturbed, so he had to flee, leaving everything behind.'

Hoshikage chided the chief inspector.

'Wait. You just said "he." Is there any evidence which points to the murderer being male?'

'No,' admitted the chief inspector.

'The culprit might very well be a woman. Anyway, I assume you have tried to find out what that disturbance could have been? The approaching footsteps of the night guard, or something even more pressing?'

'The matter has been investigated, but with no definite results.'

'I have more questions for you. Why was it necessary for the murderer to cut the body up in so many small parts? Suppose the murderer intended to take the packages to the post office to mail them. Assuming the torso, which is quite sizeable, would be accepted at the counter, why bother cutting the smaller and lighter arms and legs into multiple parts? It would only take unnecessary time and effort to cut everything up like that.'

That made perfectly sense now that Hoshikage had pointed it out.

'There's more. Assuming the murderer did open both doors, if they really did have to leave the scene in a hurry, why would they bother to lock the inside door and put the combination lock back on the first door? That seems quite absurd.'

The chief inspector had no answer to the debonair detective's point and was forced to ask:

'Mr. Hoshikage, if you know who the murderer is and how they got inside the building, please stop teasing us and tell us who it is.'

Hoshikage seemed quite amused and offered the two men Lucky Strike cigarettes before he continued.

'According to your theory, the murderer was busy wrapping the body parts when they suddenly had to leave everything behind. It was only natural you assumed that to be the case, based on the circumstances. But that was exactly what the murderer intended.'

'Huh?'

'The culprit never planned to post all of the cut-up body parts.'

The chief inspector blinked as if he had walked into a smokescreen.

'I don't see what you mean.'

'I mean that your assumption that the murderer planned to send the cut-off body parts somewhere, was exactly what the murderer wanted you to think. In fact, they were never going to send the packages anywhere.'

'So why make those packages at all?' asked Tadokoro.

'Why? Simply to make you think that the murderer was trying to wrap up the corpse in the dissection room.'

'Wha—what?'

'It was to make you believe the body had been cut up in the dissection room. The goal was to put the investigation on the wrong scent.'

'Bu—but, do you mean the murderer wasn't in the dissection room?'

'I didn't say that. The murderer went in and out of the dissection room through a normal entrance.'

'I don't get it, I don't get it all. Could you please explain it properly?'

'Hahahaha, you still don't understand?'

Hoshikage laughed and said, slowly and succinctly:

'The culprit used the ventilation opening.'

'The ventilation opening?'

'Yes. And to make sure nobody would realise that, they oiled the bolt, to make it seem as if they had used the door to get inside. The oiled bolt is what you would call a red herring. In fact, the murderer left several red herrings.'

'But what you said just now about the ventilation opening contradicts what you told me earlier. You said the murderer did not escape through the ventilation opening.'

'Please listen carefully to what I say. There was no need for the murderer to escape through the ventilation opening. They were not in the room.'

Hoshikage was speaking in riddles.

'But that contradicts what you said again. You said the culprit used a normal opening to get inside the building.'

'Just try and follow my explanation. As I said, your assumption that the body had been cut up on the dissection table was a fundamental mistake. In fact it was cut up in the cellar room to which the victim had been lured. Knowing the time difference between the time of the murder and the time the body was cut up, we can safely assume the victim was lured to the cellar and killed in the morning. The killer then returned in the afternoon to cut the body into pieces. Then they waited until the evening for a third trip. Some body parts were wrapped in oilpaper, others were left unwrapped. All the parts were taken to the roof of the dissection room, using a ladder from one of the storage units on campus. From there they were carefully placed in the room through the ventilation opening. If the culprit had simply thrown the parts inside, there would have been traces, so I think they used strings and other tools to place each body part precisely at the desired spot.'

Even the veteran Tadokoro had never heard of such a fantastic case and he cocked his head at Hoshikage's explanation.

'So the scalpels and surgical saw were also introduced through the ventilation opening?'

'Yes, to make you think the culprit had been inside the dissection room when the body was cut into pieces.'

'And that was done with everything? The oilpaper, the newspapers, the hemp strings, scissors, all of that?'

'Exactly. The goal was to create the impression the culprit had wrapped the packages in the dissection room. The bicycle lamp covered by the handkerchief was put there so you would assume the culprit had feared someone would notice the light from outside while he was busy. The switch had been left on to make it seem the culprit had fled the scene in a hurry.'

'Aha. And the shipping labels were also left there to make us believe the murderer was planning to ship the body parts elsewhere.'

'Precisely.'

The mystery was being solved one step at a time. The chief inspector appeared satisfied at first, but then a puzzled look appeared on his face.

'Wait a minute! The shipping labels were found inside the drawer of the recorder's desk. You can't put something inside a drawer while working from the ventilation opening in the ceiling. You can pull on the strings all you want, you can't place the shipping labels or the hand inside the drawer and then close it again like that.'

'Oh.'

'And there's more. The ventilation opening is only twenty centimetres square. Legs and arms might pass through it, but the torso is too large, it would never fit.'

'You are completely right, I agree with your two points. And therefore the shipping labels, torso and left hand were not introduced to the room through the ventilation opening.'

'Bu—but where did they come from then?'

'Simply through the normal entrance. They went inside through the two doors,' said Hoshikage calmly.

'But both doors were locked, either by combination lock or key.'

'And that's why they were brought inside before the doors were locked.'

'But that's impossible. Someone would have noticed.'

'It's quite possible. You just don't see it.'

Tadokoro still didn't seem to understand, so Hoshikage declared bluntly:

'The one and only possibility was to place the torso in the casket and carry it inside.'

10

Inside the casket! So that meant Enoki was the murderer. Tadokoro looked as if he had been struck by lightning, his eyes fixed on Hoshikage. He didn't know how to react to this latest revelation.

'It was Enoki's job to arrange for a casket in advance with a mortician, and then keep it in storage, meaning that there was one in some storage room on the day of the murder. Enoki brought the package with the torso in it from the cellar and hid it inside the casket. Or perhaps he had first collected the casket from the mortician, and then gone to the cellar before returning to campus. That's your job to find out. Either way, the cellar room was conveniently right next to the campus.'

The chief inspector protested once again, like a defendant desperately pleading innocence.

'Assuming he did put the torso in the casket and bring it into the dissection room, that would have to have happened before the doors were locked, so before half past four in the afternoon. But the newspaper in which the left hand had been wrapped was the late edition, which was only printed at ten to seven. Surely the newspaper proves that everything that transpired inside the dissection room, occurred after seven o'clock!'

Hoshikage didn't reply immediately, but took a few puffs before he answered with a smile.

'Oh, you are so gullible. You should consider becoming a member of one of those amateur stage magic clubs, in order to learn a few tricks and learn not to be fooled by others. The left hand package was brought in at a different time from the torso.'

'A different time?'

'Listen very carefully, the whole trick consisted of three distinct stages. The first stage was carrying the torso inside the dissection room before the doors were locked. The second stage was in the middle of the night, when most of the other parts were lowered into the dissection room through the ventilation opening. And the third stage was the following day, on the morning of the second of December when the students Enoki and Urakami entered the building. It was then that Enoki brought the left hand inside. I assume he had it hidden in a bag or something like that. After Urakami ran out in a panic, Enoki quickly put the package inside the desk drawer and then pretended to be in a panic too, so as to not attract suspicion. The shipping labels could have been placed inside the drawer at either the first or third stage, but that is of no consequence. The purpose of the charade was to create the impression, through the use of the last edition of the Nihon Keizai Shinpō, that the body had been cut up in the dissection room after seven o'clock. And that's the answer to the question I asked you earlier, of why the culprit thought it necessary to cut the limbs up into smaller parts. The package wrapped in the Nihon

214

Keizai Shinpō, destined to be placed inside the drawer, had to be small enough not to attract any attention. It needed to fit inside a bag, and not be noticed by Urakami. But had he only cut the left hand off and not done anything to the other limbs, that would have attracted the attention of the police. That is why he also cut the right hand and both feet off, and the arms and legs into two parts. Which is what actually caught my attention in the first place.'

Hoshikage gave Tadokoro a hard look, as if to ask whether he had finally understood. The chief inspector nodded without saying a word.

'The torso had been hidden in the drawer so Omagari would not see it when he placed the body of the elderly vagrant inside the casket. But the left hand was placed in the drawer for a different reason.'

'Which was...?'

'Do you remember saying, "You can't put something inside a drawer while working from the ventilation opening in the ceiling. You can pull on the strings all you want, you can't place the shipping labels or the hand inside the drawer and then close it again like that."?'

'Yes.'

'You rejected the notion of the body parts being introduced through the ventilation opening because you found the shipping labels and the hand inside that closed drawer. That was also part of the killer's plan. If he had only placed the torso in the drawer, that might have been too obvious and led to you uncovering his scheme.'

'Aha, now I get it. So those two doors were never opened.'

Now he had finally grasped the solution to the problem that had troubled him for so long, Tadokoro was quite impressed. He nodded a few times, but then another thought occurred to him.

'But Enoki had no motive, he had no reason to kill her.'

'But he did. His true goal was to frame Urakami for the murder, which would be enough to cause his downfall. Enoki would then become the one to be sent to West Germany to study. I believe that from the very moment the talented Enoki lost out to Urakami, an immense hatred and jealousy towards him festered in Enoki's heart and he plotted his revenge twenty-four hours a day.'

Hoshikage paused at that point to admire the smoke rising from his pipe.

'In order to bring about Urakami's downfall, there needed to be an incident inside the dissection room. Not an everyday incident, but a

215

locked room murder, with Urakami as the one and only possible suspect. In addition to implicating Urakami, Enoki could ensure that he himself was eliminated as a suspect, thus killing two birds with one stone. As I mentioned earlier, he oiled the bolt to make it appear as if the murderer had gone in through the doors. I assume that he would have preferred to have done the same to the lock on the inside door, but that turned out to be impossible.'

Hoshikage carefully placed his pipe on the table and crossed his legs.

'The scheme was not hatched overnight. It had to be planned meticulously and he needed to learn about Urakami's private life. Once he discovered that his rival always spent the night somewhere else on the first of the month, he knew that the murder had also to occur on the first, in order to put Urakami on the spot.'

Mizuhara had remained silent all this time, but now he spoke out angrily.

'Mr. Hoshikage, do you mean to say that he killed Emiko Katsuki just for that, someone he had no grudge against?'

'Don't be so sure. If he'd only wanted to bring Urakami down, he could simply have revealed Urakami's misconduct to the professor. I suspect that behind Enoki's apparent dislike of women lies the fact that he's impotent. The grass is always greener on the other side. To the average couple, married life might be a trial full of distress, but to an impotent person, it might appear to be a sweet, sweet life in paradise. Put yourself in his place, with a beauty like Emiko Katsuki at his side nearly all the time, a woman he would never be able to make his wife. Resignation turns into envy, envy turns to despair, and despair turns to hate.'

Thus spoke Hoshikage as he looked at his slender, well-cared for fingers.

11

Time flew by. One day in early summer, when more and more people started wearing open-necked shirts, Chief Inspector Tadokoro happened to come across Rui Itō while riding the Yamanote train line. She was wearing a neat, white outfit which made her black hair look even more beautiful.

'Oh, how nice to see you again, Chief Inspector. Have you been well?'

216

'I'm fine, thank you. How are you doing at the university?'

'A lot has changed,' replied Rui sadly. 'Professor Amano has grown old and tired. How horrible for him that his disciples were all so eccentric. He didn't have much luck.'

'And how's young Urakami?'

'He quit university at the end of the year and went back to his home town.'

It had been an expected move. Having betrayed Professor Amano's trust, he couldn't stay working there anymore.

Rui stared into the distance.

'It was like a sudden fever, becoming obsessed with someone like him,' she mumbled. She didn't seem to be making fun of herself. She had spoken the words as if she had decided time would eventually heal everything.

'And what about yourself?'

'Me?'

Her eyes flickered.

'I'm getting married in October. An ordinary *omiai* marriage.' (2)

'That's really nice to hear. Congratulations.'

The kind-hearted Tadokoro couldn't have been happier if his own daughter were about to be married. But it is doubtful whether he would have congratulated her so freely had he known that she had lost her purity of her own free will. Is there anything so absurd as a loving husband, who does not know his wife had come to him impure? In any case, the only certainty was that Rui Itō was a modern girl, in both the good and bad sense of the term.

(2) A traditional matchmaking custom, where a man and woman are introduced to each other in order to consider the possibility of a marriage. It is not an arranged marriage, but a meeting where both actors are to seriously consider a marriage together.

217

Made in the USA
Middletown, DE
17 October 2021